NEEDY LITTLE THINGS

NEEDY LITTLE THINGS

CHANNELLE DESAMOURS

BLOOMSBURY
LONDON OXFORD NEW YORK NEW DELHI SYDNEY

BLOOMSBURY YA
Bloomsbury Publishing Plc
50 Bedford Square, London WC1B 3DP, UK
Bloomsbury Publishing Ireland Limited
29 Earlsfort Terrace, Dublin 2, D02 AY28, Ireland

BLOOMSBURY, BLOOMSBURY YA and the Diana logo
are trademarks of Bloomsbury Publishing Plc

First published in the United States of America in 2025 by Wednesday Books,
an imprint of St. Martin's Publishing Group
First published in Great Britain in 2025 by Bloomsbury Publishing Plc

A catalogue record for this book is available from the British Library

ISBN: PB: 978-1-5266-7506-4; Waterstones Exclusive: 978-1-5266-9153-8;
eBook: 978-1-5266-7505-7; ePDF: 978-1-5266-7507-1

2 4 6 8 10 9 7 5 3 1

Designed by Jen Edwards

Printed and bound in Great Britain by CPI Group (UK) Ltd, Croydon CR0 4YY

To find out more about our authors and books visit www.bloomsbury.com
and sign up for our newsletters
For product safety related questions contact productsafety@bloomsbury.com

For my readers.

As strong, resilient, and magical as you are,
may you still receive the love, protection, and
softness you so very much deserve.

CHAPTER 1

· ·

I spend an unhealthy amount of time thinking about brains. It's to the point where I've started to empathize with the zombies in horror movies. Not that I have any interest in eating brains—I'm just preoccupied with how they work, how mine is different, and what it'd be like to have a normal one.

People love to be like *There's no such thing as normal*, and for the most part, I agree. I do. But let's be real, knowing what people need before they know they need it? That's some next-level stuff. And trust, I've browsed all the forums: audio hallucinators, mind readers, psychics. There may be a label out there that suits me, but I haven't found it yet.

Paper clip. Crayon. Shoelace. Chewing gum.

Dr. Stone clears her throat and side-eyes me for the third time this period. I stop tapping my pencil on my desk and angle it as if I intend to write, even though she and I both know this notebook is staying blank.

Balloon. Chewing gum. Tennis racket. Chewing gum.

I fidget in my seat. Lean forward until the back legs of my chair lift from the floor.

Chewing gum. Lanyard. Gloves. Chewing gum. Gum. GUM.

The words fill my skull until I think it may crack and spill its contents, like a broken candy machine. I scratch my neck, trying to resist before shoving my hand into my bloated red duffel, dubbed "Santa Bag" by my little brother. It's full of random items meant to save me from moments like this. My fingers grasp the familiar foil wrapper of the stick of spearmint I tossed in last week. I get out of my seat and slam it on Corbin's desk.

"Is there a problem, Sariyah?" Dr. Stone asks, her patience with me about as thin as dental floss.

"No, ma'am. Just a fly."

My bootleg little ability doesn't come with any fancy visions or reasons why people will need the things they do, so while she continues droning on about spinning objects or whatever, I watch Corbin out of the corner of my eye. There's no telling if he'll use my donation this class period, or even this week, but my curiosity quiets the other needs some. Maybe he's about to get paired up with his crush and had a garlicky lunch. Or maybe it'll help him focus. He's the only one in this class doing worse than me.

He looks around before sneaking the gum into his mouth, only to then smack on it like a cow. Little dots of saliva sprinkle his desk. If I hang around after class, no doubt I'll sense a need for disinfectant as whoever sits there next approaches. The girl in front of him leans back and stretches. She flips her ponytail over her shoulder and accidentally knocks Corbin's abstract art project onto the floor where it breaks into two sad pieces. She doesn't notice, or doesn't care, and Corbin doesn't say anything. He quietly picks it up and stares at the remains until suddenly his eyes go wide. His jaw muscles bulge and relax as he chomps the gum. I assume he's trying to work the

2

last remnants of flavor from it until I see him raise his fingers to his lips and pull away with a sticky, slobbery chunk.

"You cannot be serious," I say, as he uses the gum to repair his ugly little project.

The entire class turns their heads to look at me.

"My bad."

"Nope. Sorry, Sariyah. Two strikes, you're out. Disrupting the learning of others is where I draw the line. I'll be making a call home."

A guy in the front row takes off his hat and ruffles his hair. "Been a minute since you watched a baseball game, huh, Dr. Stone?"

Laughter erupts throughout the room and I wait for Dr. Stone to announce that he'll be getting a call home, too, but the bell rings before she can get everyone settled.

Corbin waves his unhygienic project in my face on his way out. "Hey, thanks for the gum!"

I give him a tight smile and thumbs-up, then take my time gathering my things. My mind is an endless loop of the immediate or future needs of the people around me. Tangible, everyday items . . . usually. Intrusive thoughts that pester me relentlessly until (a) I fulfill the needs, (b) they meld into a crippling migraine, or (c) the person with the need moves out of range of the anomaly that is my brain—a range that I have determined to be twenty-one feet, three inches. Such a distance is, unfortunately, impossible to achieve in the cramped classrooms of East Lake High and 100 percent the reason my grades are a mess. How am I supposed to learn about—I glance at the whiteboard—centripetal force when Nevaeh needs potting soil, Ayo needs a cotton swab, and Dr. Stone needs a stapler?

Before venturing into the hall, I toss a mini pack of Lysol

wipes on Corbin's seat, jab my squishy orange earplugs into my ears, and put my ear defenders over those. They won't drown out the needs, but at least I won't have to process them and the latest school gossip at the same time.

Toothpick. Mirror. Paper. Condom. EpiPen. Dryer sheet. Deodorant.

Funny how EpiPen tried to sneak its way in one ear and out the other while Corbin's chewing gum wanted to holler like a toddler who dropped their lollipop in the sandbox. It's no use trying to pinpoint who's walking around with some ticking time bomb allergy. Not with so many people around. And it's not like I have an EpiPen anyway. I'm pretty good at getting my hands on strange or hard-to-come-by things, but prescription meds are a territory I have no plans to trespass through.

I barge through the door of Nurse Rincon's office, panting. "Do you have EpiPens?"

He jumps and places his hand over his heart, mouth moving without words.

I yank off my headphones and dislodge the earplugs. "Do you have EpiPens?"

"I heard you the first time, Sariyah." He unlocks a cabinet and waves a little red emergency case at me.

"Sorry."

He sits on the edge of his desk, eyes sparkling. "La vidente, is there something I should know?"

I grab a juice box from the mini fridge and drink it in one long slurp. "I'm not clairvoyant."

He clicks his tongue. "Debatable, my friend. You come to me talking about EpiPen, inhaler, insulin"—he taps his temple—"I listen."

With as much time as I spend down here and all the little crystals on his bookshelves, I'm not surprised he thinks

4

there's something mystical about me. "It was just a question," I say, raiding his candy bowl.

The bell rings and Rincon raises his eyebrows when I pretend not to hear it. "You're late."

"Let me stay. It's quiet here."

"Sariyah"—he opens his desk drawer and pulls out a hall pass—"graduation will be here before you know it. Progress reports came out last week, didn't they? How'd yours look?"

"Ugly. But your grades would look like that, too, if your existence was one continuous headache."

"Do you need your medication? That's what it's here for."

The syrupy concern in his voice actually makes me want to go to class. "No, thanks. I'm good." I grab the pass and take the long way to English.

Thirty-two minutes later, an ambulance siren wails.

Fifteen minutes after that, Nurse Rincon's face appears in the doorway. He winks at me, EpiPen case wedged under his armpit.

. . .

After school, I catch sight of Deja and Malcolm in the bus lane. Her with fresh, butt-length honey-brown box braids, him sporting his signature grandpa sweater and high-waters that somehow look fashionable. Malcolm and I don't have any classes together this semester, so our reunions at the end of each day have become a whole event. I cup my hands around my mouth and shout, "Mal-col-me, my homie!"

A head taller than everyone else, he spots me easily and dances his way over, singing, "Sariyah, she fıya!"

We close the distance between us and do our eight-step greeting—one move for every year we've known each other.

Deja rolls her eyes and stifles a laugh. "All of that is so unnecessary."

"You think so?" Malcolm asks, before grinning at me and going in for a dramatic round two that makes her shield her face and act like she doesn't know us.

Deja turned our duo into a trio at the end of last summer. She fit right in and we get along great, but there's no denying we're both better friends with Malcolm than we are with each other. That I can hear her needs, and not his, is proof. I stopped hearing Malcolm's only a few months after we met and don't recall ever hearing a single need from my mom, dad, or little brother. It's like the most unique part of me refuses to share itself with the people I care about most, and I hate that. So I do my best to love them a little harder. But you don't have to have a deep soul connection with someone to enjoy their company. I throw my arm around Deja's neck and lead her back to the buses. "You need to hurry up. You know Ms. Irma will see you in the rearview chasing down the bus and press harder on the gas pedal."

She whines. "I'm not trying to go home. My mom's been on my last nerve, for real."

I laugh. "Mine, too. That's half the reason I got a job." That and restocking Santa Bag every few weeks ain't cheap.

"I shouldn't have signed up for so many AP classes." She adjusts her ginormous backpack. "I'd probably never graduate if I worked during the semester. I don't know how you do it."

"I don't take AP, and who said I'm graduating?" It's a joke that really isn't a joke, but she doesn't know that, so she laughs.

"Bye, girl." She hugs me, then shouts over her shoulder, "Call me later, Colmy!"

6

I frown a little. That nickname was once strictly used by me.

Malcolm and I wave goodbye and watch the buses roll out before starting off down the sidewalk.

"I got in trouble in class today," I say, relishing the quiet in my mind as we walk farther from the school. "My physics teacher is probably going to be calling your burner." Malcolm bought a secret extra phone last year when he kept getting his main one taken away for texting during class, but it has come in handy for me more times than it has for him.

"I'm about to start charging you for my services."

"Love you forever." I lock on to his arm. "How was your day? Hit me with the recap."

"First block was ass. No way I'm going the rest of the semester without popping *well-actually* Harold in the mouth." He scrunches up his face like something smells bad. "But second was good. Me and Deja finally figured out what to do for our social studies project. We're going to get a head start next week. I usually wouldn't condone doing schoolwork over spring break, but your boy is trying to get an A."

"I don't share your enthusiasm for social studies, but more power to you."

"Anyway. What are you about to do? Come watch a movie with me." His eyes drift to the top of my head. "I'll help you take your twists out."

I'd be offended by the offer if I hadn't been needing to redo my hair for the past week. "I have to work, but it's only a half shift. Come with. You can knock out your homework, then we can go back to your place."

"Ew," he says, catching another imaginary whiff of something foul.

"Malcolm, come on. It's been like three months."

7

"It can be three damn decades. I'm not going back to that janky little ice cream shop, even though that woman knows she owes her recent uptick in business to me. I heard about some of those new flavors. She think she woke now, I see. Needs to take ol' Chex Your Privilege and go on somewhere."

Malcolm quit his job as associate scooper at Sweet Pea's Ice Creams when he finally confronted the owner, Ms. Jess, about her sometimes problematic, puntastic flavor names. All Flavors Matter was Malcolm's breaking point. A customer got the whole ordeal on video, which promptly went viral. I even caught a few memes of my own slack-jawed face in the background. I'm not the biggest fan of Ms. Jess myself, but Malcolm's family is well-off. He wants to work—he doesn't have to. Best I could do was leave her a list of recommended reading, which she gladly accepted. But that also led to her current cringeworthy wave of socially aware flavors.

We come to the place in the road where we have to part ways. I give him one last pleading look.

"Girl, bye." He waves me off. "Love you."

• • •

Sweet Pea's is a small, freestanding shop with pale yellow walls and a green roof. Seasonal decor and ugly window art give the place a daycare kind of vibe. It's only disrupted by the faded Casey Sullivan flyers still hanging up, thanks to Ms. Jess's impossible-to-remove adhesive. Casey went to our rival high school and disappeared about four months ago. It made national news within a day. Her body was found two days after that. Malcolm was angry about Ms. Jess's stupid ice cream flavors, but mostly, I think he was sick of seeing Casey's face on the door. I know I was. And it's not because I'm cold and

8

heartless. It's because I can't look at Casey without thinking of Tessa. And thinking of Tessa hurts. She's Malcolm's twin and my first best friend. And just like Casey, Tessa vanished one day after school. But unlike Casey, the country didn't rally for her. #FindTessa wasn't a trending topic. Unlike Casey, Tessa isn't white. Unlike Casey, Tessa hasn't been found. And sure, that leaves room for hope, but Tessa taught me how painful hope can be. It's a pain I've had almost five years to learn to live with. It's a pain neither Malcolm nor I could have managed without each other. So he can be mad at Ms. Jess. There are more important things to worry over.

I enter through the back of the shop where Ms. Jess is talking with someone my age.

"Oh, Sariyah! Perfect timing!"

Nail file. Nail file. Nail file.

Her need shouts so loudly, the person's next to her is impossible to make out.

"This is Jude Abrams." She tucks her blond bobbed hair behind her ears and beams. "He'll be joining our team! I've just finished showing him the ropes."

Jude extends his hand, light brown and calloused. I shake it without making eye contact.

Ms. Jess clasps her hands together, bangles clanging. "All righty! Introductions are done and I've gotta run. Wednesday evenings are slow, but give me a buzz if you need anything." She disappears into the break room to grab her things.

I sift through Santa Bag and pull out a metal nail file. When Ms. Jess comes back out, I hand it off to her quickly, ready to be relieved of the aching in my skull. "You dropped this."

She takes it and squints. "Huh. Thanks, sweetie." She tosses it into her purse and waves as she walks out the door. "Y'all take care!"

Even when she is well out of my range, Jude's need still only presents as an annoying whisper. He says something, but I'm too busy trying to decipher the mumbles to catch it. "Sorry?"

"I said she didn't drop that."

I haven't brought myself to look him full in the face yet because he smells like he's cute—it's a thing—and I can't be any more distracted from school and work than I already am. "I know, but her nails were looking rough."

"That's weird because she said she got a manicure earlier today."

"I meant her toenails."

"She had on sneakers. You got X-ray vision?"

I look up just enough to see a small grin playing on his full, two-toned lips. "Something like that."

"Something like that, or you have a knack for predicting things people will need?"

The box of plastic spoons in my hands drops to the ground with a noisy clatter. "You came to that conclusion over a nail file?"

He begins prepping some waffle cone batter. "No. I came to that conclusion because I'm observant and I have two classes with you. Thought it was pretty cool, but after getting the cold shoulder the first few times, I stopped trying to say hello."

"I'm sorry." I gather up the dirty spoons and toss them in the trash. "This is going to sound ridiculous, but I promise I did not hear you . . . or see you."

"Is that supposed to be comforting?" He laughs and pours a ladle of batter onto the hot waffle iron. "It's all good. I may have only transferred to East Lake at the start of the semes-

10

ter, but that's long enough to process the social hierarchy. Of course someone with your celebrity status would overlook the new guy."

I snort because none of that is what it seems. Someone like me, endlessly distracted, doesn't make a good friend. I got told about myself enough times to stop trying. People know my name. I get invited to parties. I even made homecoming court in ninth and tenth grade. But I don't go to things like that anymore. Music plus everything else going on in my head turns my brain into a worthless mass not dissimilar to what Corbin pulled out of his mouth earlier. And what do I look like wearing noise-canceling headphones to a party? My popularity hasn't been earned from a stellar personality, or amazing academic performance, or innate athletic ability. People like me because I'm convenient to be around.

"I didn't overlook you. I mean, I did, but not because I think I'm something special. I have ADHD—inattentive and distractible." Not a lie, but my prescriptions do little to address the root cause. "School is hard for me." I finally look him dead in his annoyingly attractive face, and there it is. His muffled need breaks through whatever was holding it back. "You can look at my grades. You aren't the only one I haven't been paying attention to." I scrunch up my face apologetically, knowing my explanation still sounds conceited as hell.

"I can help you. With your grades, I mean." He puts two fingers to his glasses, then directs them back at me. "Laser focus." He gestures at Santa Bag, which I keep shoved under the counter by the cash register during my shifts. "So, did you get bitten by a radioactive spider or what?"

I frown. "Spider-Man? Really?"

He snaps and points at me. "You're right. X-Men would make way more sense here."

I snatch up an ice cream scoop and point it at him aggressively, a dollop of Fruity Freedom dropping to the floor.

He holds up his hands and laughs. "Sorry, sorry! But can you blame me for being curious?"

"It's just the way I am." And the way my grandmother was, but I'm not about to get into my family history with some nosy boy I just met. I don't care how cute he is. "Maybe you should target your curiosity at how to properly make waffle cones before you burn the shop down."

Jude whips around and uses the rag draped over his shoulder to fan the smoking waffle iron. While he deals with that, I sneak his need from my bag and tuck it into the pocket of my apron.

"Going to grab some more spoons. Be right back." On my way to the prep room, I slip a brand-new hairbrush into his book bag. It's got Hello Kitty all over it, but needy little things can't be choosers.

Jude and I work, finding an easy groove and getting to know each other. He even starts in on his promise to tutor me, quizzing me on Spanish verb conjugation between customers. I learn he and his mom moved here from Florida. He learns that Spanish might be a lost cause for me.

At closing, I leave him to start cleanup. There's a commotion from out back as I fill the mop bucket with fresh water. I turn off the tap for a better listen. Jude appears in the doorway.

"Did you hear that?" I ask.

We both jump when the dead bolt suddenly turns. The door opens slowly and Miss Jess stands there, white as a sheet.

"Are you okay?" I take a few quick steps toward her but freeze when I glimpse the scene behind her.

A man.

Writhing on the ground.

With a metal nail file lodged in his neck.

CHAPTER 2

· ·

"Tell me everything." Malcolm sits with me and Jude at the sun-bleached picnic table across the street from Sweet Pea's, fresh iced coffee in hand. A few people hover right at the edge of my range, but I can usually count on this park to be decently quiet. Deja sits cross-legged on a beach towel, convenience store bag full of snacks in her lap, ready for the story. Neither Jude nor I went to school today. We were caught up at the shop well past closing talking with the police. Both our moms were worried the whole thing traumatized us, and maybe it did. But it also bonded us. It sounds cheesy, but it's true. Jude's mumbling needs went dead silent the second Ms. Jess opened that back door and, despite being with him most of the day today, I haven't heard a peep. It's never happened that fast, and it hasn't happened in years. Not since Malcolm—who's currently helping himself to a handful of Jude's Takis. Any friend of mine is a friend of his.

"Well?" he pushes. "You send a few vague texts about somebody getting stabbed, leave us on read all day, and still being stingy with the details?" He sucks the dusty red seasoning from his fingers. I toss a few individually packaged wet wipes from Santa Bag onto the table.

"You've seen the news report now. We don't know much more than they've been saying there. Ms. Jess left early, came back because she forgot something, and on her way inside, this man came out of nowhere and attacked her. She defended herself."

"Was there a lot of blood?" Deja asks hesitantly, like we're sitting around a campfire sharing scary stories.

"Not much at all," Jude answers. "But there might have been if Ms. Jess had removed the nail file."

Malcolm jumps to his feet in shock. "You mean dude was just laid out with it sticking out of him?" He cuts his eyes at me as he slowly sits back down and takes out his phone. "Jude, AirDrop me your contact info because you clearly know how to tell a story better than this girl."

He does and Malcolm starts up a shiny new group chat for the four of us.

"Do they think the guy is going to wake up?" Deja asks.

"My mom's a physician's assistant at the hospital," Jude says. "They don't think it'll be long until he's coherent enough for questioning."

"Wild he's alive at all." Malcolm takes complete ownership over Jude's chips. "Nail file to the neck is pretty damn gruesome."

"I'm surprised it did the damage it did. The thing was cheap," I say. "Like ninety-nine cents from Walmart."

"Ms. Jess must have really put some oomph—Wait, how do you know that?" He slaps the table when he realizes. "Don't tell me . . ."

15

"I gave it to her right before she left."

Jude uses his hand to hide his face from Malcolm as he speaks to me. "Does he know about . . . you know?"

Malcolm cackles. "I'm sorry, was that your attempt at whispering?"

"Colmy, I know your loud mouth ain't judging nobody's ability to whisper." I turn to Jude. "But to answer your question, Malcolm's my best friend. I've known him longer than I've known the meaning of discretion. He knows everything."

"Lucky guy." Jude's eyes drift over to Deja. "And . . ."

"And I happily mind my own business," she says, staring down at her phone.

Malcolm cackles again. "Oh, we lying today? That's what we doing?"

"You know what I mean. I'm not into all that stuff. Creeps me out," Deja says. "No offense to you and your charity bag, Sariyah."

"None taken, but while we're on the topic . . ." I toss her a pocket-sized notebook and enjoy the heavy silence in my head as soon as she picks it up.

"Anyway," Malcolm drawls. "Ri, if you gave Ms. Jess that nail file, that means you saved her life."

"That's what I've been trying to tell her," Jude says.

"Saved her life is pushing it. I wasn't even out there. The man might have just been trying to rob her."

"Just?" Jude kicks one leg over the bench so he's straddling it and waits for me to look at him. "Sariyah, you keep conveniently forgetting the guy had a gun on him."

"Because he didn't have it out."

"Didn't have it out *yet*. Ms. Jess said he was reaching for it."

Malcolm clears his throat obnoxiously at that. "Women like her always swear somebody is reaching for something, stealing something, going someplace they shouldn't."

"Not going to argue with that," Jude says. "But the man looks like he could be her husband. Middle-aged white guy. The kind you'd expect her to give the benefit of the doubt. The fact that she didn't proves she must have felt legitimately threatened." He turns back to me. "You should be proud you made it so she could protect herself, Sariyah."

"I hate that I'm connected to it at all. It's like I stuck my nose in something I had no business being involved with."

"Well, that's exactly what you did," Malcolm says. "But that's what you do. You get in people's business in a way no one else can. And you doing you saved that woman's life."

I nod, but all he's done is further expose the thing that's hanging me up. Yes, I gave Ms. Jess the nail file, and sure, I can play along with the idea that it prevented something bad from happening to her. But what if I hadn't given it to her? What if I'd come in a little later, after she'd already gone? I can't stop thinking about all the needs I miss fulfilling every single day. Needs I can't trace back to the right person, items I don't have available to give. What if those people need those things as much as Ms. Jess needed that nail file? I'm so glad Mama let me stay home from school today because what I wanted, what I needed most, was to avoid people for a few hours. If I don't hear them, I can't feel guilty for not providing.

"Seriously, though," Malcolm says. "That ability has done you, and a bunch of others, a whole lot of good."

"Me? What good has it done me?"

He jerks his head back. "I know you don't think you got

17

promoted to senior scooper in your first week at Sweet Pea's all on your own merit. Comes in handy knowing what flavors customers need."

"Need?" Jude glances around at the three of us, waiting for someone to join him in laughter. "Wait, are y'all serious? My parents drilled a pretty hard line between wants and needs when I was a kid. Dessert was solidly in the *want* category."

"You're thinking about it too literally. Does ice cream bring you joy?" I rest my elbow on the table and my chin on my palm.

"Yeah."

"And you don't think joy is needed for good mental health?"

Deja, Malcolm, and I all stare him down, daring him to give the wrong answer.

He shifts back on the bench, chuckling. "Okay. Y'all got me. People need ice cream."

"And sometimes the things I give end up being compromises anyway. A stand-in when something better isn't around. I once saw these parents make a snowman out of Safe Space Sweet Cream to calm their toddler after she realized she'd lost her stuffed Olaf."

Across the street, a curvy light-skinned woman in a sundress and sky-high wedges tries to enter Sweet Pea's. The steel security door rattles loudly, interrupting our conversation.

"It's closed!" Malcolm yells. "And cursed!" He peeks at me from the corner of his eye, goading me to comment on his continued pettiness toward Ms. Jess, but I don't indulge him.

He looks back at the woman, who is now desperately tugging on the door to the shop. He stands up this time and tries again. "It's closed!" And under his breath he adds, "Is it me, or are locked doors not a sign to keep it moving?"

The woman looks at us, shading her eyes, despite already wearing sunglasses and a floppy hat. She pushes her shades down her nose, then smiles broadly before scurrying across the street, waving energetically.

"Look what you did." I glare at Malcolm, who casually inspects his fingernails.

"It's you!" the woman squeals.

I look at Jude and Malcolm and Deja, but we all know who she's talking to.

She reaches the picnic table and sets her huge tote bag on it with a clank. "I've been looking for you!" She roots around in her bag and passes me a wrinkled envelope. *Thanks for the nail polish remover. Lifesaver!* is scrawled across the front. She winks at me, then scurries her way back across the street.

"What was that about?" Jude asks.

I turn the envelope around so Malcolm can read the front.

"Oh! Need fulfillment perk!" He claps his hands as Deja rolls onto her stomach, distractedly grinning at her phone.

"Do people give you gifts often?" Jude asks.

"Not often, but it happens. A few months ago, this lady shoved two hundred dollars in my hand and ran away. Like, literally ran. I think she thought I was a witch or something."

"Do all the needs you hear fit in that bag? Never a car or a million dollars or a cure for cancer?" Jude asks.

I'm pretty sure I hear Malcolm's eyes roll into the back of his head. "Sariyah," he whines, "open the damn envelope already."

I suck my teeth at him but peek inside anyway. "Oh my God," I gasp.

Deja sits up, intrigued now. "What is it? More than two hundred?"

They all crane their necks trying to catch a glimpse.

I hold the envelope close to my body. "Malcolm Hawkins, that woman just delivered your dream birthday gift."

"Oh, give it to me on Saturday. You know I love a surprise."

"This . . . can't wait. Close your eyes and hold out your hands."

He does as instructed. I let Jude and Deja take a look first. Four tickets to Afro Alt Music Festival. Deja slaps her hand over her mouth and takes off running across the park. Jude splutters, trying to hold in his laughter. Deja and Malcolm have always wanted to go, and it starts this weekend.

I place the tickets in his waiting hands. "Open!"

Malcolm's eyes flash open. He takes a second to process what he's looking at. Then he screams.

The people nearby go silent and gawk.

"Everything's fine." Jude smiles and waves reassuringly.

When Malcolm screams again, the people decide to add more distance between us and them. His shriek is a lure for Deja, though. She sprints back toward us, her short legs moving lightning fast. It's no wonder she made varsity track in ninth grade.

"You are lying!" Malcolm shuffles through the tickets, holds them up to the sun, sniffs them. "Stop!" He flips them back and forth. "Shut up!" He breaks into a mini praise dance, then hugs my neck across the picnic table, shoving my gut against the splintery wood.

"Dang, Colmy, chill," I say with a laugh.

Deja sneaks a ticket from Malcolm's grip, her huge cheesy smile wide enough to expose every bracket of her pink braces. She gives it a good sniff, too.

"You are one of God's favorites," he says slowly. "These have been sold out for weeks. You could hustle that ability so hard. Save lives and make bank."

I open my mouth to explain for the hundredth time why I don't, but he cuts me off.

"I know, I know. You and your superstitions."

"Not wanting to become a test subject in some creep's basement laboratory and being superstitious are not the same thing. Plus, I think it'd just feel . . . wrong."

"Whatever, Mother Teresa. Let's go shopping. I know you don't have nothing to wear. And you"—he looks Jude up and down—"I accept your devotion to black, but we need to elevate this for the festival." He wags his index finger at his outfit.

Jude says, "I'm invited?" at the same time I say, "I can't go!"

"Of course," Malcolm answers Jude, and to me, "Hell yes, you can. It's my birthday."

"It's a music festival, Malcolm. There will be thousands of people and, well . . . music."

Jude looks at me like I'm a whole alien. "Wait, you don't like music?"

"You should spend some time evaluating why you find that harder to grasp than the fact that I can hear people's needs. But to be clear, it's not that I don't like it. All the noises in my head clash. Gives me migraines."

"You'll be all right," Malcolm says. "One place nobody is going to judge you over earplugs and noise cancelers is Afro Alt."

"But isn't the whole point to enjoy the music? Somebody else would appreciate the ticket more than me."

"Not as much as I would appreciate having my best

21

friend with me celebrating the best birthday gift I have ever gotten. And yes, the music is a big part of Afro Alt, but that's not all it's about." His eyelids flutter and his face goes all passionate and dreamy. "Afro Alt is about acceptance, realness, individuality. It's a place where you can be Black and awkward, Black and fat, Black and queer, Black and disabled, Black and what the hell ever and have it celebrated, Ri. It was made for a couple of strangeos like us. And you too, boo boo," he says to a random old lady paying a little too close attention to our conversation.

"Ri, once we get your outfit picked, I volunteer to snazz up your ear defender headset to match. I'm getting glam space cadet vibes already." He clutches the tickets to his chest and looks up and down the street. "Where'd Ms. Sunglasses go? I'm gonna need her to go gnatty on you if she has hookups like this."

"Gnatty?" Deja asks. "Haven't heard that one yet."

"Some people catch on to my ability and go out of their way to run into me. But after this week, I don't even care." I want to fulfill every need I can. Keeps the headaches at bay, and maybe, possibly, even saves lives.

"It's all fun and games until that gnat ends up flying up your nose cause it has zero concept of boundaries. Like that old dude," Malcolm says. "What was his name?"

"Phillip. Haven't seen him in a while." He used to stop by Sweet Pea's daily to see if I had something for him. Ms. Jess finally told him he had to buy something or stop coming. "All the ice cream he was eating probably took its toll. But at least he was generous with the tip jar."

"Not generous enough to be waiting for you outside of the school!"

"He wasn't waiting. It was a coincidence."

"Coincidence my left butt cheek." Malcolm looks at the tickets again and pokes out his lips. "But if a gnat comes bearing bomb-ass gifts like this, their faux pas are worthy of forgiveness." He grabs his iced coffee and gives it a vigorous shake. "Jude, crank up that Civic. Deja, fold up that towel. Ri, grab Santa Bag. It's time to shop."

CHAPTER 3

. . . .

I take the stairs of my apartment building to unit 3B, planting both my feet on each step like an old woman with a bad hip after a double shift. Malcolm really had us in those thrift stores like we were filming a movie makeover montage on a deadline. The hall is chilly and damp and smells like old cabbage. I enter the apartment and take a moment to give thanks to the essential oil diffuser Mama keeps on the console by the door, but before it clears my nostrils of the hallway's offenses, a Nerf football hits me square in the center of my chest. "Mama!" I draw out at the top of my lungs.

My little brother darts around the corner, laughing hysterically, but I'm not playing with his annoying behind tonight. I throw my bags down and chase after him.

"Riyah!" Mama's voice echoes through our tiny apartment. "Riyah, don't you start with him!"

I stop so short I almost fall. "Me? Jojo started it!"

He finds this so hilarious his laugh goes silent. I run into his room and pin him to his bed, my irritation quickly subsiding as I watch him gasp and writhe. I smack him upside the head with a pillow. "Ass."

"I know you not cussing in my house," Mama says from the doorway. She dries her hands on a dishrag. "Y'all stop playing and come eat."

We follow her, making faces at each other all the way to the dining table.

"Josiah, come take this medicine." Mama opens the kitchen cabinet where she keeps all the pharmaceuticals. She slips on a single latex glove, then drops a pill directly into his mouth. He promptly washes it down with a glass of water. It's hydroxyurea, part of his sickle cell pain management plan. That it isn't safe to handle it with bare hands, but Jojo can ingest it has never sat right with me, but it seems to be helping.

Sickle cell disease is a genetic disorder that causes red blood cells to be misshapen. It means Josiah's at high risk for blood vessel blockages and all the scary things that go along with them. Mama moved us from Chefly, in middle-of-nowhere Georgia, to Atlanta when he was two to have access to better medical care. Dad stayed down there to keep working his father's tiny farm. I miss him all the time, but being angry about the situation feels the same as being mad at Josiah over something he can't control. So it is what it is. I shove those feelings down and leave them for future me to deal with.

We visit Dad in the summers and he visits us for Christmas, with plenty of surprises scattered in between. It used to bother me when people would assume they are divorced, but Mama never wanted to hear me whining about it. *It's your father and me in the relationship, so it's your father and me who set the parameters* is what she would say. I didn't even know what a parameter was, but I knew they seemed more in love than most folks' parents. At some point, I decided that was good enough.

Mama sighs as she places a Stouffer's lasagna in the middle of the table. Jojo and I share a nervous glance. Neither of us mind the meal, but cooking is one of Mama's favorite things. She lives for fresh foods and trying out new recipes. The preprepared frozen stuff only comes out when she's sad. And for Mama, sad is never just sad. My strong opinions about mental health were shaped by watching her work through major ups and downs with her own. I wish I could help her. Jojo. Tessa. This ability is lacking in the worst way.

"How was work?" I ask cheerfully, hoping to kick off our usual dinner small talk. Mama's a manager at a swanky hotel downtown called the Wilhem.

"It was okay. Long day." Her voice is monotone, and she doesn't look up from her plate, which she has yet to put any food on.

"Malcolm was thinking about renting a room for a couple of nights during spring break to celebrate his eighteenth."

She scratches her scalp, further disrupting her already frizzy braid-out. "Gotta be twenty-one to book at Wilhem."

I discreetly spit out a still-frozen chunk of lasagna into my napkin. "Yeah, he figured that out. We've got better plans now anyway. This lady gave us tickets to a music festival on Saturday."

Mama's forehead wrinkles. "And why would she do that?"

"As a thank-you for fulfilling—"

She holds up her hand to stop me. "Sariyah, you know I don't like you giving handouts to strangers. It's not safe."

I bite my tongue to keep from talking back, but Jojo jumps

26

in for me. "Her head hurts if she doesn't do it. And you know she got a nasty attitude when her head hurts."

"Oh, I know," Mama says. "And that's why you have prescription migraine medication, Sariyah."

"Mama, it doesn't—"

"I don't want to hear it. You know what happened to your father's mother, parading around the way she did."

Daddy says Grandma's need-sensing started when she was eight years old, after her mom remarried and they left her to care for his three young kids. He says only a miracle could have gotten her through all of that. Other people didn't see her ability as miraculous, though. Folks down in Chefly would call her a witch in the daylight but come knocking at her basement door at night. She made them pay good money—good enough that she was attacked and robbed on more than one occasion. It took a heavy toll on her. Left her untrusting and bitter. She died only a few weeks after I was born. I wish I could go back in time and beg her not to pass her miracle down to me.

"Can I go?" Jojo asks. "To Malcolm's birthday party at the music festival?"

"No," Mama snaps. She points her fork at me. "And you're lucky if I let you do anything at all this weekend."

"What? Why?" I figured after all that mess at Sweet Pea's, she'd go easy on me for at least a week.

"I got an email from both your physics and math teachers about your grades, Sariyah."

"Ooooh," Jojo teases.

I buck at him, shaking the whole table.

Mama pushes away her empty plate. "Do I need to get you a tutor?"

"No." We can't afford one anyway. "I'll study harder. Jude even agreed to help me. His grades are perfect."

She twists her mouth to the side, skeptical. "All right, Ri. But you're more than halfway through the semester. Keep playing and you'll be watching your friends graduate without you, then settling in for some summer school up here instead of going down to visit your daddy."

"I know. I got it." I definitely don't got it, but this conversation is pointless.

"And don't think you're skipping another day of school tomorrow."

"Mama, come on! It's the last day before spring break. It's not like we're going to be doing anything in any of my classes."

"That's not what your math teacher said in that email. He said you got a quiz tomorrow."

I cross my arms. Mr. Howard would. He stays maximizing every second of class time.

"But I missed the review today. You should let me stay home and study. I can make it up after break."

"Nope. He sent me the study guide and answers. After dinner, you're going to sit right here and work on it. Use that little music festival as motivation because you ain't going unless you pass that quiz."

"But, Mama! I can't—"

She silences me with one stern look as she gets up from the table to grab her buzzing phone. "Hello? . . . Yes . . . Oh, really?" She paces and uh-huhs a few times before saying goodbye and hanging up.

"Who was that?" Josiah asks.

"What have I told you about staying out of grown folks' business?" she asks before going ahead and telling us both the business. "Looks like they've released the name of Ms. Jess's attacker. Danny Irvine. He's awake and talking."

28

I choke on a sip of water, anxiously imagining this guy at the hospital trying to convince the police that I was actually the one who stabbed him. It's stupid. I did enough Google searches to feel confident that I won't be in trouble if they find out I gave Ms. Jess the nail file. There's no way I could have known what would happen, but I still can't stop obsessing over it.

"You all right, Sariyah?" Mama asks.

"His name," I say, still trying to clear my airway, "it sounds familiar."

"Maybe he'd been by the ice cream shop before." She gives up on dinner entirely and places her clean dish in the sink. "I'm going to go lie down. I'll forward you that study guide. Don't let me come out and find you doing anything but that."

"Yes, ma'am," I say, but she never comes out to check, and I know that's not a good sign. I do study, though, harder than I have in a long time. The formulas and equations work to distract me from everything else on my mind for probably the first, and last, time ever. But my body knows when it's 10:00 P.M. I could be dead asleep. I could be out having the time of my life. But at 10:00 P.M., my world resets. At 10:00 P.M. I think of Tessa. My phone dings because Malcolm does, too. He's sent a photo of tater tots with sour cream and sriracha on top—just how Tessa likes them.

Me
Tess tots!!

I send a couple of drooling emojis. A few minutes pass before he texts again.

Malcolm
I wish we could have made people care. Can't
believe the police gaslight us to this day.
Talking about they did everything they could.

Me
You're reading about Casey
again, aren't you?

Malcolm
I can't help it.

Me
I know. I love you.

· · ·

I sit in the back of Mr. Howard's class, glaring at him while he gets everyone settled for the quiz. A few needs I missed fulfilling before the bell berate me, but I can't risk getting in trouble for disrupting class again. I convince myself that the study guide, tissue, toothpaste, and eraser circulating through my mind are not things that could easily turn into objects of self-defense. It helps ease the building guilt brought on by failing to fulfill.

"Dang, girl, fix your face," Deja whispers. "It ain't his fault they have to notify parents if your grade drops below a seventy."

"He could have waited until after spring break."

She considers this, then joins me in scowling. "True. He wrong for that. Is your mama gonna let you go to the festival?"

"She said I can go if I pass the quiz, but only because she loves Malcolm. Even if I get a one hundred on this thing, my overall grade will still be failing so I'll probably be on lock-down for the rest of break." The last part is a lie, but is it weird that I wish it wasn't? Because if Mama bothers to put me on punishment and enforce it, that means she's healthy.

Ms. McArthur, the class co-teacher, grabs a set of quizzes from Mr. Howard. "Usual crew. Let's go."

Deja and I are both part of the usual crew, only she's in it just for show and I'm in it because of my IEP. Individualized education plan. My teachers give me accommodations like extended time and small-group testing. It definitely helps, but my grades are proof that those interventions aren't enough. Not for someone like me.

The world quiets when we leave the full classroom and go down the hall to an empty one. My eyes glaze over as I scan my quiz, trying to keep up while Ms. McArthur reads the directions aloud. Written assessments exist solely to make me feel bad about myself.

"Psst."

I look over at Deja. She's angled her paper enough for me to see and her numbers are written comically large. Bless her. But I'm shocked to find I don't need her lifeline. Ms. McArthur reads the questions and they're really similar to the ones Mr. Howard put on the study guide. I still struggle with some of them, but it feels good not to be totally clueless for once. To turn in my paper knowing I at least passed. But it's not like I can rely on the doom storm that led to my rare moment of focused studying last night. Not like I'd want to.

Ms. McArthur lets me and Deja go to the media center once we've both finished. It's deserted, thank God.

"I am so hype about tomorrow, but I'm walking on eggshells around the house," Deja says. "My stepdad has been trying to talk my mom out of letting me go." She takes her phone out and smiles. Quickly types a message. She fumbles it while trying to set it down and an old jazzy song plays on full volume. A woman, crooning about some misunderstanding between her and her love. She silences it and shoves it deep into her purse.

I laugh. "What was that?"

"What? A girl can't be cultured?" she asks, strangely defensive.

I raise my hands, still laughing. "No. Do you."

She digs my physics homework out of my book bag to help me with it.

"Are you worried your stepdad will convince your mom to change her mind?"

She tucks her leg under her butt. "No. I just don't want to hear his mouth. My mom is even more annoying, though. She's been on do-whatever-you-want-since-you-think-you-grown mode since I was twelve. She lets me do stuff, even advocates for it, then gets pissed off about it later. She's going to have something to say Saturday night, and that's fine. She can go off on the walls because I sure won't be listening. It might be Mal's eighteenth we're celebrating, but I'm marking it as a new beginning for all of us. A rite of passage. A last hurrah."

I snort. "Last hurrah?"

"Mm-hmm. And hell, I might even start the festivities early." She sips her water bottle, little finger jutting out. "Tomorrow's not promised, right?"

CHAPTER 4

. . . .

Jude picks me up early Saturday morning to go get ready for the festival at Malcolm's place.

"Thanks for the ride." I toss my bags in the back seat.

"No problem." He turns off the radio and I wonder if it's because he remembers what I said about music and my headaches. "Your hair looks nice."

I tug on the mini twists I spent four hours doing last night. They've already shrunk up to my shoulders. With this humidity, they'll be up to my chin by the end of the day, but I don't mind. "Thank you," I say, trying to hide my smile.

He waits for me to buckle up, then starts driving. "I'm glad Malcolm invited me. Got me out of going to a cookout with my mom's coworkers. One of the doctors has a house at"—he taps his thumb on the steering wheel—"Lake Lanier, I think she said."

I slam my foot on my imaginary brake pedal. "Lake Lanier?"

He flinches. "What? What's wrong?"

"Oh, you sure aren't from Atlanta. Is your mom still going?"

"No. To be honest, I think she wanted an excuse to get out of it, too."

"I bet she did. Heard her ancestors whispering *Don't do it!*"

He lets out a small laugh. "What?"

"The lake is man-made, but back in 1912, part of the land it's on was a town called Oscarville. Racial tension peaked after two white women were assaulted and one of them died. No one knew for sure who all was involved, but all the Black families in the community—over a thousand people—were forced out of their homes. Churches, businesses, and even some lives were lost in the process. You can cover that land with as much water as you want, but the history can't be washed away. That lake is cursed. Everyone who grew up here knows it and yet people keep playing around like a lake ghost won't snatch their baby toe and drag them to a watery death."

"Come on, you really believe that?"

I shrug. "Some details are questionable, but facts are facts. That lake is murderous." I point at the intersection ahead. "Take a right."

Jude's jaw drops when we pull into the driveway of the Hawkins home. "Damn, I didn't know Malcolm's family had it like this."

"Yeah. They got it like that. Come on." I jog up the brick stairs leading to the front door and ring the doorbell. "You're legal!" I shout when Malcolm opens the door for us.

"Happy birthday," Jude mumbles.

I watch, humored, as he takes in the marble floors and twinkling chandelier, eagerly waiting for the change in expression when he sees Malcolm's room.

My patience is rewarded. Jude whips his head back and forth between the hallway—immaculate and luxe—and

Malcolm's bedroom with the mattress on the floor, an ancient TV, a dresser that looks like he picked it up from the side of the road, and clothes thrown all over the place.

"To be fair, stingy as they may be, my parents don't force me to live like this. I just like to do for myself. I was supposed to use the money I was making at Sweet Pea's to buy some furniture but, as you can see, I got a problem with clothes. I did buy me a cute little hooptie, but folks done lost their minds with these gas prices and road rage. Won't catch me driving nowhere."

Jude smiles widely and points at the old black pug nestled on a dog bed by the window. "Who's that?"

"Miss Doretta," Malcolm says.

"You named your dog Doretta?"

"Excuse me?" Malcolm looks him up and down. "Sariyah, get your friend."

"It's Miss Doretta, Jude. Miss."

"That's right and don't you ever get it twisted again," Malcolm says, transitioning into high-pitched doggie talk. He picks her up and kisses her head. "Miss Doretta is the perfect name. She was old when we got her. Looking like somebody's great-auntie. No teeth, white chin hairs and everything." He adjusts her pearl collar and puts her down. "Don't be shy. Get comfy." Malcolm slides a chair to Jude and the leg breaks off. We all stare at the miserable thing for a beat before bursting into laughter and frightening poor Miss Doretta.

"Anyway," Malcolm says, catching his breath, "we're already running late. Ri, Winnie-Pooh has volunteered to do your makeup."

Malcolm's little sister, Winnie, is thirteen but she's already gathered a solid following on her hair and makeup YouTube channel. I watch in the mirror as she gathers my twists into two space buns and decorates them with gold hair jewelry. After that, she grabs her makeup kit and tells me all about my hooded eyes and warm undertones and low bridge nose. She's clearly an expert, so I submit myself to her creative whims with no hesitation.

For the thirty minutes I sit in Winnie's chair, I imagine she's Tessa. It feels dirty. Like I'm willing her and her sister to swap places. But I'm not. I promise I'm not. It's just that Winnie is now the spitting image of the last memory I have of Tessa's face. Round cheeks. A small beauty mark on her left nostril. Wide-set brown eyes a shade or two lighter than her skin—Malcolm got those, too, but people always talk about how much the girls look alike. I've never seen Winnie take it as anything other than the highest compliment. She was around Jojo's age when Tessa disappeared. Young enough that her big sister was still an idol. Was still who she wanted to be when she grew up, no matter how much they teased each other. The only thing that breaks my fantasy is that I can hear Winnie's needs. Tessa was a vault.

I barely recognize myself when she's done with me and I kind of like it, even though I'm weirdly conscious of every minor movement of my eyeballs. I've never worn false lashes and the two twists Winnie left dangling to "frame my face" keep swinging into my periphery and startling me. They'll be bobby-pinned to my head before the end of the night, so I take a few selfies to preserve the look.

"Girl, if you don't come on!" Malcolm yells from downstairs, where he stands holding the front door open. He wears a chestnut-colored wide-brimmed hat with a poncho of assorted earth tones and ivory pants.

"Will you stop rushing me if I tell you you're beautiful?"

"No, but I'll smile while I do it." And he does, white teeth gleaming against his flawless dark skin as he continues to fuss.

I finish lacing up my pearlescent boots, grab my noise cancelers, and run outside, nearly plowing down Jude. He helps me find my balance, but his hands linger on my upper arms long after I'm steadied.

"Wow," he says, a little breathless.

"Wow yourself," I say, laughing off his intensity, but I mean it. It's the first time I've seen him without his glasses, and he has a cute constellation of dark brown freckles across the bridge of his nose. His curls are popping, too. Hydrated and freshly finger-coiled.

He offers his hand to help me down the front steps, and I wonder how obvious it is that I never wear heels. Not even one-point-five-inch block heels.

"Thanks," I say.

"My pleasure," he replies, grinning like a complete fool.

"Can y'all stop flirting or whatever the hell it is you're doing and get in this car?"

I drop Jude's hand. "Nobody is flirting, Malcolm."

"Speak for yourself," Jude says as he jogs to the driver's seat, leaving a delicate trail of cologne in his wake. He slips on a pair of dark sunglasses once he sits down and I try not to stare at him in the rearview mirror.

It's a quick ride to Deja's place. Malcolm texts her as we pull up outside and catcalls when she appears in the doorway. "Ladies and gentlemen and all the magnificent folks outside of and somewhere in between the binary: Deja Nelson!"

We all hop out of the car as she gives a curtsy in her

platform sneakers. She's adorned her already glorious braids with a flower crown. Her outfit is a white, off-the-shoulders romper that contrasts with her complexion beautifully. A bandanna with QUEEN printed across it in cursive is tied neatly around her neck.

Malcolm goes to her while Jude and I wait by the curb. "Ça va?" He air-kisses her cheeks.

"Bien. Joyeux anniversaire!"

"Merci. You're killing it, as always."

"Y'all take one semester of French together and think you're something special," I shout.

"Maybe, or maybe you are just a hater," Deja says, putting on her best French accent.

Malcolm escorts her across the weedy yard, both looking like Black royalty. As soon as she's in my range, I'm bombarded.

Pepper spray. Pepper spray. Pepper spray.

It puts my stomach on spin cycle. Why the hell would Deja need pepper spray?

When Jude asks her about her sunglasses, I use the opportunity to pull Malcolm to the side.

"Hey, I'm getting a weird need off Dej." I scan our surroundings, like some creep might jump out from behind a bush any second.

"What even qualifies as a weird need?"

"Pepper spray," I say plainly. "It's making me really nervous. Especially after . . . you know."

His eyebrows pinch together like he's trying to figure out a complicated test question. "Pepper spray? As in *back-up-off-me* pepper spray?"

I nod and run my tongue along the back side of my teeth, anxiously fixating on the small gap between the front two.

38

"Mal, maybe we should just go inside her place and chill. We can order pizza."

"Pizza? For my eighteenth birthday? Are you kidding me? Ri, Deja and I have been wanting to go to this festival for years. Half the time people don't even use what you give them in the way you'd expect. What happened Wednesday night is a perfect example."

"Yeah, but—"

"Don't get your panties all bunched up. She'll probably use it to . . . season her food."

I frown. "One, pepper spray is not an aerosol flavor enhancer and two, we're going to a Black music festival. The food is seasoned, Colmy."

"Okay, regarding point one, you've clearly not found yourself deep down into the depths of YouTube at three in the morning."

"Malcolm, I'm serious."

He sighs. "Do you have some on you?"

"Yeah." I turn so he can see Santa Bag perched on my back like a turtle shell. It would never get through the security check, but my plan is to hide it in the woods and jump the blockades to grab it once we're in.

"Well, there you go. Nothing horrible is going to happen while we are all together. Give it to her later and don't make a big deal over it."

I think it over, trying to convince myself he's right. "Okay, but she doesn't leave our sight all night. I'll tell Jude, too."

Malcolm pulls a face like he can't understand why this has me so stressed.

"I can't go if you don't promise."

"Okay, Sariyah, jeez. Buddy system. Scout's honor."

I squint at him. "I know you think scout vests are high

39

fashion, but since you never actually were one, I'm going to need a little something else."

He throws his head back and stomps his foot. "If you don't take this pinky."

He sticks out his little finger and I lock it with mine.

CHAPTER 5

. . . .

Malcolm's a kid at Disney World once we make it to the security check at Hyde Park where the festival is being held. He admires the outfit of every single person in the vicinity, dishing out compliments that make people grin, twirl, and strike poses. He even smiles pleasantly at the bones of a discarded chicken wing and an empty bag of Flamin' Hot Cheetos on the ground. "I love Atlanta." He gives me a hug and a wet kiss on my temple, which I promptly wipe away. "Bless you and that freaky little brain, girl."

Inside the park, the air smells like incense, shea butter, weed, and barbecue. The vibes are everything Malcolm said they would be. Black people showing off the infinite varieties we come in, with an extra-large shout-out to the subcultures you don't often see us represented in, and the ones you do. Punk and hip-hop forced so close together that the line between them blurs. It's everything. Natural hair, relaxed hair, head wraps, and wigs. Bald heads, silk presses, locs, twists, and braids. Hair every color of the rainbow. Outfits equally diverse. Glam and edgy and boho and goth. Everyone so different. Everyone the same. It's all beautiful, but my brain won't let me be great. It won't let me meld with this moment. I slip on my bedazzled noise cancelers, leaving one ear out so I can hear my friends. It defeats the purpose, but I can't relax until I get Deja what she needs—if screeching speakers and the nonstop needs of everyone else is considered relaxing.

Bookmark. Pad. Pepper spray. Spoon. Ice. Safety pin. Charger.

I preemptively pop some migraine meds. It's going to be a long night, but Malcolm's joy, all of theirs, is worth it. "I'm going to grab Santa Bag," I say to the group. I tossed it in some bushes next to a decaying fence behind the food trucks.

"I'll go with you," Jude says. "Probably best if none of us goes our own way."

Deja happily agrees with this, like the rest of us hoped she would.

I take Jude by the hand so we won't get separated in the thick crowd. Once we are in the woods, the sounds from the festival fade and I'm comfortable enough to free my covered ear. "It's way too easy to smuggle stuff into places."

He gives me a goofy smirk.

"What?" I ask with a laugh.

He shrugs, still grinning. "You held my hand."

I snatch up Santa Bag with a snort and check inside to make sure nobody's been snooping. "I didn't hold your hand," I mock. "I was . . . guiding you."

"Same difference." He tucks his thumbs into the front pockets of his black jeans. "You look really nice today."

My stomach does a couple of back handsprings. "You said that already."

"Well, I'm saying it again."

Maybe it's the energy here, but I feel more sure of myself

42

than I have in a long time. "I like it," I say, as I brush by him, heading back for the park.

"You like what?"

"I like it when you tell me I look nice. You clean up well, too."

He looks down at his fit. "Step up from the Sweet Pea's apron?"

"Might be a tie." He looks damn good in that apron and I'm sure he knows it. I turn and walk backward, extend my hand for him to take again. "Come on."

• • •

I fulfill every need I can as Jude and I casually search for Malcolm and Deja. Some people are hesitant to take random offerings from a stranger, but I've gotten pretty good at convincing them to accept. *Your friend dropped this* and *Might come in handy* has been particularly effective today. After a solid thirty minutes of giving and wandering, the stabbing sensation behind my left eye drops from a nine to a somewhat-manageable four. We find our friends near the front of stage two and I stealthily pass off a mint-green key chain pepper spray to Deja. She's confused until I point out the hot-pink one clipped to my belt, which I put there hoping she'd see me as a safety-first friend, and not an ominous, need-fulfilling weirdo. It works.

"Good looking out!" she shouts over the music.

We vibe to a few sets from a couple of artists, then crash the food trucks, each getting something different so we can sample everything. Vegan soul food, fresh beignets, jerk chicken tacos, massive cups of juice and iced herbal teas. I sneak-purchase a decadent-looking banana pudding cupcake and hide it in another bag filled with desserts.

We make a picnic on some fabricated seating. A lady behind Malcolm taps his shoulder and compliments his hat. He compliments her nails and they dive into a conversation about accessories. Perfect timing. I nudge Jude and Deja with my elbows before grabbing the number-shaped birthday candles and lighter I have stashed in Santa Bag. Deja shoves a waxy one and an eight into the whipped cream and I light them while Jude hides our shenanigans with his body. When Malcolm turns back around, we present him with the cupcake and burst out in a chorus of "Happy Birthday"—the classic version immediately followed by the Stevie Wonder version. Random people around us join in and Malcolm is happier than I've seen him in years. He reaches out and grips my hand. The others don't know that Malcolm's favorite cupcake flavor is red velvet. But Tessa, her favorite dessert is banana pudding. And it's her birthday, too. A few fat tears escape his eyes.

"Everything I do is for you, Tess." He mouths the words like a prayer, but I know what he's saying without having to hear it. It's his fifth birthday without her and he's said the same thing every year. He blows out the candles, then plucks a vanilla wafer from the top of the treat and pops it into his mouth.

The sun begins to set, painting the sky my favorite colors. Once it dips below the horizon, Deja and I visit booths with handmade art, jewelry, and hair and skin products, all lit with sparkly colored lights. Strong scents like tea tree oil and sage assault us as I fulfill more random needs. Eventually, Malcolm stands up on a stack of pallets and shouts for us to come back. I don't hear him, but I see his long arms waving us over. Deja grabs my hand and we run back to him and Jude.

"Come on. I want to check out this metal band they've got going up next." Malcolm makes a sign of the horns and sticks out his tongue. No one looks impressed. "Haters. Y'all never heard of faking it till you make it?"

We get a spot right up front. The music begins with a loud squeal from an electric guitar and there is only one need breaking through.

Earplugs. Earplugs. Earplugs.

I rustle through Santa Bag until I find a handful of the squishy orange plugs, then I shove them into each of my friends' ears and into the hands of anyone who will accept them. Once that's taken care of, I join in on the feral jumping and dancing. The music is muted, but the bass pounding through me is a worthy experience. Some people wedge their way between our group, separating the boys and me from Deja, but I can see her long braids whipping through the air as she gives headbanging a go—dozens of golden beacons pinpointing her exact location.

Malcolm fishes her from the crowd when the song ends. She comes out panting, looking happy and so damn full of life. Malcolm leans over and says something in her ear. Her smile breaks briefly, but then she hugs him.

Plate. Bucket. Extension cord. Soap. The needs grow louder now that the live music is paused, but I can't pinpoint any of them. I'm exhausted.

"Sariyah!" Deja whines. It's not the first time she's called me. "You're out there in la-la land while I'm about to pee my pants." She puts her hands over her crotch and mimes an urgent need to go to the restroom. "Come on!"

I tap Jude's shoulder and point to the porta-potties. He gives me a thumbs-up.

The line is tragically long when we get there. This festival has treated my nose to some mysterious scents, but porta-potties have never been anything but up front about exactly what they are. There are ten of them, each with lines at least fifteen deep, and based on the look on her face, it's going to be a long, hard wait for Deja.

She wiggles next to me. "Don't you have to go?"

"I've been limiting the liquids. You see these tights Malcolm talked me into wearing? I don't want to have to roll them down inside one of them cramped, stank things."

She pinches the front of her romper. "At least you don't have to get naked in it!"

I do have to go, actually, but the noise in my head is an endless distraction.

Phone. Hairpin. Potato. Scissors. Aloe vera. Potato. I survey the crowd, trying to figure out who on earth urgently needs a potato, but there's no use. It's dark and almost everyone is drunk or high. Still, it nags at me. *Potato, potato, potato.* In my searching for the source, I notice the line at the end of the row has gotten short.

"Hey, Dej, that line—"

She's not next to me anymore. I scan the lines to my left and right, but she's not there. She's gone. I tear off the noise cancelers, but it only makes my ability to hear worse. Music blasting. People singing. Somewhere, a dog barking. I pound the sides of my head with the heel of my hand, trying to focus. "Deja!" I abandon our place in line. "Deja!" My heart thunders in my chest. I text and call her several times back-to-back but get no response. Maybe someone let her cut them. I wait and watch as person after person leaves the porta-potties. She never emerges. It's possible she couldn't hold it and decided to go in the woods.

I trot over to the trees and call out for her, but there's no answer. This is not good. I need to find Jude and Malcolm. I text them, but my phone dies shortly after. Based on the number of songs that play, way too much time passes. I'm near tears when I hear someone shout my name.

"Sariyah!"

The voice is familiar, but it's not Jude or Malcolm or Deja.

"Sariyah!" Closer this time, but I still don't see whoever it is.

I spin until I make myself dizzy.

A pair of hands grip my upper arms to steady me. "Easy. Are you okay?"

"Nurse Rincon?"

He chuckles. "Don't look so surprised. I have a life outside of East Lake, you know."

I want to hug him. "It's not that. I got separated from my friends. I've been looking for them."

"Yes, sweetie. I could see your distress from well across the way. I'd been purposely keeping my distance before that."

"You saw me earlier?"

"Yes. You and your little friends. I trust you, but I wasn't trying to end up on anyone's socials. I don't think Principal Mayjack is ready for this outfit."

I note his chain mail shirt dotted with decorative pins of Africa, Colombian flags, and . . . herbs and avoid eye contact. "Have you seen them?"

He points. "Over there by the food trucks."

The news is like a shot of espresso straight into my veins. "Thank you, Rincon! See you after break!" I run off before he can even say goodbye.

Sticky with sweat, I crash into Malcolm. "I've been looking for you guys."

"You found us," he says, peeling me from his body.

47

"What happened to you?" I ask Jude. His eyes are watery, red, and puffy.

"Uh"—he scratches his arm—"I partook in some . . ." He pinches his index finger and thumb together and brings them to his mouth.

I roll my eyes. "Well, I guess you and Rincon would make great friends."

He laughs. "Huh? The school nurse? What's that supposed to mean?"

I shake my head. "Nothing at all. Just mildly annoyed that you've been off getting high while I've been worried out of my mind. Where's Deja?"

"What do you mean?" Malcolm asks. "Why are you asking us when she left with you?"

"Nurse Rincon said . . ." I trail off, realizing he never said *who* he saw. My chest constricts, making it difficult to take a complete breath.

"You weren't supposed to leave her alone," Malcolm says. "That was your idea, remember?"

"I didn't," I snap. "She walked off while we were waiting for the toilet. At this point, we should separate and look for her. Give me your spare phone. Mine is dead."

His hand moves to his back pocket, but he hesitates. "My mom found out about it. She took it."

I'd bet my last dollar he's lying to me, but now isn't the time to get into why. "Deja!" I yell as loud as I can.

"I can't believe you let her wander off," Malcolm mumbles.

"I didn't let her do anything, Malcolm. I told you I didn't want to come here! My head is aching. I can't focus on anything and now—"

He jogs off, shouting her name.

"What time is it?" I ask Jude.

48

He checks his watch. "Nine thirty-seven."

My stomach lurches and I sprint in the direction opposite of Malcolm. I call for Deja frantically. A few well-meaning people ask me what's wrong, try to see if they can help, but I can't say anything but her name. I need to find her before ten o'clock. Like some bastardization of Cinderella, I convince myself that if we can just find her before ten, everything will be okay. We have to find her before ten. That hour already took Tessa. It can't take another friend from me.

"Deja!" I scream, dodging thoughts of her fending off an attacker with that pepper spray. I'm so stupid. I got slapped in the face with a red flag the size of my whole body and still let her come.

My bones know as soon as ten o'clock strikes and I beg Tessa for help, something I never do because it makes me feel like she's dead. Like she's high in the sky, able to pull some strings that affect my life. I hate myself for it, but I do it.

The music on stage three cuts, making me freeze in place. "Deja Nelson. Deja Nelson. Your friends are looking for you. Meet 'em at the security tent."

I race for the tent, feet aching. Jude's already there. The all-call was his idea. Malcolm shows up next. Then Rincon. We wait. Two minutes. Five. Ten. I instinctively check my phone over and over, even though it's dead.

"Had she been drinking?" Rincon asks discreetly. "You aren't in trouble. Be honest."

"No," Malcolm answers.

"Okay. Come on, I'll help y'all look."

We search until the crowd thins after the final set and it becomes undeniably clear that Deja is not here.

Jude places a hand on my shoulder. "Maybe she went home."

I shrug him off. "Why would she do that without saying anything?"

"I don't know! But I don't want to assume something horrible happened."

"No," Malcolm says, ready to jump down his throat. "That's exactly what we need to do. We tried that *oh maybe she just* mess with Tess and where'd that get us?"

Jude's face wrinkles. "Who is Tess?"

Malcolm's posture straightens. His fists clench, nails biting pale lines into his palms. Agitation evident in every muscle.

Rincon steps between him and Jude. "Hey, settle down. Take some deep breaths. Go home. See if she is there. If not, have her parents call the police. Just as a precaution. She'll turn up."

We shoot each other anxious glances at the mention of the police. It adds a layer of realness to this situation that I don't want, but she's been gone for hours now. Rincon doesn't even know about the pepper spray and still thinks we might need to get the police involved.

"I have to relieve my son's babysitter," he says. "Do you guys need a ride?"

"No." Malcolm says, refusing to look at anyone.

"Okay. Everything is going to be all right. Let me know when you find her, okay?"

I nod, holding back tears. Rincon gives Jude his number and leaves the park.

"Well, what are y'all waiting for? Let's go." Malcolm storms off, but whips around when he realizes we aren't following him. "We need to go back to her house right now."

"Jude, give me your keys," I say.

"I can drive. It was just weed."

I glare into his bloodshot eyes. "Is that what you're going to say when we get pulled over?"

His expression grows panicked, like he'd forgotten that was even a possibility.

"Forget y'all. We don't have time for this," Malcolm says. "I'll get my own ride."

He disappears into the night.

CHAPTER 6

. . . .

Police cars are already outside Deja's house when I turn Jude's car onto her street. We checked all the fast-food restaurants and convenience stores near the park before coming back. Nothing. No one has seen her.

Jude has tucked himself deep into the passenger seat. "Sariyah, please take me home. I don't do well around cops."

He said the same thing Wednesday night at Sweet Pea's, but I don't want to hear it. "You're so put off by cops that you thought driving high was a good idea. Got it."

"I don't think that. I just—"

"And I'm kind of mad you're more worried about being around cops than you are about where Deja is."

"I'm not, Sariyah." He points at his head. "This stuff just has me paranoid."

He's still talking when I get out of the car and slam the door. I'm not trying to sit around arguing with him.

I only make it halfway down the sidewalk before I have to take the ridiculous boots off my blistered feet. The drive here allowed a horrible ache to set in and I can't take even one more step in them. I walk up to Deja's duplex in my socks. It seems like every light in the entire house is on. A guidepost calling her home.

Malcolm sits on the front porch staring at the ground. He shakes his head when he looks up. A nonverbal request to not mention the only other person who could be at the forefront of both our minds on a night like this. We were still in middle school when Tessa vanished, so the adults didn't share many details. But we know what this is like. Missing someone. Worrying over them. Waiting for them.

"We shouldn't have gone," he says.

"We don't know if not going would have changed anything. How would you feel if we stayed home and this still happened? Then it would have been *Oh, if we'd only gone to the festival.*" I say the words only to comfort him. In reality, I wish with my entire heart that we hadn't gone.

"Her mom wants to file a missing person report," he says, looking over his shoulder and through the storm door.

My breaths come faster, more shallow. "What? Already? I mean, do you think—I thought someone had to be gone for at least twenty-four hours for that."

"Hollywood myth. Plus, she's still a minor. Her stepdad and a couple of officers just drove back down there to see if they can find her. They think maybe she got turned around or made some new friends or something."

I scrunch up my face. "Made some new friends? And what, left with them?"

"I know. That's why her mom wants to go ahead with the report. Deja wouldn't do something like that." He exhales and rests his head in his hands. "You need to go inside and talk to them. You were the last one to see her."

My armpits dampen. "Is that bad? Is it bad I was the last one to see her?"

"No. Just go get it over with. It'll help. They just asked me what she was wearing and stuff."

I open the door and it creaks loudly, causing all eyes—and a smattering of needs—to land on me. Deja's mom, Ms. Jasmine, holds a tissue to her nose. Her eyelids are already swollen from crying. I've never been inside the house. Deja always preferred to meet up at a park or restaurant. It feels so wrong to be in here now. Under these circumstances.

"Hi there, I'm Officer Lucas Penby." A short man in uniform holds out a meaty hand and I shake it weakly. "Are you a friend of Deja's?"

Toothpick. Toothpick. Toothpick.

"Yes, sir."

He smiles kindly and motions toward the dining room, shoving the last remnants of a protein bar into his mouth. The action is so frustratingly casual, like this is just another day at the office for him. And I guess that's because it is.

"Come chat with me," he says. "It won't take long and there's nothing for you to worry about. I'm just going to ask you a few questions that might help me find your friend, okay?"

"Should I call my mom?" I ask, trying to ignore the bit of food trapped next to his upper right canine.

"It's okay, Sariyah. Tell him what you know," Ms. Jasmine pleads, face wet with fresh tears.

I sit across from Officer Penby and he takes out a notepad. "Can I get your full name?"

"Sariyah Lee Bryant."

"Spell that for me."

I do as he asks.

"Got it. Thank you." He clicks the tab on the back of his

pen a few times and smiles again. "Decided to go have some early spring break fun with your friends tonight, huh?"

I look over at Ms. Jasmine, who encourages me as she pops a pill into her mouth and swallows it dry.

"Yes, sir. We went to the Afro Alt Music Festival."

"Any adults go with you?"

"No. I mean, Malcolm turned eighteen today, but no."

Ms. Jasmine cries harder and something about it irks me. I feel bad for wishing she'd go do that somewhere else, but it's hard to talk about Deja when her mother is sobbing like she's never coming back.

"Can you describe what Deja was wearing tonight?" Officer Penby asks.

"She had on a white romper and a bandanna that said 'queen.'" He doesn't look like he even knows what a romper is. "I have pictures."

"Even better. We'll make sure to get those from you." He closes his mouth and runs his tongue across the front of his teeth, makes a loud sucking sound. His need goes silent. "When exactly did you guys lose sight of Deja?"

I swallow hard and can't remember the last time I drank any water. "She had to go to the bathroom. I went with her, but the lines were really long. I zoned out a little and then I couldn't find her. I thought maybe someone let her cut in line, but she never came out."

Officer Penby makes wild scribbles across his paper that surely only he can decipher. "Do you know around what time this was?"

"A few hours ago. Like nine o'clock I think."

He nods. "Did she seem upset at all? Scared? Worried?"

"No," I answer quickly. "She was fine. We were having a good time. She just had to pee."

Friendly crinkles appear next to his eyes. "Music festivals are always a good time." He glances at Ms. Jasmine, then lowers his voice a bit. "Do you know if Deja maybe did anything to enhance the fun?" He raises his eyebrows suggestively.

"No, she didn't do anything like that." I think of Jude's red eyes and loopy smile. I don't think she did anything. It didn't seem like it. I had eyes on her most of the night. But she did go off with Jude once. And once with Malcolm, too. I force my brain to replay those moments by the porta-potties. Did she seem sober? I'm not sure anymore.

"Don't worry," Officer Penby says. "None of you will get in trouble if she did. We just want to make sure we get her home safe."

I sink into my seat, fiddling with the pendant on my necklace. "I mean, I don't know for sure, but I don't think so."

He presses the button on the back of his pen again and scoots back his chair. "Okay, Sariyah. Thank you so much. The information you provided was very helpful. That's all I need from you for now. Wasn't too bad, was it?"

"No, sir. But um . . ." I tug at a twist by my ear.

"Yes?"

"I—I gave her some pepper spray earlier." I take off mine and slide it across the table. "Like this, but light green."

He jots this information down. "You're a good friend. I'm sure it gives you peace of mind to know she has something to protect herself with."

It doesn't. Not when I could have prevented her from needing to protect herself at all. "Are you guys going to find her?"

"I bet she'll turn up any minute now, but until then, I assure you we've got the best people on the job. But let me have another chat with her mom here. I'm sure your own mother will be expecting you home soon."

He's right. I slip out of the room and back onto the porch where Malcolm still sits.

"How was it?" he asks.

"I told him about the pepper spray."

"Guessing you left out a few details."

"I don't think making him doubt my sanity would help matters."

He puts his hand on the back of his neck and rolls it until it cracks. "Probably not. You about to drive Jude home?"

"Is he still here?" I step off the stoop and look down the street. Sure enough, his stupid little car is still sitting there. "Call me if you hear anything, Colmy."

I head off down the sidewalk and wait for a car to pass so I can cross the road. A moth flutters around the streetlight and the crooked sign on the corner catches my eye. Irvine Street. I study it, trying to figure out why it has grabbed my attention now when I've probably seen it a hundred times. I take a steadying breath and step off the curb.

Then I remember.

Danny Irvine. The man who attacked Ms. Jess. His name was familiar because my most notorious gnat, Phillip, has mentioned it before. Now with both their faces floating in my mind, I see the resemblance. Danny is Phillip's brother. I don't know if it counts for much, but he always spoke so kindly of him. I look up at the sign again. As annoying as Phillip is, or was—I haven't seen him in months—something about the connection makes me feel like there might be more to what happened that night at Sweet Pea's. And if this night has taught me anything, it's that I should trust my intuition.

"Any news?" Jude asks when I get in the car.

"You'd know if you came in."

He hangs his head and shoves his fingers into his now puffy curls.

"I'm sorry," I say with a deep exhale. "The police seemed chill, but I guess that's how they're supposed to seem. They think she got lost or met someone, but I don't know. What if she's hurt or something? What if—"

"It's probably best not to play the what-if game. The police and her family will contact all the local hospitals. But if you want, I can check with my mom. She's working right now."

I forgot she works at the hospital. "Could you?"

"Sure."

He types out a long text. Moms need details if you're hitting them up to ask if your friend has shown up in the emergency room.

"Do you think you could get me in there?"

"In where? The hospital?"

"Yeah."

"My mom hasn't even texted back yet."

"It's not that, and I don't mean right now." I nibble at my thumbnail. "I need to talk to Danny Irvine and I assume he doesn't have the same visitation rights as everyone else."

"Danny Irvine as in that dude Ms. Jess stabbed at Sweet Pea's?"

"Yes. Can you make it happen?" Because maybe if I talk to him, maybe if I find out he truly deserved what happened, it'll relieve me of this sense that I'm cursed or something. Cursed in a way that makes people get stabbed. Cursed in a way that made my friend disappear. And I don't know, maybe my ability has always been connected to things like this. But if so, I would have been happy to be kept in the dark.

• • •

58

Mama opens the door before I even get my key in the lock. She yanks me into a hug so hard it knocks the breath from me.

She presses her palms to my cheeks, scanning my body, looking for anything amiss. "I fell asleep and woke up at half past midnight to a dozen missed calls from Deja's and Malcolm's parents. Your phone was going straight to voicemail." She lets go of my face and places one hand over her heart. "Terrified me."

"I'm fine." A lump forms in my throat.

She leads me to the couch and makes me tell her everything, even though it's clear the important parts have already been relayed. This time I can't get through it without tears.

She squeezes my hands. "Don't worry, baby. I'm sure she'll turn up home any minute now."

The more people say that, the harder it is to believe. Because time keeps passing and Deja still hasn't turned up.

Mama stands and rubs her hands down her torso, trying to smooth the wrinkles in her Wilhem Hotel polo. "She will come home, but you won't see her all spring break because she'll be on punishment for a month."

I wipe my tears and laugh a little at that, but it's hollow. I don't share my mother's confidence, if it's even real. Something is wrong. The question is, how wrong?

Jojo's standing in the hallway when I head for my bedroom. "Eavesdropping is rude."

"I wasn't. I was going to the bathroom."

"The bathroom is behind you." I move past him and into my room. He follows.

"You guys were talking too quietly for me to hear. What's going on? What happened?"

"Sorry our private conversation was too quiet for you." I plop down on the foot of my bed.

59

"You never tell me anything."

I rub my forehead and look up at him. I don't want to tell him because I don't want to worry him, but he's already looking around wide-eyed, anxiously shifting from left foot to right. "One of my friends, Deja, you've met her—"

"Yeah, I know Deja. She always gives me watermelon Sour Patch Kids."

"That sounds right. Well, Deja . . . got lost at the music festival."

"Got lost?"

"Yes. And I don't really want to talk about it because it makes me sad, okay?"

Josiah twists his bottom lip with his index finger and thumb, thinking. He disappears and returns with Tibby, the stuffed pig I let him adopt from me during a rough thunderstorm when he was six. "I don't need it anymore. You can have it back."

I reach for the pig and pull Josiah to me in the process. I squeeze his fat head, dropping tears all over him. He squirms and struggles for a few seconds before succumbing and accepting my rarely provided physical affection. We stay like that for a solid minute before I playfully push him away. "Get out of my room."

He goes but leaves Tibby behind.

I plug my phone into the charger and will it to light up with a call or text from Deja. I'm too scared to reach out to her again. Too scared she'll try me at the exact moment I try her and she won't get through. Too scared that this time will be the time it goes straight to voicemail. That it'll mean her phone has died. That she has no way of getting help if she needs it.

I open my laptop and DM Jude.

Me: I feel like I'm stuck in a really, really bad dream.

Part of me feels guilty for choosing him over Malcolm, but I'm worried I don't have the words to interact with Malcolm tonight. This will hit differently for him, after Tessa. Shame washes over me because I know, as his best friend, I should try. But I hope, as my best friend, he won't knock me for waiting until morning. And maybe, hopefully, by then, there won't be anything to discuss.

Jude: Not gonna lie, the police being involved is scary af, but it's a better safe than sorry thing, right?
Me: I don't know.

And I don't know if his hang-up about the police has to do with his lingering high, or genuine concern over Deja. Not that I think he's some empathy-lacking jerk, but he doesn't know her like Malcolm and I do. He hasn't been here before, like Malcolm and I have. And maybe that's part of the disconnect here.

Me: If this goes on beyond tonight, there are things you need to know that I don't have the capacity to explain to you right now. I'm going to send you a link. I don't want to talk about it. I don't want to answer questions. I don't want condolences or encouraging words, okay?
Jude: Okay.
Me: www.findcontessahawkins.org

I push my laptop aside and pull the covers over my head. The DMs lead me into a lucid dream. Tessa sits beside me, singing and painting her toenails. She wears a stretchy tie-dyed headband with her hair in a high puff as big as her head. She hasn't visited me in a while, but I knew she'd come tonight. She speaks to me, but the words are always recycled parts of old conversations that long ago ingrained themselves into my memory. My best friend turned Magic 8 Ball, dishing out canned responses.

Usually, I'd draw the dream out by exchanging pleasantries and small talk, but tonight I'm frustrated and anxious. Tonight, I want answers.

"Where are you, Tess?" It's not the first time I've asked, and like every other time, I still hope for a fresh response. A combination of words I've never heard. Something new and valuable. "Where are you, Tess? I need you."

She disappears and the sound of her giggles echoes across the room. *"You're getting warmer! Follow Miss Doretta."* We were twelve then. A little old to still be playing hide-and-seek, but the Hawkins family had just moved into their current house. It was cavernous and full of boxes and begging us to indulge in a childhood favorite.

"Are you safe, Tess? Are you alive?" I try instead.

The room warps around us until it's the best replica of Mr. Frank's middle school English class my memory can cook up.

"You ask too many questions, you know that? You probably wouldn't even hear the answers if someone gave them because you're too busy thinking up the next question." That one was from sixth grade—when the needs got louder and more persistent and school got harder. I'd realized running my mouth helped quiet things in my head. I didn't want to get in trouble for talking to other kids, so I'd ask my teachers questions incessantly. Tessa's comment had hurt my feelings at the time. Mostly because it was true.

"Something bad happened today. Bad things happened this week."

"Tell me the good news first." I used to tease her about that. Why would anyone take the good news first, only to be sent crashing back down to Earth after?

I think and think, desperate for something positive to share. But before I can come up with anything, Tessa dissolves into blackness.

CHAPTER 7

· ·

A car alarm wakes me in the morning and I am immediately pummeled by scenes from last night. My chest is tight and my legs are sweaty under my sheets. I kick them off and reach for my buzzing phone, accidentally yanking the charger from the wall.

Malcolm
Are you up?

Me
Yeah. Anything??

Typing bubbles appear and disappear three times before another text comes through.

Malcolm
She's still not home.

A rush of anger courses through me—an emotion I don't really mess with—and I'm surprised to find it directed at

Deja. Like she's done this on purpose. Like she's playing some awful joke.

"Hey, Siri, call Deja," I say into my phone like I have countless times before. Like doing this perfectly boring, typical, average little thing might set everything back in order.

"Calling Deja, mobile."

It goes straight to voicemail and I think I might vomit. She was obviously going to get into some kind of trouble and I let her speed straight for it. I didn't even let her decide for herself. I pace around my room, fidgeting with things, making a mess. I can't stay in this house all day. For once, I want to be around people. I want the noise of their needs to fill my brain and distract me because this silence, this waiting, will eat me alive. And if the waiting doesn't do it, I'll do it myself. My fingernails are chewed ragged. I reach for the emery board nail file on my dresser and pause once it's in my grasp. It's time to visit Danny Irvine.

Jude picks me up thirty minutes later. He reaches across the passenger seat to open the door for me. The moment I glimpse his face, I know he's viewed the link I sent. He saw the elementary school pictures of me and Tessa. The newborn photos of her and Malcolm. The grainy convenience store security photo of her and a stranger. Most likely the same stranger she'd been secretly chatting with online for three months. Time stamp, 10:00 P.M. Six hours after she failed to show up home from school.

"Still no word on Deja?" he asks.

"No." I'm grateful he stuck to our agreement from last night, but I'm not in the headspace to talk about Deja, either. "How's this going to work?"

"You're lucky Danny's in my mom's department, or this might be harder. Helps that it's early in the day, too. I bought her and her coworkers breakfast. If there are no emergencies, that'll distract them for a few. But you better hope there's not an officer posted at his door." He puts the car in drive.

The lobby of the hospital is deserted, except for a security guard outside of my range. We take the elevator to the eighth floor. Once we start passing patient rooms and hospital workers, needs creep into my mind. I welcome them like a six-year-old welcomes a cold glass of Kool-Aid after playing outside all day.

Coffee. Insoles. Cigarette. Coffee. Pen. Contact solution.

I don't have time to run in and out of hospital rooms fulfilling needs, and I don't feel guilty about it. If something bad happens to someone here, there are people trained to help them who have real medical instruments and medicines. They won't need my janky solutions.

We come up on a nursing station where a pretty woman with short cropped, bleach-blond coils types on a computer. She couldn't deny that Jude's her son if she wanted to. He stole her whole face, right down to the freckles across her nose.

"There's my mom. Try that way first." He points down the hall and I dip off in that direction.

"Got you guys those grits you love from the Ornery Omelet!" I hear him say. His mom and a few other people squeal in the distance.

I focus on the needs as I slip by each room, looking for a sign that Danny may be nearby.

807 Tennis ball.

808 Paintbrush.

809 Tweezers.

In the end, it's not a need that clues me in. It's a disposable coffee cup and chair outside room 817 that I can only assume had been occupied by a cop. One that may return any minute. I slip into the room without knocking.

A solidly built, salt-and-pepper-haired white man with a short beard looks up from a magazine. Danny. "Was wondering when you'd come see me."

"You—you remember me?" I stay close to the door.

"Not from that night, if that's what you're thinking. But Philly said you'd put two and two together eventually. Said you were smart like that." His voice is deep, with a strong southern drawl, so different from his brother's high-pitched twang.

I scratch the crook of my arm nervously. "You wouldn't say that if you saw my grades."

"What's grades got to do with smarts?" he asks seriously. But then he winks and waves me over. "I don't bite."

I keep my feet firmly planted where they are. "Why did you attack Ms. Jess?"

"Straight to the point, I see." He adjusts himself in bed so he is sitting up straighter. "I think you know I didn't attack her. You wouldn't be here if you thought I did."

"Then what happened?"

He takes a deep breath, like he's preparing for a long story. "Philly's rheumatism has been acting up. It's been hard for him to get around. Been stuck in the house, mostly."

That'd explain why I haven't seen him in a few months.

"I been taking care of him. You know, grabbing groceries, picking up prescriptions and such. Well, a few weeks ago he starts carrying on about this psychic at the ice cream shop he used to go see. I thought he was bored and telling stories like he tends to do. But he got himself all worked up thinking if he could go see her, she'd give him exactly what he needed to get better." He scoots himself a little higher up the bed and winces. "Pass me that water, will ya?"

My wariness is dumb. The man can barely keep himself upright. I give him his water and he guzzles it, wiping his mouth with the back of his hand when he finishes.

"I told Philly I wasn't hauling his ass out the house and into my truck to go talk to no ice cream psychic. Told him he didn't need to make up such wild tales to get a scoop of Gelato Fun. But his birthday came around and being the thoughtful older brother I am, I stopped by Sweet Pea's after work to pick him up something special." He wags his finger at me. "I seen you straight away. You looked exactly like he described—lots of hair, big old headphones—only he ain't say you were just a kid. My brother's a kind soul. Wouldn't hurt a fly. Wouldn't think a mean or wrong thing about nobody. But it makes him naive. He wouldn't even fathom it. What some folks would think about him approaching you so often."

He pauses when my phone dings.

Jude
Everything okay? You find him?

Me
Yeah. Room 817.

I return my attention to Danny. "Sorry about that."

He bats his hand at me. "Anyway, Philly's always watching this old sitcom about a teen psychic. Black girl, like you. I was standing there in line wondering if I needed to get the man some professional help. He done convinced himself the show was real!" He laughs, but it instantly turns into a painful coughing fit.

I pour him some more water.

He takes a minute to recover before continuing his story.

"I thought my brother had finally taken a dive off the deep end, but then I saw you give a little boy a whistle with his ice cream. I stepped outside and not two minutes later, that little boy's dog tugged free of his leash and darted out into the street. It was fixing to get run over, but the boy blew that whistle and it froze in place. Froze right as a car sped by in the other lane. I might have thought it was a coincidence or the hand of God himself if Philly hadn't told me the things he did. That's when I knew you could help him."

"I'm not a psychic, Danny."

He smiles and his eyes sparkle a bit. "I ain't got no fancy degree or nothing like that, but I'm sure this is what they call 'semantics.'" He winks. "It was busy at the shop that day, so I figured I'd come back during a slow evening when I could talk to you without holding up the line. But the night I came, y'all had closed up early. Philly'd had a bad day, and I didn't want to put it off any longer, so I decided to wait in my truck until you came out. Plus, I swear I seen some weirdo creeping round back by the fence. Y'all need to replace the security light back there. Would do many people some good." He touches the bandage on his neck. "Anyway, I'd had a hard day myself and ended up dozing off. Wasn't until Ms. Jess pulled into the parking lot that I woke up. I figured that was my chance and hurried out the car to catch her before the door wound up shut in my face, but I frightened her. I frightened her real bad. Her shouting and carrying on—it made me nervous, you know. I just wanted her to settle down, but everything I tried worked her up more. In the confusion, she caught sight of my gun and well. You know what happened from there."

"Do the police believe you?" It wouldn't surprise me if they do. There's something likable about him. He's got a trustworthy vibe for someone who allegedly threatened a tiny, middle-aged woman with a gun.

"Lived here my whole life. No record. Licensed to carry. Ms. Jess don't got a visible wound to speak of. My lawyer thinks I'll be fine. Thinks I could press charges on *her*. But I'm content to drop it all. Here's hoping she will be, too."

"I gave her the nail file." Word vomit. It comes out without any preemptive thought, and I don't know why.

He studies me. "Well, ain't that something?"

"Danny, like I said, I'm not a psychic. What I do—it's not always right. It doesn't always make sense."

"Or maybe it does. Maybe I would have hurt her," he says matter-of-factly.

"You just said—"

"Maybe not on purpose. But maybe it would have happened. Maybe you stopped it."

I gesture to his neck. "Pretty violent solution."

He grins. "Just a scratch. Would have been out by now if it hadn't gotten infected."

"Well, I feel like I should apologize or something."

"No, no. Never that, but I may take you up on the *or something*."

"You want me to go see Philly."

He places his hand on his chest. "We'd both appreciate it."

"Danny, there's no guarantee I have something that will help the way he expects or wants. Both of you need to understand that."

"Sure, of course. But you stopping by will at least lift his spirits some, and that's worth plenty."

I take out my phone. "What's his address?"

"402 Milner Place, Atlanta."

I type it into my Maps app and the red target centralizes

almost directly on top of Hyde Park, where Afro Alt was held. My hand trembles as I try to contain my shock. "Thanks for talking with me."

"Nothing but a thing. You take care."

"You too." On my way out, I place a fly swatter on his bedside table.

Jude's in the hall waiting, back against the wall, one foot propped up. "Figured I'd keep a lookout. How'd it go?"

"Fine. I think the whole thing was a misunderstanding, but he did tell me something kind of strange. Maybe coincidental. Will you drive me somewhere? I'll explain on the way."

"Sure. Where to?"

I hold up my index finger and glance down at my ringing phone. "One second, it's Malcolm—hello?"

"Turn on the news."

I pop back into Danny's room. "Hey, can I use your TV for a minute?" I ask, a little breathless.

"Be my guest." He points to the remote sitting on his breakfast tray.

Jude hovers behind me as I turn it on and flick through the stations. When I get to channel 2, we are greeted by Deja's senior photo.

CHAPTER 8

· ·

We missed most of the news report, so Jude drives us straight to Malcolm's. I enter through the front door without ringing the bell like I have so many times before, but this time I find a dozen people gathered around the coffee table holding hands. Malcolm's parents are rarely home. He says they work hard to pay for a house they never spend any time in. He says work and providing a comfortable life for him and Winnie has been their get-out-of-parenting-free card ever since Tessa disappeared. I think it's partly why he rejects most of the material things they try to provide. If he doesn't want them, doesn't need them, doesn't use them, what excuse do they have then? But they're here today. Solemn faced, eyes closed, and heads bowed. Mr. Hawkins leads the group in prayer, his wife to his left, and Derrick, Deja's stepdad, to his right.

"And we ask you, Father God, protector of the helpless, be with Deja. Guide her safely back to us."

Malcolm leans against the large kitchen island, looking on, arms crossed, jaw set. I lock eyes with him and point upstairs.

He meets us in his bedroom a couple of minutes later. "I

ain't mad at them for praying. I just don't know why they can't do it in the car on the way to search for her. They're wasting valuable time. My parents know that. They've been through this. That's why everyone is here."

"Malcolm, what happened?" Deja making the news might mean we find her sooner, but there's a reason they are running the story when she's been gone less than a day. And I know it's not a good one.

He squats down onto his faux-fur footstool. "They found something."

"Found what?" Jude asks hesitantly.

"Police went back out to the festival site this morning to search in the daylight. One of them found her phone in the woods. It was dead. Screen smashed." He gnaws at his bottom lip. "They also found that pepper spray you gave her, Ri."

"Can they tell if she used it?" I ask.

He rubs the heels of his palms over his denim-covered thighs. "Yeah."

My nose burns and Jude looks between Malcolm and me like he's missing something. "Okay, they can tell, but did she? Did she use it?" he asks.

Malcolm's nod is almost imperceptible. No one speaks for over a minute, but the room is loud. The reality of what this might mean screams. It rages. Bouncing from wall to wall, knocking the breath from each of us as it goes.

Jude speaks first. "It's good that she made the news, though, right? Getting the media involved will help."

"One would hope," Malcolm says. "But they didn't even pick the story up on their own. As soon as the police had a reason to suspect foul play, my dad reached out to his media contact on behalf of Deja's mom, Ms. Jasmine."

"That's great," Jude says. "Not everyone who goes missing knows someone who knows someone."

Malcolm gives a sarcastic snort, then mumbles, "Right. Too bad Dad didn't know this lady when it might have helped his own daughter." He clears his throat, then speaks at a normal volume. "She said it might be to Deja's advantage that this happened at such a well-known event. Might be able to get the organizers to make a statement. They have reach." He studies the dusty picture of him and Tessa on his windowsill. It seems to strike some fury in him, some energy. "We have to get this to go viral. That's how we find her quick. And we have to find her quick. I already drafted up some posts for all the socials. If y'all don't have accounts everywhere, make them. Even Facebook. It's mostly old folks on there, but them aunties and godmommies know how to hit that share button. We should make posters, too. Hard copies and digital. Be useful, you know. The whole nation needs to be shouting 'Find Deja' ASAP."

I frown, and Malcolm cocks his head to the side.

"I'm sorry," I say. "There's just something really foul about reducing her to a hashtag."

"No, what's foul is girls who never come home," he retorts. "The hashtag worked for Casey. We need to do whatever it takes to get Deja's name out there. We can't rely on anyone to care as much as we do."

No one mentions the elephant in the room, which is that yes, the country rallied for Casey, but it didn't save her life. Part of me wondered if all the noise might have actually been the thing that led to her murder, but the autopsy showed she was killed the night she went missing. Which also provides no comfort in this situation.

"Hopefully this is over and Deja's home before we have to

worry about anything going viral." Jude takes his glasses off and rubs his eyes. The skin around them is red. I'm not sure if it's because he's emotional, or if it's been like that all day. Since last night.

There's a knock on Malcolm's door and his mom lets herself in. "Hey, you guys. Officer Penby said they've already faxed the missing person information along with Deja's photo to all the local precincts." Malcolm opens his mouth, but she cuts him off with a quickness. "I'm not saying y'all can't make your posters. The more we can get her face out there, the better. Just letting you know. The detective on her case is named Habib." She puts a business card on Malcolm's dresser. "Run anything you make by him first. There are certain things they don't want the public to know."

"Yes, ma'am," Malcolm answers.

I glance at him, silently asking permission to engage his mother in conversation. He picks up his laptop and I take it as a go-ahead. "Do you know anything else? Malcolm told us what they found this morning, but that's not enough to assume something bad happened, is it?"

"Assume the worst and hope for the best is never more relevant than with a missing child."

"I know, but other than the phone and pepper spray, do they have actual reasons to assume the worst?" The panic building inside me makes the words come out sharp and impatient. "Sorry. It's just that this went from she'll-turn-up-soon to suspected-foul-play so fast. How do we know something else wasn't going on with her? Maybe Penby was on to something."

Malcolm scoffs. "You know Deja better than that. She didn't run off with some stranger she met last night."

"No, I don't mean that. But like, maybe there was something going on at home. Maybe she ran away."

75

"Did she seem like she wanted to run away to you?" He leans forward, one brow raised. "Is that what you were thinking about Tess? Were you secretly agreeing with the cops when they wasted time spinning that bs about her being a troubled kid who 'wanted space' from her family?"

I narrow my eyes at him. "Don't. Don't act like these two things are the same. Deja and Tessa are different people."

"But will the police see them that way? Or will they see just another missing Black girl? You sure you want this runaway narrative escaping your mouth?"

"I just want hope, Malcolm! We know barely anything and everyone seems to be jumping straight to worst-case scenarios. I want to be sure there isn't something we're missing. *This time* I want to be sure there isn't something we're missing."

He concedes, for now, with a slight nod. It's always zero to one hundred and back with him.

Mrs. Hawkins places her hand on my upper back. Gives it a consoling rub. "I hear you, sweetheart. But you know the cops aren't going to share every little thing they know with us. The best we can do is cooperate with them and control the things we can control."

Malcolm fails to keep his expression neutral at that.

"Do we have a problem?" Mrs. Hawkins asks her son, hands on her hips, locs swaying with the sharp movement of her head.

He rolls his lips together and releases them with a small smack. "No, ma'am."

She pauses to make sure before slowly turning her attention back to us as a group. "Now, I came up here because Derrick told me they found something else at the scene. A brush. Her mother didn't recognize it. They can run DNA, but it'll take a while. White and red. Cartoon cat on it. Sound familiar?"

Jude fidgets next to me, still messing with his eyes, with hands that I now notice are just as irritated.

"No," Malcolm answers resolutely enough for all three of us.

"Well, look, all of you are going to need to go up to the station to give formal statements. I've called your mothers. Told them you were here and that I'll drive. Give me a few minutes to get ready." She excuses herself.

"You probably want to start talking right now," I say to the floor.

"Huh?" Malcolm rummages through a basket of clean laundry.

"Not talking to you."

"You gave it to me." Jude's voice is barely a whisper as he makes the revelation.

"What the hell are y'all talking about?" Malcolm asks, shaking out a wrinkled T-shirt.

"Look at his face. It's all red," I say, gesturing toward Jude. "Look at his hands. They weren't like that until last night."

Malcolm laughs out loud but stops when neither of us joins in. "Sariyah. Come on now. What are you saying? You think Jude attacked Deja? Mama, I promise you he didn't. I do want to know why he isn't more upset about the accusation, though." He crosses his arms, tilts his head to the side, and waits for Jude to explain.

"Because I know it looks bad. It looks like I got pepper sprayed in the face."

Malcolm laughs again. "Y'all are really serious? Listen, Ri, that stuff wears off in like twenty minutes. The boy smoked some good herb last night and frankly, I don't blame him if he smoked some more this morning." He looks at Jude's hands. "And that's just . . . eczema?"

"Were you with him?" I ask. "When he was supposedly smoking at the festival?"

"No, but—"

"But you screamed at me for leaving Deja alone, when you two didn't even hold up your end of the deal?"

The muscles in Malcolm's neck go stiff and he speaks slowly. "Okay, but we weren't the ones generating needs that made it seem like we were about to get jumped or something."

"Maybe you were! I can't hear your needs!" Tears drip from my eyes. "I worry about all of you. Constantly." I turn to Jude. "And I don't know why. I don't know why my brain decided you were something special because you're a liar. You didn't smoke anything, did you?"

"Ri, I swear to God I was high out of my mind. It's why I didn't realize I was sitting in a bunch of poison ivy while I was smoking. When I stood up it got all on my hands, then I rubbed my face and . . ." He shrugs. "I was embarrassed."

I cross my arms. "Why don't you tell us both how Deja got your brush?"

Realization spreads across Malcolm's face. "You have a brush with a cartoon cat on it?"

"Yes," I answer for him. "I know because I gave it to him. Need fulfillment. The only need of his I ever clearly heard. The first night we met."

"I had it in my pocket. Leaned against a brick wall and it snapped in half. Probably would have cracked my phone screen if it weren't in there, so . . . thanks. Deja snatched the half I pulled out to touch up her edges."

"Where's the rest of it?"

He reaches into his pocket and pulls out the other half of the brush, palm sweaty. "I know how it looks."

"It don't look like nothing," Malcolm says. "It's not weird to let your friend borrow your brush and I'm sure a doctor can confirm you've got poison ivy."

"If that's the truth, it'd look a mess of a lot better if you explain it all to the police before they have to ask," I say.

"What if they don't believe me?" He looks like he might puke.

I want to tell him he has nothing to fear if he has nothing to hide, but Black boys, even Spanish speaking light-skinned ones like Jude, even in the city of Atlanta with a bunch of Black cops, are smart to be wary of the police.

"What if they don't believe me?" he asks again, more urgently. "You don't even believe me!"

I press my thumb and index finger to my forehead and close my eyes, exhale deeply. "I do believe you, Jude, and we'll be there to support you." I feel bad for getting him worked up, but I don't apologize. I truly don't think he had anything to do with whatever has happened to Deja, but I have a good sense for when people are keeping things from me and he is lighting it up. And if I'm honest, Malcolm is, too. But he has an excuse. As her best friend in the entire world, Tessa's disappearance crushed me. But Malcolm shared a womb with her. There are layers to his hurt I'll never be able to access. This situation is both devastating and triggering.

"Jude, let's take your car and go down to the station right now," I say. "Your mom is probably already there. You should talk through it with her before we go in." I turn to Malcolm. "We'll meet you and your mom there, okay? We can work on the posters as soon as we get back."

CHAPTER 9

· ·

We pull up to the precinct and Jude's mother is by the car before he can even get the door open. She pulls him into a hug, then steps back and grabs his chin, looking him directly in the eye. "Everything is going to be okay." She glances at me, then looks back to her son. "Come talk to me for a minute." She leads him by the wrist, both disappearing behind an overgrown bush.

Mama waits for me by the door. She's working a night shift and should be asleep right now, and it shows in the form of dark circles under her eyes. She has no words of encouragement for me, but I don't need them. She's here. I know how hard it is for her to get out of bed some days, but she's here. That's enough.

Once Malcolm and his mother arrive, we all go inside together. Ms. Jasmine is in the lobby speaking with an officer but stops midsentence when she sees us. Her eyes narrow, and she charges straight for us, teeth bared. The aggression is jarring. She wasn't like this last night.

"I ought to beat each and every one of y'alls asses!" she screams, jabbing a finger in our faces. A few people in the waiting area gasp as the officer grips her shoulder, easily holding back her small frame. She's sweaty and shaky like she exercised on an empty stomach, but the only need coming off her is for painkillers. I don't offer any. There is nothing in Santa Bag that could ease her pain.

"How could you leave my baby out there?" Ms. Jasmine cries. I don't know if it means something that she looks directly at me when she says it. "How could you leave her all alone?" She begins to outright wail. Maybe it's my own defensiveness, but there's something off about it. Something put on.

"They found blood out in them woods," she sneers in between sobs.

"Blood?" My mouth forms the word but no sound escapes my lips. "B-blood?" I stammer.

Jude's skin takes on a grayish hue as the officers usher Ms. Jasmine down the hall.

"Still want to convince them she ran away?" Malcolm asks with a nasty scowl. His voice is like nails on a chalkboard, instantly enraging me.

"Shut the hell up, Malcolm. Shut—"

"Hey!" our mothers scream all at once.

Mrs. Hawkins gets in her son's face. "We ain't doing that. Not now. Not ever. Go sit your ass down. All of you."

We take a seat on the old orange terry cloth chairs, our heads bowed in shame.

Mrs. Hawkins straightens her shirt. "Now, I didn't want to mention it at the house because I didn't want to get y'all worked up before we know all the facts. Yes, they found some blood. We don't even know if it's hers, but even if it is—babies, it wasn't much. You hear me? Not enough to start catastrophizing."

No one speaks.

"I said, do you hear me?" Mrs. Hawkins's tone is even sharper now.

"Yes, ma'am," we all mumble.

"What we not gon do"—she pauses to look at my mom and Jude's mom—"is tolerate y'all fighting among yourselves. You think Deja wants that? Huh? You think that's helpful?"

"No, ma'am."

"I'm sorry," Malcolm whispers to me, head still bowed.

"Me too," I say, even though I don't feel ready to.

We all sit in silence for over half an hour before two different detectives come out. One takes Jude, the other takes Malcolm. Their mothers go with them and I'm left waiting. I get one last glimpse of Jude's red, irritated hand before he disappears into a private room.

I want to believe Jude's story, but I'd be lying if what Ms. Jasmine said didn't arouse new suspicion in me. I take out my phone, careful to angle it so Mama can't see, and deep dive into Google searches about pepper spray and poison ivy. A small bit of relief washes over me when I read that Malcolm was right about how long the effect of pepper spray lasts—until I find some images on Reddit of someone who had an allergic reaction to it. The pictures are indistinguishable from a reaction to poison ivy. People in the comments even suggest the original poster made up their story about pepper spray and rolled around in the woods somewhere.

I switch gears, this time typing *Jude Abrams* into the search bar. Of course, I get nothing. His name isn't unique enough. I try *Jude Abrams Florida*. There's an obituary for someone named Desiderio Moreno. The Google preview says he leaves behind his sons, Joaquin and Elian Moreno, his daughter-in-law Evie Abrams-Moreno, and his grandson Jude Moreno.

I know this is Jude's family. Coincidences don't come in this size. But it doesn't have to mean he is hiding some horrible secret. His parents are probably divorced. Maybe it was ugly and he wanted to take his mom's name. Or maybe not. I erase Abrams from the search bar and replace it with Moreno. There's a hit on a Jude Moreno in the news section. An article about some school fight gone wrong. But it was in Texas, not Florida. My thumb hovers over the link, but before I tap it, Detective Habib calls my name. I wonder how odd it is to be relieved by his timing. To be more eager to discuss Deja's disappearance with a detective than to potentially uncover some ugly truth about my new friend. A new friend I never asked for, but one my brain—with no good reason—has categorized with the un-rivaled likes of Malcolm, Tessa, and my need-silent family.

Detective Habib welcomes Mama into the small room with me. He offers us drinks and snacks and assures us over and over that I'm not in trouble, that he just wants to make sure they have every piece of information that might help them find Deja. I offer him a stain remover pen from Santa Bag. His questions aren't much different from Officer Penby's last night and despite his assurances, I wonder if he's asking me the same ones to see if I still have the same answers. He gives me his card so I can contact him if I think of anything else worth sharing.

"Text your father," Mama says as soon as we're done. "He's worried about you." There's a familiar detachment in her voice. I would recognize even the faintest hint of it, but it's not faint at all today.

"Yes, ma'am." I sound young and eager to please. A pattern I slip into whenever I sense her falling. It never keeps her above water, but I'll probably always try. "Thank you for going in with me."

"I'm your mother, Sariyah. You expected me to sit on my behind at home while you got questioned by the police?"

"No, I mean—I'm glad you're here."

She places her hand on my back, directing me down the hall, and sighs. "I know what you meant, baby. I'm sorry. I can't believe we're going through this again. I don't even know what to say to Jasmine. She's inconsolable."

It's probably best if she says nothing to her. There aren't words for these sorts of things.

We make it back to the lobby, but Jude and Malcolm haven't come back out yet. "Can we wait for them?" I ask Mama.

"No telling how long they'll be. I'm tired and I need to pick up a prescription for your brother. Let's get going."

· · ·

Mama parallel parks outside Chapman's Pharmacy and I jog across the street to the entrance. My stomach knots up when I see the windows have already been tagged with Deja's missing posters. This is real.

I pull open the door and the little bell above it dings. *Drinking straw. Drinking straw. Drinking straw.* A tired-looking Nurse Rincon waves at me as he bags some cough syrup for the person at the counter. He works here part-time. The customer leaves and I snatch a bag of paper straws from the shelf and place it in his outstretched hand.

"A blessing from you to me. Thank you."

"Not a blessing. I noticed you were low last time I was in your snack drawer," I say, hoping to calm his Spidey-senses about me. "Where'd those posters of Deja come from?"

"I didn't hear from any of you after I left the park last night. Caught the news report this morning and stopped by the police station before my shift."

I turn around so I can use my arms to hoist myself onto the counter for a sit. He hates when I do it, but I could see in his eyes from the moment I walked in that he'd let me get away with anything today. I fiddle with the ring on my thumb. "Do you think they'll find her?"

"Yes," he says plainly.

I watch as he sifts through a box of prefilled prescriptions labeled with a *B*. "Do you think they'll find her alive?"

His fingers freeze in place, index outstretched, ready to flick over to the next bag. "It has only been a few hours, Sariyah. Not even a day. She's okay."

"How can you say it with so much confidence?"

"How can you have such little faith?"

Tessa is the answer to that question, but he never knew her. "I want to believe something else. Be positive. I've been trying all morning. But you were there. All those people from all over. She could be anywhere with anyone right now. And you know how things go. You know how things go when it's us."

His brown eyes melt. "Yes. I know. And those stories, those sad ones, they stand out. Justice not served—it will shout at us forever. It will shout so loud that it drowns out all the other stories. The odds are in her favor, Sariyah. Most missing kids return home. Ninety-nine percent. I looked it up. And I gave the officers a statement about what I saw. It will help, and I'll see all four of you back at school next week." He hands me two prescription bags. "Had one for your mother, too."

I peek in Mama's bag. It's her antidepressants. I wonder how much they are helping her, if she might need a different dose. She doesn't check in with her doctor often enough.

"Thanks, Rincon. See you later." I hop off the counter.

"Bye, sweetie."

I go back to the car and Mama takes the white paper bags from me. "What's this?"

"You had your antidepressants on auto-refill, remember?"

She throws the bag in the back seat. "Funny how I'm the one on antidepressants when Jasmine has a missing daughter. When Felicia Hawkins hasn't seen her baby girl in almost five years. Strange, ain't it? What do you think that says about me?"

I know I shouldn't answer, that the questions are rhetorical, but I do anyway. "It doesn't say anything, Mama. I know for a fact Malcolm's mom sees a therapist. For all we know, she's on antidepressants, too. There's nothing to be—"

"Don't, Sariyah." She turns on the radio. Turns it up loud.

Anita Baker croons at us and I make myself small in the passenger seat. I want to defend her against herself and I don't even know why anymore. Maybe it's because when she's healthy, she's literally the best mom on the planet. So good it more than makes up for the occasional wave of . . . this. But I know that line of thinking is toxic. I know this back and forth with her will damage me eventually. Maybe it already has. But what am I supposed to do? She's my mother. I love her.

CHAPTER 10

· ·

The alarm on my phone blares the most jarring jingle I could find in the sounds list. It's spring break and I'm up at six thirty in the morning. There's no real reason, other than an all-encompassing fear that I'll miss something while I'm dreaming, or that I'll dream of someone I'm missing—and have to wake to the reality that they still aren't here. I should be laid up in the bed for at least three more hours. And then I should laze around the house without a care in the world, deciding whether I want to spend my first day of vacation chilling or getting into something fun with my friends. But my life never really gave a damn about should. Somehow my life has become a horror movie with unnecessary early mornings. With stabbings. With missing girls.

Both Malcolm and Jude gave me choppy responses when I asked about their meetings with the detectives while we put together Deja's posters. They said enough to prove they weren't on the brink of crisis, but not enough to settle the twitching in my stomach. The feeling that won't let me sit still. The feeling that drove me to visit Danny yesterday, and the one that's guiding me to Phillip's today.

I look in the mirror and prep myself for a battle against my now-frizzy twists, which broke free of their bonnet last night, but the sound of cartoons draws me to the living room before I can get started. Josiah sits cross-legged on the couch, a blanket draped across him like a cape, a big Tupperware filled with cereal milk in his lap. Without making eye contact, he moves the Miles Morales pillow he dragged from his bedroom out of the way to make room for me to sit. A casual assumption that I intend to join him. A reminder that, at nine years old, the world could be falling down around you, but it's no excuse to miss *SpongeBob* reruns.

Maybe Phillip Irvine can wait. It's super early anyway. I detour to the kitchen, grab the carton of almond milk and a bowl, then take a seat next to my brother. "You seen Mama this morning?"

"She came home from work a little while ago and went straight to her room."

"She's tired. She didn't get to sleep much before her shift last night."

He downs his milk, burps and places his bowl on the coffee table. "Want to play some video games with me?"

"I don't know if I'm up for games, Jo. But you can turn up the TV and pass me that box of cereal." I put on a pleasant enough face for my brother, but on the inside it's all panic, worry, and dread. An ugly contrast to the bright, cheerful sounds coming from the TV.

The cereal is overly sweet and goes soggy too quickly, setting off my gag reflex. I double-check the box to see what abomination my brother convinced Mama to buy—some off-brand thing called Poppin' Pogo Puffs. I put my bowl down and nudge it away from me. Jojo snatches it up and begins to devour the mushy remains.

"That's disgusting."

He smiles, proud of himself, then watches an hour and a half of cartoons while I stress over how early would be too early to show up at Phillip's house. Josiah groans when the *SpongeBob* marathon ends and a show he doesn't like comes on. He reaches for the remote with his foot. He's got some impressively fingerlike toes, but all he manages to do is knock the thing to the floor. I pick it up and flick through the channels while he climbs all over me, trying to snatch it away. I'm holding it high in the air, completely out of his reach, when I see Deja's mom on the news. Josiah whines and I shush him.

He drops back onto his bottom and looks at the TV. "Who's that?"

I grab my phone and hit the group chat with Jude and Malcolm—the new one Malcolm made that doesn't include Deja. I'd wondered what he thought when he made it. If it felt like some kind of betrayal. It's not that I don't get why he chose to—it was weird talking about her in the other one, knowing she wouldn't be chiming in. It was weird to imagine her reading through all of it once she comes home. But I know it was also weird to start a new chat without her. People usually do that when one friend is annoying or can't keep a secret. Deja isn't either of those things.

> **Me**
> Are y'all aware Ms. Jasmine is
> on the news right now??

Jude
What?! This is big, right?
This is what we want?

"Who's that?" Josiah asks again.

"Shh!" I turn my phone face down so I can pay attention. "It's Deja's mom."

"She looks different." He squints at the screen. "She get a haircut or she forget to put her wig on?"

I shove him as Ms. Jasmine wipes her eyes and speaks to the reporter outside of the police precinct. They must have recorded this yesterday.

"Deja baby, if you see this, if you hear me, come home, love. Come home. Please, if anyone has any information. If you were at the festival that day and saw her. Photos. Anything. Please come forward." She breaks down into sobs and the reporter gently pats her shoulder.

"She's fake crying," Jojo says, picking at his toenails.

"What?"

"Look," he points with his chin. "There aren't even any tears coming out."

"Josiah, that's rude." He's not wrong, but I don't know. She's probably cried herself dry.

"I don't like her."

"You don't know her, Jo. You don't understand what she's going through."

This offends him enough that he drops his foot and gapes at me. "I do too! I wasn't born yesterday. No mom wants their kid to disappear, but I still don't like her."

"Why not?"

"Because she's mean. She was a substitute in our class. It was right before Christmas and she made us go on silent lunch."

"There's a difference between mean and strict, Josiah. Y'all were probably bad." I've heard stories about some of those wild behind kids in his class. They probably traumatized her.

I stare at the TV, trying to shake the uneasy feeling Jojo's comments left in my gut while he's busy defending his class's honor.

My phone rings. A FaceTime call with Jude and Malcolm. I answer. Malcolm's sitting on his bed with Miss Doretta tucked under his chin. Jude's in his kitchen, a Pop-Tarts package dangling from his mouth.

"Did y'all catch it?" I ask.

"Barely," Jude says, briefly setting his phone down and showing us his ceiling while he opens his sad breakfast.

"Did Deja ever say much about her relationship with her mom?" I ask, looking at Malcolm.

His eyes shift away from his TV and to his phone. "Why are you asking that?"

"Because Ms. Jasmine is mean!" Jojo yells.

I shove the remote deep between the couch cushions just to annoy him and go to my room.

"Your little brother putting you on to conspiracy theories?" Malcolm asks.

"No. And why would it have to be a conspiracy? You think it's unheard of for a teen not to get along with their parents?"

"I don't, but what are you saying? You think Ms. Jasmine had something to do with her disappearance?"

"No. I don't know. I just think it's important to know what all was going on with her."

Malcolm runs his hand down his face. "Sariyah, we went over this yesterday. Getting Deja's name out there is a better use of our time than trying to piece together little clues to figure out what happened. One viral post will do way more than you finding out the last thing she and her mama fought over. Only we're going to need more than local news reports to get her the kind of exposure she needs."

"This segment is proof that people are paying attention though, right? That they want to know more?" Jude asks.

"It's proof my family has money and connections and empathizes with Ms. Jasmine's situation," Malcolm says. "The real question is if my family has *enough* money and the *right* connections."

I prop my phone up on Tibby so I can pick out some clothes while I talk. "Exactly. Not sure how much weight we can give these reports. They run one or two non-primetime, thirty-second stories. Get their missing person diversity plug for the month and then they let everyone forget."

"And not saying those stories aren't a privilege," Malcolm says. "It's more than most people get, regardless of race. But I've seen what didn't work for Tessa, and what did work for Casey. We need to do more."

I perk up, put my face back in frame. "How about a rally at the school?"

Malcolm perks up, too. "I'm listening. When?"

"A couple of days from now. Wednesday? Hopefully she'll be home before we even have to go through with it, but if not, it's enough time to plan and spread the word."

"That's a good idea," Jude says.

"It doesn't have to be some fancy thing with speeches and political statements. We can get people from the school and community to pass out flyers and get Find Deja trending."

"Let's do it," Malcolm says.

We end the call and I get dressed, still thinking about what Jojo said about Ms. Jasmine. Still thinking about her strange behavior. Dredging my mind. Trying to recover anything I can from the conversation Deja and I had in the media center the day before the festival. She'd talked about her mom and stepdad. She'd said he didn't want her to go, that her mom was going to have something to say after. That she wouldn't be listening when she did. Was it because she knew she'd be gone? Or am I clinging to that idea to make myself feel better? Because I feel like shit. I feel like a horrible friend. I am a horrible friend. She never should have set foot in Hyde Park and I knew that. So it's my responsibility to do everything I can, to explore every angle possible to bring her home. I couldn't do it for Tess. But I'm going to do it for Deja.

• • •

I ride the bus to Hyde Park. Jude would have driven me, but I never got around to telling him what Danny and I talked about and I wasn't in the mood to answer twenty-one questions. The bus drops me off right where the security check for the festival was. It's bizarre knowing I existed in this exact spot less than two days ago under entirely different circumstances with entirely different feelings. I picture little holograms of the four of us, laughing and carrying on. Me thinking I could circumvent whatever fate had in store.

Phillip's house is right around the corner, all rotting wood and chipped butter-yellow paint. It looks harmless enough, sitting on a big open plot of land, but just in case, I take out my phone and share my location with Jude. He immediately sends me a text.

Jude
What are you doing at the park?

Me
Not the park. Danny's brother's house.

Jude

What the hell are you doing there??
Are you by yourself?
Is that where you wanted me
to drive you yesterday?

Question one, two, and three of twenty-one.

Jude

Never mind. On my way.

I thumbs-up his last message. If something goes sideways, my getaway vehicle is en route.

I maneuver my way up the front steps, dodging foot-sized holes, and ring the doorbell. There's no sound, so I rap a few times on the metal bit of the screen door. No one answers after a few seconds, so I do it again. This time, a grumpy voice responds from deep inside the long, skinny home.

"Who's that?"

"Um. Hi, Phillip," I holler through the door. "It's me, Sariyah. Your brother Danny said you wanted me to come by."

There's some rustling, then a shadowy figure appears in the hall.

Air horn. Air horn. Air horn.

He leans heavily on a cane, looking more like Danny's father than his little brother, even though he can't be older than fifty. "Well, aren't you a sight for sore eyes?" He unlocks the door and pushes it open. "Come on in. Come on in. And call me Philly. I'm back here in the kitchen having a sandwich. You want something?"

A roach scurries across my path looking a little too brave and familiar with the place. "No, thank you." How an air horn could be more useful to him than bug spray, I don't know. I'll leave him some anyway.

He leads me down the hall. A dusty box fan sits wedged in the kitchen window, but it does little to cool the place. The heat is stifling even though it's still early. He pulls out a rickety kitchen chair for me. "Go on and have a seat. Make yourself at home." A cigarette sits in the tab of a Coke can, almost burned to the butt. He picks it up and takes a final draw before sinking his teeth into what looks like an egg salad sandwich. Watching him eat it in the hot, cramped, buggy space makes me queasy.

"I'm sorry about what happened to Danny," I say, once I get control of my stomach contents.

He looks up at me, a glob of sleep still stuck in the corner of his eye. "Why would you be sorry?"

If Danny didn't choose to tell him the details of my involvement, I don't feel comfortable doing it, either. "I mean, it's really unfortunate. He said it was all a misunderstanding."

"Of course it was! Danny wouldn't hurt nobody. You come all the way over here to say that?"

"No."

"I didn't think so." He grins and eyes Santa Bag nestled in my lap. "Let's get to it."

I scowl at him and he checks himself.

"My bad, my bad. But like I've always said, I'm happy to pay ya. You can make good money off this. I can help you make good money off this."

No, this man is *not* sitting here trying to pimp out my ability. Gnats always take it this direction. Malcolm, too. And I'm tired of it. I get up to leave.

"Wait a minute. Where you going? You can't take a little joke? Come on." He adjusts his tone. More apologetic now. "I didn't mean to insult you. I just want to show my appreciation. That's the real reason I wanted to see you."

I twist my lips, skeptical.

"I'm serious. You been nothing but kind to me when you didn't have to be. And the stuff you've given me, I could tell story after story about what they've meant to me. Messes they help me avoid. Not sure I ever said thank you."

"You don't need to do that, Philly." It makes me uncomfortable when people talk about what I do like it's a completely selfless and random act of kindness.

"I figured you wouldn't take money, so I was thinking about what I could do," he says like he didn't even hear me. "Then I remembered how you mentioned school wasn't your thing. What plans you got after graduation?"

I shrug. "I'm just trying to make it to graduation first."

He chuckles. "You know, before this rheumatoid arthritis of mine started acting up, I was an electrician. Can make a solid living for yourself if you learn a trade. I've made a whole bunch of connections over the years and I'd be well honored to help you out if you think you might want to go that direction."

Trade school actually is something I've been considering on and off, but I've been nervous to bring it up to my parents. I know how much Mama wants me to get a degree.

"Ain't gotta take me up on it right now," Philly says. "Just putting it out there. You think on it and let me know. Or if you think of some other way I can help you, alls you need to do is ask."

I take a few steps back in his direction. The floorboards are loose and creaky under my feet. "Well, I did have a question for you."

"Oh?" Intrigue adds a little youthfulness to his voice.

"Have you heard about that missing girl on TV?"

His demeanor shifts hard toward annoyance and he hacks out a few wet coughs. "I hear about a lot of missing girls on TV. This world got problems, and I tell you what, it all started with the invention of that doggone internet."

"The world's problems started with the internet?" I ask, deadpan.

"You heard me. Won't ever find me paying for that mess. Gives you cancer and they use it to spy on folks." He clears some phlegm from his throat, grimaces. "Not that I got anything to hide."

I need to redirect this conversation before it goes full tinfoil hat. "Did you hear about the girl who went missing around the corner from here? Her name is Deja Nelson. It was Saturday night. During the music festival."

"Heard that music all damn day. If you could even call it music. Noise, more like."

"Right, well, she's a friend of mine and I was hoping I could leave you with some missing person flyers to share around. Danny says you aren't getting out much but—"

"Excuse me for a minute. Need the john." He scoots by me and down the hall. "I got IBS, darlin. When nature calls, you get a move on!"

Really? Once the bathroom door clicks shut, I peek into the living room. The muted TV plays the Weather Channel and the local paper is spread open on the coffee table. I take a step into the room, the squeaky floor threatening to expose my creeping. Philly needs an intervention before he ends up on an episode of *Hoarders*. There are hip-high mounds of random things scattered all around the living space, leaving only a narrow path to walk. The path forks, one portion leading toward the couch, the other to a wood plank door. I look over my shoulder to check for Philly. I haven't heard a toilet flush or the faucet running, but to be honest, I'm not sure if he's the type to bother with any of that. I shake out my hands, hoping my sense of unease flings off and gets tangled up in one of the teetering piles of junk. I consider where the door may lead. Maybe it's his bedroom or a closet, but I need to see. I place my hand on the knob and actually scream when a loud *clank!* echoes up from beneath my feet. There's a large gap between the floor panels, exposing the cement floor of the basement below. Something's moving down there. I squat for a closer look, but almost lose my balance when Philly appears behind me. He spits into his Coke can, then wipes his mouth with a bandanna that has the word QUEEN printed across it in cursive.

"The hell you doing, girl?"

CHAPTER 11

. . . .

"Where did you get that?" Every muscle in my body tenses.

"Get what?" He looks far less frail than he did a few minutes ago. He's taller than I realized, has more weight on him.

"That bandanna." My eyes scan the room, darting from left to right like someone might jump out from behind one of the many places to hide.

"You come here just to ask me the same damn questions the police already done asked?"

He takes a step toward me and I take two back, accidentally knocking over a stack of magazines. "W-Why did the police come here?"

He laughs out loud, revealing a gap where his bottom left premolar should be. "Your friend. They're saying they think she's been abducted, maybe killed."

My skin goes instantly clammy because I hadn't heard words like that out loud yet. Not in reference to Deja. And not by a man holding what might be her bandanna.

Philly clears his sinuses with a stiff snort. "I'm a single

man living not a stone's throw away from where that girl vanished. You know why the police came here."

He suddenly reaches for a grocery bag on the end table beside me. I flinch, but he ignores it. "Danny thinks I'm dense, but I bet ya a dollar and two cans of soup he had something to say about me always seeking you out. He thinks I don't know how it looks, but I do. I just figure it's worth the risk. Considering what you can do." He shoves the bag at my chest. "Go on and open it up."

My hands tremble violently, but I do as he says. Inside are dozens of individually wrapped bandannas with various words and phrases. CUTIE PIE. BOSS. FLIRT. QUEEN.

"If I would've known they'd cause me so much drama, I never would've bought them. Bulk order from six months ago. Been selling them around town. Never going to get rid of them. Gave my niece a bunch to sell at her school, but I still got a thousand more in the basement."

I look at the floor, wondering what else he has down there.

He huffs, fed up with me now. "It's an old house for crying out loud! You folks get real suspicious over a water heater and Bear."

"Bear?"

"Yes, Bear. My dog. Got to keep him down there or else that boy will run me over and I ain't got no Life Alert."

"Then this may come in handy one day." I take the air horn from Santa Bag and give it to him. A new need immediately replaces the former.

Gemstones. Gemstones. Gemstones.

I purse my lips. This needy behind. I pull a small bag of assorted faux gems from my bag. "This, too. Thanks for talking to me, but I better get going."

He inspects the synthetic stones and turns the air horn

over in his hands a few times, then waves it at me, smiling. "Tell you what, you're always welcome in the Irvine household. Come on back to visit soon."

He follows me out to the front porch, waving until I make it down the driveway. The fresh air is such a relief after breathing in the stale, stuffy air of his house. A car horn honks. Two soft, quick beeps to get my attention. Jude waves at me from where he's parked down the street.

"Hey. Malcolm just called," he says when I open the passenger door. "He wants to meet up to make plans for the rally."

I buckle my seat belt. "That's fine."

He puts the car in drive but keeps his foot on the brake. "What were you doing here?"

"Do you remember that gnat Malcolm and I were talking about? Phillip?"

"Yeah. Vaguely."

A light rain starts up. My eyes linger on the wiry muscles of his forearm a little too long as he reaches to click on the windshield wipers. "He's Danny's brother. He asked me to come here and I felt guilty about everything so I said yes."

"But isn't he some kind of creep?"

"Malcolm said that, not me." I position Santa Bag comfortably between my feet. "But I guess his feelings rubbed off on me because a few minutes ago I thought maybe Phillip had Deja in the basement."

Jude laughs awkwardly, like I've made a bad joke. "Wait." He turns his upper body to face me. "You're serious?"

"Yeah." I raise my eyebrows and pop my lips. "I wouldn't kid around about my missing friend."

He presses his palm to his forehead. "I'm sorry. That was a stupid thing to say."

"It's fine. I hear how it sounds, but the police really did question him."

He opens and closes his mouth a few times, like he needs to chew on this information to process it. A couple of seconds pass before he wrinkles his nose and frowns. "Did you know that before you went in there?"

"Hell no. Some stuff crossed my mind when I saw how close he lives to the park, but no."

"Why'd they question him?"

"Probably a combination of things, but he sells bandannas just like the one Deja was wearing. He buys them in bulk." I blow out a puff of air. "Of course, I saw him use one before I knew all that, then I heard something moving in his basement and my mind ran with it. Almost peed my pants."

"Do you think he could have been involved?"

"No. He's kind of weird, but he's always been like that. And the police didn't arrest him, so there's that." The last part doesn't comfort me as much as it should, but it does help.

Jude begins to drive. "What was moving in the basement?"

"His dog."

"What kind was it?" he asks all eagerly, the way dog lovers always do.

"I—" My blood goes a little icy. I didn't see the dog. But did I hear it? Did I see water or food bowls? A leash? Pet hair? I can't remember and I'm embarrassed to admit I left without even confirming if what Philly said was true.

"Ri?"

"I don't know. Big dog named Bear. Could knock him over. That's why he has it down there."

Good thing Philly said I'm welcome anytime because it looks like I'll be making another trip to the Irvine residence really soon. No chance my brain will let this go until I do. But for now, I can address something else my brain won't drop.

"I know you didn't really want to talk about it last night, but were you able to clear up the whole hairbrush, poison ivy thing with the police?"

"I think saying *clear up*"—he flicks on his turn signal—"makes it seem like there was something they had the wrong idea about. That was my first time talking to them. I just told the truth. Like I should have told you from the jump. Might have avoided you looking at me like some kind of criminal. But what can I say? I was really embarrassed."

"Why would you be embarrassed about that?" I ask, wondering if it might have anything to do with what I saw on Google.

He fiddles with the cord of his phone charger at a stoplight, smiling a little. "You started calling me your friend right after the Danny thing."

I scrunch my brows, confused by where he's going with this. "Yeah. I told you why."

"Because my needs went silent."

"Right." It's my turn to be embarrassed. "Was that awkward? I'm not well-versed in the making-new-friends department."

He laughs. "Yeah, it was a little awkward, but not for the reason you think."

"Then why?"

He licks his lips and keeps his eyes trained on the road. "I get embarrassed around you because I care what you think of me. I noticed you months before you noticed me. I don't think I was ever interested in just being your friend."

The temperature in the car seems to spike twenty degrees

and I'm tempted to open the door and throw myself into the road just to feel a little breeze. "Jesus, Jude." I pull at the collar of my shirt. "Don't people, you know, usually beat around the bush with that sort of thing? Ease into it?"

"I don't know." He smiles. "You asked. But also, to be clear, I'm not asking you anything. You don't have to say anything. There are way bigger things going on right now. But you should also know that I'm here for you however you need me to be. Okay?"

My heart threatens to hammer its way completely out of my chest because I like this boy. I do. But do I deserve this excitement fluttering in the pit of my stomach? The warm flush he gives my cheeks? Do I deserve that while Deja is out there somewhere? Hurt or in danger? Do I deserve it when it was choices I made, tickets I was given, needs I heard that led to it?

I settle back into my seat and whisper, "Okay."

CHAPTER 12

· ·

Jojo's sprawled across the living room floor on his belly when I get home later that afternoon. An empty carton of orange juice sits on the coffee table and some Oreos are crushed into the rug. He lazily presses buttons on his game controller.

"Really, Jo?" I collect a couple of pieces of trash. "Where's Mama?"

"In her room," he says without looking away from the screen.

"When's the last time you checked on her?" I don't wait for him to answer. If she'd seen this mess, he'd be scrubbing the walls instead of playing games. I tap on her bedroom door before letting myself in. "Mama?"

The lump on the bed shifts but does not speak.

"Mama, did you give Jojo his medicine?" Her bedroom is worse off than the living room. Aside from a narrow passage from the door to her bed, the floor is covered with random stuff. It's not filthy, like Philly's place, but it's equally cluttered. "Shouldn't you be getting ready for work?"

"Mind your business, Sariyah."

"I'm not trying to be nosy, but the house is a mess and Josiah—"

She sits up, makeup smudged across her face, headscarf barely hanging on. "If the house is a mess, go clean it up. Don't come back in here. Not going to work tonight. I called in."

I glimpse some NyQuil and Kleenex on her end table. "Are you sick?"

"I'm tired, Sariyah. I'm tired. You can entertain your brother for a little while, can't you? And let me catch up on some sleep?"

"Yes, ma'am." I grab an overturned laundry basket and fill it with as much as I can, but it barely makes a dent in the mess. "Can I bring you something to eat?"

"No, I'm all right. I need to be alone for a little while, then I'll be good as new."

I leave her room wishing I could believe her. Wishing for the one millionth time that my ability extended to the people I care about most. She says it doesn't work with her and Dad and Jojo because all they need from me is love. But that's not true at all. It's not true for them and it wasn't true for Tessa. It isn't true for anyone.

"Play *Mario Kart* with me," Josiah says before I can make it across the living room.

"No."

"Please," he begs.

"I said no."

"You never want to do anything fun."

I grit my teeth to keep from popping off on him when it's other things that have me in a mood.

"I'm hungry. And my leg hurts. And I need help with my extra-credit project."

"Josiah," I whine. "Go play outside for like"—I check the

time—"an hour. When you get back, I'll fix you something to eat."

"I want pizza."

"You got pizza money?" My skin crawls when I realize how much I sound like our mother.

Josiah throws back his head and stomps off down the hall. A few seconds later, the front door opens and shuts.

I try cleaning the mess he made, but I'm preoccupied with planning my next visit to Philly's. All I need to do is peek in a basement window and see that dog. That's all I need to relieve this stupid doubt. I should have turned around and done it before we even left. Not that it should matter. If the police missed something that obvious, the world can go ahead and get swallowed by a black hole.

Resigned to spending the day googling the Irvine family and boosting social media posts about Deja, I go to my bedroom and open my laptop. *Never read the comments* has been Malcolm's motto ever since the incident between him and Ms. Jess at Sweet Pea's and I'd adopted it, no questions asked. Until now. Because what if someone's seen her? What if we miss it? I scroll until my eyes hurt and Josiah comes back from the playground asking for food. I make sure he takes his medicine while I scramble us some eggs. He eats his in front of the TV and I take mine back to my room. I'm scarfing down my last bite when my phone rings. I snatch it, hopeful, but it's just Dad.

"Dad's calling!" I shout to my brother.

Josiah busts open my bedroom door and leaps straight from the threshold to my bed, which gives an angry groan in response. He grabs the phone from me and angles the camera at his toes before accepting the FaceTime call.

"Hello!" my father draws out joyfully. "Now, I can't quite

put my finger on it," he says to Jojo's feet, "but Sariyah, something looks different about you."

"Y'all are not cute."

Dad chuckles and I seize the phone from my brother.

"Spring break means the countdown is on until I got my favorite farmhands in town. I'm ready to put y'all to work."

"Y'all? You mean Jojo."

"I'm ready, Dad!"

"I know you are, son. And your sister is ready to lie up by the creek with some books."

That farm is the quietest place on Earth for me. Summers there are the only time of the year I can go days without hearing a need.

"Josiah, why don't you let me talk to your sister alone for a few minutes?"

I shake my head, knowing he wants to talk about Deja. "It's okay, Daddy. He's been asking to FaceTime with you for days." Deja is the last person I want to talk about with Daddy. He's hurt by this and I can tell. He feels like I never talk about real stuff with him. Sure, we've texted about it, but texts don't count as communication in his mind. But speaking about what happened, out loud, with him—that will make it real. And I already know it is, but it's real here. In this world. In Atlanta. If I don't talk about it with Dad, Chefly can stay clean. If I don't talk about it with him, our calls can be a magical bubble where there are no stabbed men and no missing girls.

He presses his lips together and moves on. "You bringing Malcolm down again this summer? If so, I might really see about getting that rental cleaned up."

"Actually, that's a project I wouldn't mind helping with." I think about my conversation with Philly before things got weird and figure it's time I'm straight with at least one of my parents about what I want to do with my life. "I've been thinking I might like to be a contractor or something one day."

"Contractor, huh? I can see you in a hard hat. What's Mom think about it?"

"She wants me to enroll in one of the local community colleges in the fall and transfer to a bigger school later. But I don't think all that is for me. I'll be lucky to make it out of high school." With Tessa, and Casey, and now Deja, I can't say things like that without hearing another, darker, meaning.

"Have your grades gotten that bad? Is it old Izzy the Intuition giving you trouble?" Izzy the Intuition is what he calls my ability.

"Yeah, that's a big part of it. It's hard to stay focused."

He frowns. He gets really down on himself sometimes. Like he was supposed to anticipate that I'd be like Grandma and unearth some useful clue about how to deal with it before she passed. But I don't need all that from him. I just need him to answer the phone when I call, and he always does.

"Put your mother on. Trade school is an option more of you young folks should consider. Little debt. Good job security. Maybe I can warm her up to the idea. Lots of opportunities down here for you to get some hands-on experience."

"Mama's not feeling too good. She took the night off to get some rest." I glance at Jojo, then back at Dad, hoping he'll pick up what I'm putting down without me having to be too direct.

He nods. "I'll give her a call later on."

"What's new down there?" I ask, eager to pull the conversation in a different direction. "How's Auntie Cheryl?"

"Good, good. Everybody's doing well. Cheryl's got her hands full with your little cousins." He snaps his fingers. "You know who's back in town?"

"Who?" I ask, not expecting to recognize the name. He stays talking about people I met once when I was three, like I'm supposed to remember who they are.

"Fitzgerald Davis. Kenny's boy. He's taking a little break from college."

I can't resist the grin that springs to my face. "Fitz?"

Dad grimaces. "Yeah, but don't smile so hard. He was too old for you when you were eleven and he's too old for you now."

I scrunch up my nose. "First of all, he's only a year and a half older than me. Second, ain't nobody trying to date him, Daddy. He's my friend." His sister Ella, on the other hand, was my first crush.

"Good, because he's fixing to propose to his high school sweetheart. What's her name—Crystelle."

I never met her, but I heard stories. "Didn't she cheat on him and dump him at their prom?"

"Hell if I know. I don't be in young folks' business like that. Ran into him and his buddy Jed at the grocery store. Told him I'd tell you he said hello."

Fitz is what I like to call a seasonal friend. The only communication we have between the months of September and May is a check-in via text around Christmastime. When I'd asked Fitz what he wanted for Christmas, he'd said he wanted to be happy. I assumed that meant he was still struggling with the breakup, and maybe I should have asked, but I guess they worked it out. Or Dad's got something mixed up. Especially if Fitz is hanging around Jed. He couldn't stand Crystelle and it almost ruined their friendship.

"Hey, Dad, did you know Sariyah's friend Deja is missing?" Josiah asks, casual as ever.

He runs his hand over his beard. "Yes, son. I did."

"Did Sariyah tell you, or did you hear it on the news?"

"Your mother told me first. Then your sister. Hasn't made the news down here yet."

I frown. "Of course it hasn't."

"Why do you say that?" Jojo asks. "Everybody's talking about Deja. Everybody! Her pictures are all over the neighborhood. Her mama was on TV today!"

Dad catches my eye, silently telling me that Josiah is too young. Too young to understand that the people talking about Deja in *our* neighborhood will never have the same reach as the people who talked about Casey in hers.

"That's good, Josiah. You keep talking until we find her," Dad says to him. "And you." He pauses until I look at the screen. "You know how it is. You know how things go. Email the information and a copy of the flyer, and I'll spread word down here."

Chefly's a small, close-knit, mostly Black town. The people there are good for gathering behind things like this. But Dad will need help. It might be time to upgrade my seasonal friend to a full-timer.

CHAPTER 13

. . . .

Tuesday morning I lie in bed and draft a DM to Afro Alt. I include a few pictures of Deja from the festival, along with a strong plea to share. After that I get to work creating social media posts about the rally. I tag them all with #FindDeja, desperately hoping I'll have to update them later to announce that she's back home, and the rally has been canceled. My notifications pile up right away. I'm clearing them when my door smacks against the doorstop with a loud *thwong*. I sit up just enough to see Josiah flying through the air, lips curved into the evilest grin. I open my mouth to scream, but the weight of his body landing on my chest knocks the air out of me before I can get it out. He laughs hysterically as I attempt to fight my way from beneath the blankets. He tries to run for it when I break free, but I grab his ankle and tickle the bottom of his foot. It's a dangerous move. He kicks at me violently, but I dip and dodge and don't let up until he hollers for mercy.

"Punk." I shove him hard into the mattress and stand up.

"Your breath stanks!" he shouts to my back as I walk to the bathroom.

He's waiting for me in the hall when I come out. I blow my minty-fresh breath in his face.

"Can we do something fun today?"

"Josiah. You know what's been going on. It's not a good—"

"But it's spring break! Mama said we could go to the zoo today."

Do-not-enter vibes ooze from her bedroom door. I look up the zoo admission fee on my phone. "How much money you got? Because it's going to cost us fifty dollars to get in."

Jojo runs to the kitchen like something's chasing him. He opens every single drawer, searching and searching, until he finds what he's looking for. "Here they are!" Two free passes to Zoo Atlanta. "Please, Riyah. Can we go? Can you take me? It's going to rain tomorrow. I want to see"—he looks at the tickets carefully—"the new reptile exhibit!"

"Josiah—"

"Please!" he begs, dark eyes glistening like two black marbles.

The look on his face puts my heart in a chokehold. Little brat.

"And we can go get stuff for Santa Bag," he adds. "It's looking kind of low."

I take an unnecessary peek inside my bag. Afro Alt left it pretty depleted, and with the way things have been going, this is not the time for me to be packing light on things that people need.

"Okay. We can go."

• • •

Jojo and I hit up the dollar store, where I drop twenty precious dollars on random stuff. It hurts, but it doesn't feel like

I have a choice. Not since the headaches started. It was easier when I was a kid. When the needs were just whispers that I could tune out. Now the only way to shut them up is to fulfill, and that means Santa Bag needs to stay stocked. I take Jojo to Grant Park next door to the zoo, hoping we can stumble upon a few useful, and free, extras. He launches straight into Operation Find Stuff. He creeps through the grass, eyes trained on the ground, stopping abruptly here and there when he thinks he's spotted something good. Half a mile into our walk, he comes to me with a handful of items. Bottle caps, pens, receipts, a couple of keys, rubber bands, and a gold ring that looks like it got separated from its owner a decade ago.

I use the hem of my shirt to rub some grime off the ring. "Dang, Jo. You did good. I should start paying you for this."

"Yeah. You should." He grins widely and darts off to the playground to search some more.

I plop down on a hot plastic bench and check our group chat. I agree with Malcolm's suggestion that we all meet at Retro Diner for dinner later tonight. Then I check the Atlanta Police Department's Facebook page. They posted about Deja yesterday morning. The same senior picture on all the hard copy posters smiles back at me.

Seventeen-year-old Deja Brielle Nelson was last seen Saturday evening at approximately 9:30 P.M. at Hyde Park, the location of the annual Afro Alt Music Festival. Deja was wearing a white shorts outfit and platform sneakers with her hair styled in long golden-brown braids. She stands five foot two inches and weighs one hundred and twenty pounds. If you have any information about the disappearance or whereabouts of Deja, please contact the Atlanta Police Department immediately.

There are eighty-seven comments, twenty-six shares, and almost two hundred reactions, sad emojis leading the pack. I add a comment about the rally and end it with #FindDeja. Then I scroll down the page until I find Casey Sullivan's missing person post.

Sixteen-year-old varsity athlete and honor student Casey Ann Sullivan . . .

I stop reading there. Deja's an athlete and honor student, too. It's little things like that. Little things that alter people's perception in little ways. We hit all of Deja's brag points on our posters, but I hate that it even matters. Should people care less about her disappearance if she were a C student? I'm sitting at a 1.9 GPA this semester and participate in zero extracurriculars. What if it'd been me? Casey's post has over seventy thousand reactions and I don't know if it's a good or bad thing that I can't compare the stats of her post when it was twenty-four hours old to Deja's.

"Sariyah?" comes a voice from behind me.

Ms. Jess's corgi waddles over and happily sniffs my feet.

"Oh. Hi, Ms. Jess." I'm beyond thankful the only thing radiating off her is the floral scent of her perfume.

She looks out at the playground. "Big sister duty?"

"Yes, ma'am. We're going to the zoo in a few."

"That'll be nice." Her words come out far less enthusiastic than usual. Like speaking is a great effort.

"How are you?" I ask.

She continues to look at Josiah. Her huge sunglasses block the upper half of her face. "Oh, you know. It's been a lot." The dog takes a big poop and she pauses to pick it up. "I'm sure you're eager to get back to work and cash in on all the spring break tips. I was thinking about opening back up next week. Probably leave most of it to you and Jude for a while. I still need some time off."

I watch an ant carry a crumb across the seat of the bench, not sure what to say. Is she so overwhelmed by what happened with Danny that she doesn't know what happened to Deja? Deja, who she hired to work in the shop last summer while Malcolm and I were in Chefly. I guess it's possible she hasn't heard. Or maybe she just doesn't know what to say, either.

She lets out a long breath and drags the toe of her shoe across the mulch. "I'm going to drop the charges. I'm not sure I completely buy Danny's version of things, but I know the Irvine family. They're decent people. Maybe Danny already got his just deserts."

I study her, wondering what the heck Danny's family has to do with what happened that night. Wondering if she would have awarded that get-out-of-jail-free card to anyone from a decent family. Wondering what even makes a family decent.

She pushes her sunglasses up on her head and looks me in the eye for a few brutal seconds. "You said I dropped that nail file that day. That wasn't true."

I stare back at her, expressionless, unsure of where she means to take this. Is she thankful? Upset? Her face gives nothing away.

"Everything about that night was a little strange. Don't you think?" She turns her gaze back to the playground. "And everything since." She tugs the dog's leash. "C'mon on, Julia."

The dog saunters over.

"Take care, Sariyah."

• • •

Jojo darts straight for the flamingos when we enter the zoo.

"Look!" He stretches his index finger over the fencing. "That one is young. Know how I know?"

I do, but decide to let him have the joy of telling me. "How?"

"Cause its head isn't pink yet. The chicks are light gray. It can take a couple of years for them to get like those over there." He points at a cluster of older flamingos. "Their color is from all the brine shrimp and algae they eat!"

A zoo worker in a visor, navy polo, and khaki shorts joins us, along with her need for a bobby pin. Her name tag says TARA. "You know, that animal knowledge could get you a pretty cool job when you grow up."

"I know." Josiah beams. "I want to be a herpetologist."

"Oh, really? You should talk to your parents about signing up for our Young Zookeeper and Conservationist Summer Program!"

Jojo looks at me, eyes the size of dinner plates, obnoxiously long lashes fluttering. "Can I sign up?" he asks, but his face quickly falls, like he just realized I'm not Mama. He looks back at Tara. "My mom isn't here."

"That's okay. Registration is open all week!" She looks up at me and smiles. "We have brochures in the gift shop."

I hand Tara a bobby pin and one of Deja's flyers as Josiah pulls me to the shop. He shoves one of every available brochure into Santa Bag, then drags me out again, rambling excitedly about fossas, warthogs, and diamondback terrapins. I feel bad for being resistant to bringing him here. The zoo is to him what Afro Alt was to Malcolm and Deja. He is so full of glee and excitement, it's near impossible for me to feel anything else. Unfortunately, near isn't quite good enough and the weight of everything I'm ignoring right now follows us like an angry, attention-demanding storm cloud. And I know once I look back at it, it'll rain. And it won't stop.

So I don't look back. I let my brother tug me all around the zoo, fulfilling needs and passing out Deja's flyers the whole time. We work up a good appetite and gorge ourselves on mediocre, overpriced pizza and ice-cold sodas before setting off to look at more animals. Jojo runs up to the fence to get a better look at the gorillas and I take a rest on a bench. I find the brochure for summer programs and flip through it. Jojo would eat this up, but it's four hundred dollars for one week, due this Sunday. Mama would never go for that. Especially not right now. I have some money saved from Sweet Pea's and birthdays and holidays over the years. I'd gladly drop four hundred on this for Josiah. Finding out he gets to go might be enough to keep him from noticing how much Mama and I are spiraling. But I can't access my money. My checking account is shared with Mama and she transfers most of what I earn directly to a savings account I can't touch until I'm eighteen—and that was at my request. I have some cash hidden in my room, but it's barely a third of what I need. I tuck the brochure back in Santa Bag and hope my brother will forget about camp.

I lean back and roll out my ankles. It's hot and I should have worn more comfortable shoes. A man in a pair of well-loved Grill Master 3000s walks by and, as unattractive as the brown leather sandal and crew socks combo is, all the middle-aged Black uncles in America must be on to something. A young couple, no more shoe wise than me, takes a kissing selfie together in front of a gorilla statue. I do a double take as they pull away from each other.

Deja.

I jump up from my seat and realize my mistake almost

immediately. The girl looks so much like Deja. But it's not her. She's too tall, and her hair isn't the same, but the resemblance is uncanny. I wonder if she's noticed it. I wonder if she's seen Deja's picture on the news. If she gasped and thought how easily it could have been her. She catches me staring, my eyes flooded with unshed tears, and raises her eyebrows. I quickly look away and go find Josiah.

CHAPTER 14

It's an hour and a half until I'm supposed to meet Jude and Malcolm for dinner. Just enough time for me to swing by Philly's. The bus drops me off in front of Hyde Park again, but this time I don't linger long enough to be assaulted by memories. This trip serves one purpose, and it's to set my mind at ease by glimpsing that damn dog. The last vestiges of daylight disappear in the short time it takes to reach his street. The only light coming from the house flickers and I assume it's Philly in his living room watching TV. I trot over to the side of the house, crouching a bit, for sure looking like I'm up to no good. I straighten and slow down because I'm not doing anything wrong. He said I was welcome whenever. But people like me have been shot dead for walking around their own property, let alone some white dude's.

The outer walls of the basement are made of a ruddy brick that contrasts with the yellow panels of the rest of the place. There are some concerning cracks in the masonry. Perfect for spying. But it's no surprise that I see nothing when I peek through one. If I can see in, anyone being held captive could see out and call out. I walk around to the back of the house anyway, curiosity driving me as hard as a white girl in a horror film. A *pop!* makes me jump as I turn the corner, but it's just a muffler backfiring. I laugh, realizing how ridiculous it was that I even entertained the idea that Philly had Deja down here. The basement is so busted up, it couldn't keep a dog in. Didn't keep a dog in. There are food and water bowls, but I don't see this Bear anywhere. He probably trotted off happily into the sunset through the giant hole in the wall. Upstairs, Philly begins to cough. He hacks for so long, I'm pulling his need from my bag before it officially forms.

Cough drops. Cough drops. Cough drops.

I walk around to his front porch, set them on the stoop, knock, and run.

• • •

Retro Diner isn't really retro. It was built only three years ago. They decorated it to look like some 1950s soda fountain. It's corny as all get-out, but the food makes up for it. Cheap, greasy, satisfying. Inside, I can almost feel the scent of burnt coffee latch itself to my clothes and hair. I choose a booth way in the back where I can't pick up on any needs. At least until the server approaches.

"Just you tonight?"

Sharpie. Sharpie. Sharpie.

"No, I have two more people joining me." I slip a blue Sharpie from the side pocket of Santa Bag.

"Okay, I'll grab some waters and then have Lizette take over for me. My shift is ending."

I smile politely. This guy seems nice, but Ms. Lizette is our favorite. "Sounds good. Thank you."

121

It's easy to discreetly drop the marker into a pocket on his apron when he leans over to set down our waters a few minutes later. Jude shows up as he walks off. His glasses are dirty and his curls are flat on one side, but the skin around his eyes is finally calming down.

"Hey." I take a microfiber cloth from my bag and pass it to him. "For your glasses."

He slides onto the bench across from me and takes the cloth. "You hearing my needs now?"

"No. You just look like you sprayed oil sheen on your lenses. Might need to wash them with dish soap."

"It's from the lotion for my rash. I don't have a greasy face, promise." He tilts his head to the side. "Well, not that greasy." He glances at Santa Bag to my left. "You don't got soap in there, do you?"

I side-eye him for asking such a dumb question before pulling out a travel-sized bottle of Dawn. He moistens the cloth with the condensation on the outside of his glass of ice water and gets to work. Something about the action makes my insides go all tingly. My body is betraying me. It's betraying Deja. It feels so impossibly wrong that it's made space to feel an attraction toward this boy when there are things so much bigger, so much more important, than some stupid crush on someone I barely know.

He raises his glasses to the light, inspecting them with a frown. "Yep. Definitely made it worse." He folds them up and sets them aside.

"Are they not prescription?"

"They are," he says, sounding a little offended before cracking a small smile. "But to be fair, I'm only mildly nearsighted. I mostly wear them to distract from my fivehead."

"You don't—" I squint, taking in the proportions of his face. "I mean, it's a four point five at most."

"See. I knew you were a real one." He sips his water. "Saw your text on the way in. Why'd you go back to Phillip Irvine's place?"

I nod to the door. "Tell you later. Malcolm's here." It's only after the words exit my mouth that I realize I've been keeping the Philly and Danny stuff from him, but I'm definitely not interested in examining why. Not right now.

He sits on my side of the booth, slides across the bench until our thighs are pressed against each other, then throws a comforting arm around my shoulder and squeezes. "Hey, y'all."

"How you doing, Mal?" I push the remaining glass of water closer to him.

He scratches the underside of his chin. "It's been three days. They'd found Casey by now."

"I'll take the longer wait if it means we get a better outcome than Casey did," I say, even though I know what the stats show after more than seventy-two hours pass.

"Of course." Malcolm bangs his straw on the table a couple of times before sliding it out of the wrapper. "Social media is so much bigger than it was when Tessa disappeared. I really thought Deja's face would be viral by now."

"Will Afro Alt be making a statement?" Jude asks.

"Think they are set to release it tomorrow, actually. And that's huge, but I don't know . . ." He waits for the words to find him.

"But Casey didn't need a statement by Coachella to go viral?" I offer.

Malcolm slaps his palm on the table. "Exactly. Casey

didn't have to disappear at some high-profile event to matter. And I'm not saying people don't care about Deja. The local news segments helped, folks are talking, they're sharing posts. But it's not enough."

The server, Ms. Lizette, comes over and brings no needs with her. "Look who it is, my favorite East Lake crew. Grabbing the usual tonight?" She gives Jude a second glance. "Oh! I'm sorry. Got a new musketeer over here. Where's Deja?"

"See what I mean?" Malcolm mumbles.

I straighten up in my seat and lean forward a little so she can see me better. "Ms. Lizette, Deja's been missing since Saturday night."

Her mini clipboard and pen clatter to the ground. Her left hand creeps over her mouth and her right grips Malcolm's wrist. "Oh my word, I'm so sorry, babies. Dear God. I'd heard a local girl went missing, but I hadn't realized it was—oh my heart." She squats down so only her head pokes above the table. "What do y'all want to eat? On me tonight. Least I can do is feed you."

"It's okay, Ms.—"

She holds out her hand to silence Malcolm. "Let me do it. And do y'all got a poster or something I can put out front?"

I take three from Santa Bag and hand them to her.

Ms. Lizette picks her clipboard off the floor and stands up. "Jerry!" she yells toward the kitchen. "Jerry!"

A sweaty, round-faced man sticks his head out the swing door.

"Jerry baby, go hang these up for me." She passes him the papers, then puts her hands on her hips, attention back on us. "What'll it be, sweeties?"

"Their usual is fine with me," Jude says. "I'm not picky."

"It'll be right out. Y'all holler if you need anything else in

124

the meantime, okay?" She walks back to the counter whispering, "Bless their hearts."

Jude and Malcolm pick up the conversation where it left off before Ms. Lizette interrupted. Names stand out—*Deja. Casey. Tessa. Deja. Casey. Tessa*—but I can't follow the details. More people trickle into the diner and the names intermingle with needs. Deja. *Scarf.* Casey. *Sugar.* Tessa. *Pacifier.* A pulsating heaviness develops in the upper right quadrant of my head. A brewing migraine.

Malcolm catches me taking my medicine. He stands and waves me out of the booth so he can sit on the inside instead. "Were you just going to sit there in pain?"

"I know it's frustrating when I fulfill needs in the middle of a conversation. I didn't want you to think I wasn't listening."

"And I'm supposed to believe you can focus while your head is pounding? Jude can listen to me run my mouth. Go do your thing." He initiates the condensed version of our handshake, then I grab Santa Bag.

Putting other people's needs before my own is so ingrained in me. But I'm glad to have a best friend who looks out for me when I struggle to do it myself.

I fulfill a few needs and come back to the table ready to actually participate in the conversation. "I thought I saw her today. Deja."

Malcolm stiffens. "What? Where?"

Jude's eyes are bulging and I wonder if he thinks I mean at Philly's.

"It was at the zoo. I took Josiah. This girl looked so much like her. I felt like a freak when she caught me staring at her." I tear at a napkin, stalling before I bring up something else I've been thinking about. "Guys, the days are flying by. We've heard nothing new from the police. How do we know they're doing anything? Tessa was only thirteen and managed to keep a huge secret from everyone. A secret that took the cops way too long to dig up. I need to know the same won't happen for Deja. We need to search for answers on our own."

"I don't disagree, but is anyone else mad as hell that we have to? It's not that I expect the police to do all of the work. That's not how it went down for Casey. Strangers, random folks on the internet. They gathered up the puzzle pieces and handed them to the authorities on a silver platter. Hundreds of thousands, maybe millions of people showed up and out for her. That was the difference maker. Where is Tessa's army? Where's Deja's?"

"At this table," I say. "It's not fair, but until the rally tomorrow, until Afro Alt releases their statement, that's the reality of the situation. We can be mad about it or do something. We owe it to her to investigate. To explore every rabbit hole that comes up." I don't mention that I've already gone down one that led me to Phillip Irvine. I need to make that make sense to me before I share it with him.

Ms. Lizette brings over our food. Potato hash with bell peppers, onions, and a fried egg for me, a spinach omelet and bacon for Malcolm, and a stack of chocolate chip pancakes drizzled in chocolate sauce, and topped with whipped cream, strawberries, and sprinkles for Jude.

"Oh." He regards the outrageous concoction in front of him. "Y'all couldn't warn me?"

Malcolm unrolls his napkin-wrapped silverware. "Hey, man, you said it was all right."

"Don't worry. We always share."

We arrange all the entrées in the middle of the table so everyone can easily help themselves to whatever they'd like.

126

As I adjust the pile of pancakes, a fresh need sneaks into my range.

Pepper.

I freeze. Focus on it. Make sure I heard the complete thing.

Pepper. Pepper. Pepper.

A server places a condiment caddy in the center of a crowded table and the need disappears, but it leaves behind the same dread I felt when I first heard Deja's need Saturday afternoon. "I hope she's okay," I say so quietly I'm not sure Jude or Malcolm can even hear, but a moment later Malcolm's arm is back around my shoulder and Jude's hand is gripping mine across the table.

"She's going to be okay." Malcolm removes his arm and taps my chin. "Look at me."

I turn to him.

"I know I stay pointing out differences between Casey's case and hers, but the most important difference is that Deja is going to be okay." He says it with such confidence and authority, I feel like it'd be an insult not to take him at his word. He breaks the eye contact and snatches up a piece of bacon. "But you know she'd be pissed at us for letting this happy stack get cold, so let's get on with it."

I sniff and allow a small laugh to escape. Malcolm's good for getting those out of people wherever, whenever.

We demolish the food. It's the kind of good where you know there will be a price to pay in the bathroom soon, but you don't even care. We're all slouched in the booth, letting our stomach acids do their thing when a phone buzzes. Malcolm jumps and pats his pocket.

"Relax. Your phone is never on vibrate. It's Jude's."

Malcolm laughs, but there's something uneasy about it. "Right. Think I was falling asleep to be honest. Scared me."

"We did just tear up a put-you-to-sleep kind of meal," I say.

"I'll be right back. Need to call my mom real quick." Jude slides out of the booth and wanders toward the restrooms. He returns barely a minute later, head bowed, scratching his neck nervously.

"What's wrong?" I try to stand, but my knee hits the table, knocking over a glass of water. "Is it Deja?"

He motions for me to stay seated. "No, no. It's Danny Irvine."

"What about him?" Malcolm asks, but I already know what. I can see it on Jude's face.

"He just had a massive heart attack. He's dead."

CHAPTER 15

. . . .

The booth feels tiny. Jude stands there mumbling something, blocking my way out. "Move." I nudge him, try to force him out of my way while keeping the rapidly building nausea at bay.

"Sariyah, wait. Calm down first."

"Move!" The chocolate sauce and eggs and sprinkles and bacon battle in my stomach.

He steps aside and I run straight for the restroom. My meal reappears in the toilet only seconds later.

"Sariyah?" There's a gentle tap on my stall door.

I turn enough to see Ms. Lizette's tiny classic black Reeboks.

"Is she okay?" Jude calls from the doorway.

"Is anyone else in there?" Malcolm asks before his Doc Martens step into view. He whispers something.

"Okay, sweetie." Ms. Lizette's shoes squeak across the tiles as she leaves.

"Riyah, don't make me get down on this nasty ass floor."

"It's not that bad," I mutter before standing, flushing, and sliding open the lock.

Jude hands me a glass of water.

I take a huge gulp and swish it around my mouth before spitting it into the sink. "He's really dead?" I ask their reflections in the mirror.

Malcolm turns my body to face his. "A heart attack." He scans my face for understanding. "Say it with me, girl."

"A heart attack," we say together.

"But—"

"Aht." He holds up his index finger. "But nothing, Sariyah. I know you and that brain. This is America. The land of heart disease. He had a heart attack. It's sad and the timing sure as hell leaves something to be desired, but don't go where I know you're going."

His statement has strong end-of-conversation vibes and I don't know if it's because it's that simple and obvious to him, or if it's because he doesn't have the capacity to deal with me and my guilty conscience right now. But that conscience is raging. It's raging completely out of control. "Malcolm, Danny got stabbed with a nail file I provided. Then he got an infection. Infections can put strain on your heart. Can't they?"

"What infection? What are you talking about?"

"From the nail file. It's why he's still been in the hospital. My mom told me," Jude says, saving me from having to admit the things I've been keeping from my best friend.

Malcolm gently taps my jaw, forcing eye contact. "It doesn't matter. Did you hear the chain of events you stormed through to take the blame for this? If some sweet old lady gave a kid a piece of candy that the kid later gave to their friend who later had an allergic reaction to it, would you be demanding the old lady be put on trial?"

No. I wouldn't. But me and this hypothetical old lady are

130

not the same. There was no voice in her head compelling her to give that specific child the candy. No voice telling her the child needed the candy. Nothing guiding her to pick exactly the type that would end up making the other child sick. My bottom lip trembles uncontrollably. And then I'm surrounded by a weighted blanket. A weighted blanket in the shape of my friends, minus one. Minus two.

· · ·

I'm surprised to find Mama on the couch when I get home from the diner. Tears instantly cloud my vision because seeing your mom when you're sad, when you don't know what to do or say, when you've had to go without her for a couple of really hard days—it's like opening a tap on full blast.

I drop Santa Bag on the floor. The sound makes her snap her head up.

"Sorry. I didn't mean to scare you." I wipe the moisture from my face because if she notices that, it'll only scare her more. "Where's Josiah?" The apartment is eerily quiet.

"He's at his friend's house. Can't remember his name. Mama's name is Angela."

"Mario?"

"That's right. He's staying there for a few days. He was driving me up the wall."

I know Jojo has a lot of energy, but something about the comment offends me. She hasn't even tried to entertain him. I've barely seen her face since the trip to the police station. "Did he pack his medicine? Does he know when to take it?"

She raises her brows. "I may be going through my own shit right now, but you think I'd really send my son off somewhere without taking care of all that?"

"You don't even know the name of the kid he's staying with," I say under my breath.

Somehow her brows go even higher, way up near her hairline. "You say something?"

"No, ma'am."

"I didn't think so because I know you wouldn't stand there and judge me for letting that little boy's name slip my mind. I met Angela at the sickle cell center. I don't let Jojo stay just anywhere."

"I know."

"Then why you acting like you forgot?"

"I'm sorry, Mama. Really," I say for being rude, but not for being fiercely protective of my brother. "It was a good idea to let him go over there."

"I don't need you to tell me what's a good idea when it comes to my own child."

"That's not what I meant." The words come out fast and panicked because all I want to do is backtrack this conversation. To somehow un-offend her. "I meant he usually looks forward to doing things with me during school breaks, but I've been caught up in everything else going on right now." I don't know if she knows I took him to the zoo today and I don't mention it. I stand there, playing with my fingernails, hoping she'll sense my desire, my need, to talk to her. *Ask for what you want.* It's something she has drilled into me and Josiah our whole lives. *Don't expect people to read your mind.* Jojo gets it, but it's been a constant struggle for me, a girl who can hear what most people need without them having to ask. And it seems like now even that can't be trusted. Trusting that gets people killed. It gets people put on missing persons lists.

Mama stands. Takes a step toward me. For half a second,

132

I think she might reach for me. Pull me into a hug. But she takes a hard left and disappears into her bedroom.

I leave the apartment before the air inside it suffocates me. My neighborhood isn't bad—only the occasional car break-in or stolen package. But I do live in the city, and there are certain rules you're taught to follow to stay out of trouble. Sometimes people follow all the rules and trouble still finds them. Sometimes people break all the rules and get on just fine. I think the law of probability would put me in the latter group. If there's a missing-girl quota, my friend group has met it. So I'm not scared as I walk down the street near midnight. It's just me and Santa Bag, but I'm not afraid. If anything, I'm the one who should be feared. Creeping around windows. *Ladle. Helmet. Lotion.* Hovering by backdoors. *Salt. Ruler. Detergent.* Hiding behind shrubbery. *Washcloth. Graph paper. Hanger.* Leaving behind gifts with a missing flyer as a greeting card. Use at your own risk.

I fulfill needs until I'm numb to my own. When I slip into my cool sheets and close my eyes, I see Danny lying in his hospital bed. Danny lying on the ground outside of Sweet Pea's. Danny in a coffin. I see Philly graciously accepting gifts from me, oblivious to my involvement in the death of his brother. I see myself passing the pepper spray to Deja. These conscious thoughts fade into a dream. Me. A corrupt Santa Claus screaming *trick or treat.*

• • •

Jude and I ride to the rally together. We decided to hold it on the soccer practice field next to the student parking lot for visibility. There's a traffic light at the corner and rush hour is the perfect opportunity to get Deja's face out there.

Corbin, from my physics class, is the first person to greet us. "Morning! Me and my grandma made these." He gives Jude and me a handful of pins with Deja's face and hashtag.

"Wow, Corbin, these look great. Thank you."

"Five hundred more where those came from. East Lake rides for our own! You know that."

He jogs off to pass out more, leaving me feeling guilty for thinking some of the things I've thought about him in the past.

"There's Malcolm," Jude says.

He and his family are huddled up with Detective Habib and a representative from an organization for missing BIPOC children. His mother waves Ms. Jasmine over and Malcolm slips away to join us.

"Hey, y'all."

"Avoiding Ms. Jasmine?" I ask.

"After the way she spoke to us at the station? Yes. I'm not about to willingly subject myself to more of her wrath." He points to a group of elderly people settled in lawn chairs around a folding table. "I'm going to help them make signs. Want to come?"

I chew the inside of my cheek. "I think I'll take the box of ones they've already finished and start setting them up by the road." It's productive, and it'll keep me far away from everyone else. After the nightmares I had last night, Santa Bag got shoved underneath my bed for the day. Plus, this rally is about Deja and if I spend the whole time fulfilling needs, I won't get anything important done. I took my migraine meds this morning and brought my noise cancelers. That, and keeping my distance from the thicker parts of the crowd, will have to do for a few hours.

Jude passes me the box of signs and a mallet. Someone

has set up a tent with grocery store glazed doughnut holes and orange juice. I never understood why those two items are so often served together in minimal continental breakfast spreads, but I fuel up on sugar and head to the edge of the field to get to work. When I finish, the parking lot is crowded with cars. Students, teachers, school admin. Random folks taking flyers and buying T-shirts. I pause to check all my socials, typing #FindDeja into the search bars. There are hundreds of posts made within the last hour. Dozens of people tagging Afro Alt, asking them to share. I go to their page and I'm greeted by the beautiful picture of my friend I sent them via DM. Deja poses with Malcolm's birthday cupcake, toothy grin plastered on her face. Shared only two minutes ago, the post reads: This queen disappeared from our Atlanta Fest Saturday night. Like. Comment. Share. Let's bring her home fam. #FindDeja. I watch in real time as the likes jump by the dozens. When I look up, Malcolm and Winnie are sprinting across the field toward me, grinning.

I meet them halfway. "Did you see?"

"Yes!" Malcolm answers, thumbs flying a hundred miles per hour on his phone. "They posted on all their platforms."

"I made a short video that's getting a lot of hits, too," Winnie says.

"I'm going to tell everyone to keep posting and sharing," Malcolm says. "If we can get her trending, maybe she'll get some national attention."

They trot off as quickly as they appeared, straight by Ms. Jasmine who stands alone in an oversized #FindDeja T-shirt—Nurse Rincon is making them to order with his heat press machine. She raises her hand to the height of her face, but doesn't quite wave at me. I take my chances and approach her. She's probably still angry with me and I don't blame her.

But if I want to know for sure if Deja was hiding something, I need to get into her bedroom. That requires making nice with her mother first.

My head fills with her need for a sleeping aid as I get closer. "Hi, Ms. Jasmine."

She looks at me, but her bloodshot eyes don't seem to focus, and she sways on her feet. I'd think she was under the influence of . . . something, if her need hadn't revealed her sleep troubles. "Appreciate you organizing this, Sariyah."

There's an unspoken *it's the least you could do* hanging in the air, so I offer more. "I was wondering if there's anything else I could do to help? Even little things. I could run errands for you or bring some meals by."

She scratches the dry skin of her forearm and toes anxiously at the soft ground. "I've been meaning to have you and Malcolm over. Chat with you two for a bit."

There's nothing aggressive in her words and I wouldn't care if there were. I just want to get into her house.

"Can y'all come by for an early dinner tomorrow?"

"Yes, ma'am. We'll be there."

• • •

I go to the student parking lot to wait for Jude by his car. On the way, my phone lights up with an incoming call. Fitzgerald Davis.

"Hello?" I answer, not even trying to hide my shock.

"Hey, Atlanta."

I wedge the phone between my ear and shoulder, grinning. "It's so wild you called. I'd actually been meaning to reach out, but it's got to be breaking some cardinal rule of the universe for us to speak to each other outside of summertime."

"Maybe, but I heard from your dad that you're going through it right now. Consequences for rule-breaking are suspended under such circumstances."

"Guess that means he told you about Deja?"

"Yeah. Me, Ella, and my boy Jed helped him put some flyers up around town."

"Thanks for that. We're actually just wrapping up a rally to help spread the word about her."

"Oh yeah? Anything else we can do to help from down here?"

"I know social media isn't your thing, but if you have friends who are active, could you get them to share Deja's posts? We're using #FindDeja. Trying to get it to go viral."

He sighs. "Seems like the only way to make sure people get found these days."

"I hate it, but we need to do everything we can."

"I'll let folks know."

"Thank you, Fitz." I lean against Jude's car. "It's been forever. How have you been? How's post–high school life?" I ask, happy to change the subject.

"Not what I expected, to be honest. Fall semester was rough. I'm taking a break. Working. But it ain't all bad. I'm gonna ask Crystelle to marry me."

"Wow. My dad mentioned it, but I thought he had something mixed up. "

"Nope. Sounds like he had it right," he says with a chuckle.

"You're only nineteen. What's the rush?"

"You ask what's the rush, I ask why delay?"

"I can give you a hundred reasons, but I'm going to guess you've heard them all."

"Probably. But you know this is how we do down here. Your mom and pop jumped the broom young, didn't they?"

"Yeah."

"And look at them. Marriage tight enough to survive years of distance."

I appreciate that he sees that as a strength. Most people assume it was relationship trouble that led to our move. "Got me there, I guess." I spot Jude making his way toward me. "How's your sister?"

"If this is you finally getting the courage to ask her out, I'm afraid you're too late. She's dating Jed. Speaking of, Jed stays on Instagram. He has a lot of followers. I'll definitely get him to share some posts about Deja."

"Thanks so much, Fitz. That'd be really helpful. I gotta run, but send me some pics of you and Crystelle once you make her your fiancée! Can't believe I never met her."

"Will do, Ri. Take care."

I hang up feeling a little worried for Fitz. If I were him, I would have been done with Crystelle the second all the messy rumors about her cheating were confirmed. He always seemed way too caught up on that girl. But maybe I just don't get it. I've had my share of crushes—hell, I've got a big inconvenient one right now—but romantic relationships are as foreign to me as the stuff Dr. Stone scribbles on the whiteboard each day.

CHAPTER 16

· ·

Jude joins me at his car. "Check your email," he says.

Concerned by the look on his face, I quickly tap over to my Mail app, where one new message from Ms. Jess sits waiting.

From: Jessica Kent msjess@sweetpeasicecreams.com
To: Sariyah Lee Bryant Ribryant18@zeemail.com,
Jude Abrams heyitsjude@mailme.net

Dear Sariyah and Jude,
I apologize for sending something so sensitive via email, but in light of recent events, I hope you'll be understanding. My mother has been ill for quite a while now and I've put off visiting her for too long. I need some time away, so I've decided her home in Savannah is as good as any other for me to gather my bearings. Unfortunately, this means that Sweet Pea's will be closed indefinitely. Since this is coming on such short notice, and at no fault of either of yours,

your next paycheck will include the wages for all the
hours I had you each scheduled for this week.

Be Blessed,
Jessica Kent
Owner and CEO of Sweet Pea's Ice Creams
Atlanta, Georgia
Find us on Instagram!

I read the line about neither of us being at fault several
times, but it doesn't make it any more believable. Not after
yesterday at the park. Not after the way she looked at me. Not
after what she said.

I lock my phone and put it in my pocket. "Can't say I'm
surprised."

He agrees with me without truly understanding what he's
agreeing with, but it makes me feel better anyway. Makes me
feel validated in carrying the blame. Not that I need anyone's
permission. I'd be carrying it either way.

"I want to visit Philly again. Give my condolences."

Jude hesitates, only pulling his car keys halfway from his
pocket.

"You don't think I should."

"No. But I suspect you're going to do it anyway, so I'll
drive you." He unlocks the doors and we get inside. "I know
I've said this several times already, but in case you forgot,
what happened to Danny isn't your fault."

I turn away from him and stare out the window.

"It's not," he insists. "You say it all the time. You can't
predict how people will use what you give them. You aren't
picking and choosing what to pull from Santa Bag. It's *their*

need. It's nice of you to give this man condolences, but I hope you don't feel indebted or something."

"I don't," I say, even though I do. He's incapable of fully grasping my perspective. Everyone else on the planet is, too.

· · ·

Philly opens the door for me, television remote gripped in one hand, his cane in the other. He immediately turns around, heading back down the hall to the kitchen. "Knew you'd come."

"I can't stay long. My friend is waiting for me."

We sit at the tiny kitchen table. My arms stick to the plastic tablecloth. It's quiet for a moment and then we speak at the same time. Me paying my respects; him telling me he's already used everything I gave him last time I was here.

"Hold on one sec." He shuffles out of the room and returns with a dusty shoebox. He opens it and inside are at least two dozen old-fashioned steel hair combs. "My mother used to collect them. She was a mean old bag. Gonna see what I can get for 'em at the pawn shop, but this one is for you. To show my appreciation."

He passes me one that's been neatly repaired with some of the gems I gave him the other day. It's small, but heavy. Pretty, too, but not really my style and the pointy teeth seem like they'd scratch the mess out of my scalp. "Thank you, Philly."

"It's nothing. You want some tea?" He lifts a plastic pitcher, undissolved sugar swimming at the bottom.

"No, thank you."

"Suit yourself." He fills his battered Braves cup to the

brim, chugs half of it, then tops it off again. "Never did get to make it up to see him in the hospital, but I spoke to him yesterday afternoon. He sounded good. Like he always sounds. I wasn't thinking it'd be my last chance to talk to him." He swipes a tear from the corner of his eye and sniffs.

"I'm sorry," I say again.

"You love apologizing for things that don't got nothing to do with you, don't you?"

"That's the thing, though. It does have something to do with me."

"Why? Because he was at the shop to see you? You're forgetting he was there on my behalf, and I tell you what, I won't be losing any sleep over it. Danny wouldn't want me to, and he sure as hell wouldn't want that for you."

"It's not just that—"

He hocks a loogie. "It's that hoity-toity bitch who owns the ice cream shop that owes me an apology, that's who."

"Why?" I prod, hopeful to gauge his reaction to the truth without having to say it.

"What do you mean, why? That woman murdered my brother."

The word "murder" travels through my ear canals and lodges itself in the middle of my brain. It shudders there, nauseating me like the worst migraine ever. Malcolm and I are back in the bathroom of Retro Diner. *Say it with me.*

"He had a heart attack." I stutter the words out, needing Philly to agree. "He had a heart attack."

"Yuh. Well. I would have had a heart attack, too, if someone stabbed me in the neck with a nail file." He spits into his Coke can.

"He'd forgiven her." I don't say it for her benefit. I'm greedily searching for my own absolution here.

"Don't mean I got to." A firm, cold anger settles into the lines on his face.

Batteries, batteries, batteries.

The new intrusion into my mental space comes on strong enough to kick the word "murder" out, but it disappears as rapidly as it came on.

Philly's eyes go wide. "I've seen that look before. You got something else for me? Where's that goodie bag of yours?"

The need continues to come and go, dancing on the boundary of my range. "Philly, is there someone else here?" Because this need, most certainly, is not coming from him.

He opens his mouth but seems to rethink whatever he was going to say. "Bear's here."

"Bear, your dog?"

He points at the wall between us and the living room.

I scoot back in my chair, experiencing some déjà vu. There's a tiny dog sleeping on the back of the couch. "That's Bear?"

"Yeah."

"But he's a chihuahua."

"What's your point?"

"You said your dog could knock you over. I thought it'd be a big dog."

"Nope. That ankle biter will get underfoot and trip you up real quick. Felt bad keeping him in the basement, but after you gave me the air horn, I figured it was safe to bring him up."

Batteries, batteries, batteries.

"Right," I say softly.

"Something wrong?"

Everything is wrong, and it's probably stupid to answer him, but the words tumble from my mouth. "I don't hear the needs of animals."

143

"Well, it's only you and me here, girl, so go on and hand over whatever it is." His voice has a grating, desperate edge to it.

I stand. Put more space between us because I can't tell if he's trying to fool me. Distrust, maybe paranoia even, makes the hairs on my arms stand erect. There is definitely someone else here. It makes my heart race. Makes my mouth dry. Maybe I keep being drawn to this place for a reason.

Batteries. Batteries. Batteries.

Bear barks and I make several decisions all at once. I snatch the remote control from the table and shove my way past Philly. I dart out the back door, following the direction of the need. Whoever it's coming from can't be far away.

"What on God's green Earth?" he calls after me. "Get back here!"

I'm only a few feet from the house, but the trees are thick. It'll take Philly forever to work his way through the woods with that cane.

"Deja!" I call out. "Deja!" I shout her name over and over because finding her now, right here by home—it'd make all this make sense. Danny's death, everything that led to it, all cogs in the machine, leading to a moment maybe only seconds away. A few more paces through the forest, I find a tree with small planks of wood nailed to it. A ladder. I look up and see a trapdoor to a tree house.

Batteries. Batteries. Batteries.

"Deja! Are you up there?" When there's no answer, I climb. I'm three steps from the top when the trapdoor swings open. A pink-faced girl from my math class, Charlie McKinny, pokes her head out like an opossum.

"Sariyah?"

My foot slips, and I plummet to the ground.

144

"Oh my God! Are you okay?" She starts to climb down, but I tell her to stop.

"I'm fine." My tailbone throbs and I wince, calling out my lie. "I want to come up."

Charlie moves out of the way so I can hoist myself into the small, dim space. There are a few gallon jugs of water, an obviously slept-in sleeping bag, and some grocery bags with snacks.

"Are you living up here?" I wonder for a moment if this is a choice she made of her own will. "Are you okay?"

"I'm fine." She blushes. "My mom wouldn't take me camping for spring break, so this is the next best thing."

I take another look around, trying to understand how this setup could be desirable. I want to ask her if she knows she's "camping" in Philly Irvine's backyard, but she isn't hurting anyone and it's not my job to police trespassing.

"Why were you shouting for Deja?"

"I thought she was here."

"Why would she be here?"

"I thought someone . . . put her here." It feels ridiculous when I say it. But part of me hoped it was true. Because despite the disdain on his face when he spoke of Ms. Jess, I don't believe Philly would hurt anyone. I don't believe he could. If he'd somehow put Deja here, I for sure would have found her safe and alive.

Philly's voice finally reaches us, echoing through the trees. Charlie's mouth pops open. "You thought my uncle . . ."

"Your uncle?"

She nods slowly, like I'm dumb or something. "You thought I was crashing in a random dude's treehouse?"

"No. I don't know. I didn't know what to think."

She clicks her tongue. "To be fair, he doesn't know I'm up here."

145

"Sariyah!" Philly shouts, closer now.

"Well, he's about to."

"That's okay. He won't care. I just wanted to avoid talking about Uncle Danny."

"I'm sorry, Charlie." I leach every bit of sincerity in my bones into the words. They land heavy and thick, and I hope her subconscious somehow processes why. "These past few days must have been hell for you and your family."

She grins darkly. "Hell is pretty standard for us. But yeah. It's been worse than usual." She briefly rests her hand on my shoulder. "Worse for all of us. Shall we go talk to Uncle Philly before he has a heart attack, too?"

"Sariyah!" This time, it's Jude's voice echoing through the trees. He must have heard all the shouting.

"Let's go."

I remove the two triple-A batteries from the remote, place them next to her snacks, then follow her down the ladder.

. . .

The first thing I do when I get home is slip the hair comb Philly gave me into Santa Bag. I don't imagine he'd mind. Someone will need it. After that, I look up Charlie online and end up finding a link to a fundraiser started by her mother for Daniel T. Irvine's medical expenses.

You may have heard my brother Danny's name in the news recently. I want the world to know that all charges against him were dropped. The entire thing was a horrible misunderstanding and the Irvine family holds no ill will against Jessica Kent or vice versa. Our dear Danny had been battling severe heart disease for over a decade. Doctors had warned us of his need for a coronary bypass, but he couldn't get the funds together in time. Danny wished to be put to rest quietly, so there will be no public service, but we are raising funds to pay off his medical debt. Please, if you have the means, even a dollar will go a long way and be greatly appreciated. If you cannot give financially, your prayers for our family are more than enough.

Thank you,
Melissa McKinny

The progress bar on the ten-thousand-dollar goal is barely visible. There have been only two donations. Ten dollars from a Stephen McKinny and five hundred from Jessica Kent with no comment added. I scan the post again. Melissa McKinny should check with Philly about that no ill will part.

I click on the green donate button and give twenty dollars anonymously. It feels like nothing. It's not enough to move the progress bar and not enough to relieve any guilt.

My phone dings.

Jojo
If I do your chores until summer break,
can you give me some money?

Me
No. And you're only supposed to
use your phone for emergencies.

Mama got him some kid-friendly phone that can't do anything but call and text certain numbers.

Jojo
This is an emergency! Riyah pleeeeeease

Me
What do you need money for?

Jojo
For zoo camp! I asked Mama but she said no.
She said it costs too much money.

I could have told him that much.

Me
I'll talk to her

Jojo
Okay but you have to hurry because
you gotta pay by Sunday

I send him a thumbs-up. He replies with a dozen smiley faces and prayer hands, and I frown at them. Mama's not likely to be up for negotiation by Sunday. Her highs and lows are measured in weeks, sometimes months. I'm confident I can talk her into allowing him to attend by summer break, but I'm going to have to come up with the money myself. The progress bar on the fundraiser taunts me as a seed plants itself deep in my brain. A seed that has tried to take root there a hundred times before. Finally, I allow it. I don't have a job, and who knows when my final Sweet Pea's check will hit my account, but I'll always have a way to make money. If I hustle my ability for cash, Jojo could go to camp. I could donate to Danny's fundraising account, start one for Deja—do some good as penance for the bad that I have no control over. I crack my knuckles and pat my cheeks, trying to physically rid myself of the idea. This exact

148

thing ended in disaster for Grandma Bryant, but she tried to make a career out of it. I just need a temporary side hustle. Malcolm gets onto me about the missed opportunity about once a month.

Maybe it's time I follow his advice.

CHAPTER 17

. . . .

"Do we have to do this?" Malcolm asks as I drag him down the sidewalk toward Ms. Jasmine's house.

"Yes. We do. It's just dinner and Deja would do it if it were either of us. Our moms probably wouldn't have even had to ask her."

He plants his feet. "Our moms wouldn't have bitten her head off the way she did us at the police station."

I get behind him and push his back until he starts walking again. "Are you sure about that?"

All he offers is a noncommittal grunt.

"Plus, the things she said that day—they weren't wrong. I did leave Deja by herself."

"No, you didn't. You said she walked off."

"That answer wasn't good enough for you on Saturday." I don't know why I say it. It makes me feel dirty and needy, fishing for an apology.

"It is today." He picks up a rock and tries to skip it down the sidewalk. It lands with a bored thud a few yards away. We take turns kicking it. "You think Ms. Jasmine even remembers yelling at us?" he asks after we lose the rock under a parked car.

"Yes, and I think it's why she asked us to come over."

"To apologize?"

I snort. "Her generation doesn't apologize. They feed you and act like nothing happened."

"True. Let's get on with it, then."

We walk up the driveway of the duplex, dandelions sprouting up through cracks in the concrete. Ms. Jasmine opens the door before we reach the front step.

Lip balm. Lip balm. Lip balm.

She dabs her nose with a wadded-up tissue. "Y'all come on inside. Get out of this heat," she says, even though it's not especially hot today.

It takes my eyes a moment to adjust to how dark it is inside. Unlike the night Deja disappeared. The heavy burgundy drapes are drawn. The lamps are shrouded. The house itself seems to grieve Deja's absence.

"Y'all hungry?" she asks. "Food's hot."

"I could eat," Malcolm says in a way that I know stirs up something primal in the hearts of all mothers.

She leads us to the dining room where a few Styrofoam containers of chicken wings sit on top of the smiley face plastic bags they came in.

Malcolm's body goes rigid with the effort to hold in his laugh.

"Don't start," I whisper through clenched teeth.

Ms. Jasmine disappears into the kitchen and I dig a sealed tube of cherry lip balm from Santa Bag.

"Mm-hmm," Malcolm says. "She sho needs that."

"Malcolm," I hiss. "Really?"

"Listen to me good, Sariyah. I don't care what I'm going

through. If my lips are dry, if my hands are ashy, if my breath is stank, you better tell me. You can have empathy and still be straight with folks." He takes the lip balm from my hand and tosses it into a little glass bowl filled with keys and pens and coins.

I stare at the nickels and dimes, as the seed that planted itself in my brain last night finally begins to sprout.

"I thought this woman was cooking," Malcolm says, peering at the wings. "Where she get these tiny things from?"

"Malcolm!" I whisper-shout. No time, place, or situation is safe from his jokes, especially when he is even remotely uncomfortable—which is what these comments are really about.

"I'm just saying, if you're—Oh, shh. Here she come." He straightens up and tries trading his wing-judging eyes for sympathetic ones, but if I had to pinpoint an emotion in them, it'd be . . . shame?

Ms. Jasmine tosses a small stack of dessert-sized paper plates on the table before easing herself into a creaky chair. She has a rash on her cheek and her tiny frame looks even smaller than usual. "Y'all go on and help yourselves." Her fingers twitch as she motions toward the takeout bags.

We take five or six wings each and sit across from her.

She clears her throat and I peek at Malcolm out of the corner of my eye. She's preparing for her non-apology.

"Y'all are Deja's best friends. All she ever talks about." She fidgets in her seat like she can't get comfortable. "I've been hurting, and Malcolm, I know you've been here before. You've been here for years."

It hurts my feelings that she excluded me. I feel like a jerk for it, but I love Tessa, too. I lost her, too.

"Wouldn't wish this on nobody," Ms. Jasmine continues.

"It's a good thing what y'all been doing to spread the word, get folks looking for her, talking about her. Keep it up for me, because I need my baby home." She gives her scalp a few hard slaps and a vigorous scratch, grabs the lip balm from the bowl and smears some across her lips. "I need y'all to help me raise some money, too. That's what I really need." She says this, but all I'm sensing is a fresh need for painkillers. Again.

"I want to hire one of them fancy private investigators, you know? Someone paid to put all their time on Deja. Those cops, they are overworked. They got a dozen cases exactly like Deja's." She lets out a little sob and all I can think is that Josiah had a point. This woman cries without tears.

The front door squeaks open and heavy boots clunk across the floor. Ms. Jasmine smooths her blouse and pats her dry face.

"Jas?" A deep, irritated male voice booms. A need for a black light comes with it.

"In the dining room!"

A tall man in a dirty white tank top appears in the door-frame. He looks at me and Malcolm, then cuts his eyes at Ms. Jasmine. "What are they doing here?"

"Don't be rude, Derrick. They're Deja's friends. They came for a little visit with me. Sit down and have some wings."

He drapes his belt over the back of one of the dining chairs, looking us up and down. "Friends, huh? That word don't mean what it meant when I was coming up."

"Derrick!"

"It ain't nothing personal. But this world isn't what it used to be. My mother"—his eyes burn through Ms. Jasmine—"didn't let me go to weird-ass music festivals with smoking and drinking."

Malcolm fidgets awkwardly, picking at his chicken wings

while I mentally plead for him to make eye contact with me, wishing I could get telepathic confirmation that needing a black light is suspect.

"I didn't know it was that kind of festival," she says, scratching her head again.

"Probably would have got yourself a ticket if you did, huh?"

She laughs even though there is zero indication he's joking.

Derrick turns his attention back to us. "She ask y'all for money yet?"

"That's enough," Ms. Jasmine says. "We need it, Derrick. We're going to need it if we want to find her."

He leaves the room like she didn't speak to him at all and I catch Malcolm glaring in his wake.

Ms. Jasmine forces a smile. "He's Deja's stepfather, but he loves her like his own. He's taking this pretty hard." She wipes the spotless area in front of her with a napkin and sniffs. "All of us are. But I appreciate you two checking up on me. He does, too."

"Have you heard anything new from the detectives?" Malcolm asks.

"'We're doing everything we can. We'll let you know if there are any developments.' That's all they keep saying." She wrings her hands, scratches her neck. "But there haven't been any developments. They've brought in a few people for questioning, but it's all come to nothing. That's why we need to raise some money. Quick."

I don't know how much a PI costs, but I'll do what I have to do to help raise the funds. Until then, though, I'll do my own investigating. "May I use your restroom?"

Ms. Jasmine looks over her shoulder toward the sound of

running water in the main floor bathroom. "Upstairs. Can't miss it."

I give Malcolm a pointed stare, which he acknowledges with the slightest nod, before walking through the tiny living room and back into the cramped hall. The stairs are steep and creaky and I see what Ms. Jasmine meant when I reach the top. No way to get turned around up here. Straight ahead is a narrow door, a closet, I guess. To my left and right, full-sized doors. That's it. The landing is only big enough for two people to stand comfortably. Moving furniture into Deja's room must have been a hands-on experiment in physics and geometry. The bathroom door is cracked open, but I don't go into it. Instead, I gently push open the door to her bedroom. It smells like her and I hate myself for wondering how long it'll take for the scent to fade. Wondering if it has started to already. I peer down the stairs and once I confirm no one has followed me, I slip inside her room. It's small and messy, like mine. Not messy in the way I'd expect it to look after a police search, though. They should have turned the room inside out. And I don't know, maybe they did. Maybe Ms. Jasmine straightened it back up so Deja could come home to something normal. I poke around without knowing what I'm looking for, or if I'm looking for anything at all. She has a lot of books, but I don't think I've ever seen her reading. Most of them are newer bestsellers that have blockbuster movies to accompany them or old classics. The corner of a red envelope peeks out from between *Their Eyes Were Watching God* and *The Great Gatsby*. It's barely noticeable, but I'm drawn to it the way I'm drawn to items in Santa Bag when there's a need to be fulfilled. I slide it out and hesitate only a moment before removing the card inside. It says HAPPY VALENTINE'S DAY on the front. Must be a platonic one because I distinctly remember Malcolm asking her about her Valentine situation. She'd said there was no situation and she liked it that way, so the inside of the card catches me by surprise.

DEAR DEJA,
YOU'RE EVERYTHING I WANT AND NEED. COUNTING DOWN THE
DAYS TILL WE'RE TOGETHER.
FOREVER,
J.

"J.?" The first face to pop in my head is Jude's, but I looked at his class notes long enough to know this isn't his handwriting. Not to mention the idea of him and Deja being in a secret relationship before he moved here is absurd. Almost as absurd as the next *J* name that comes to mind. Josiah. I laugh out loud at that because, while I wouldn't put it past my brother to crush on one of my friends, he's not out here buying and sending greeting cards. I pick at a pimple on my forehead, racking my brain. There are two J-A-Y Jays that I know of at East Lake, but ain't no way Deja would be involved with either of them. I slip the card into my purse, planning to cross-reference it with my yearbook later. Malcolm's voice suddenly grows louder from downstairs. I take it as a signal to go back down, but my breath catches when I reach for the door.

There's a chain lock on it. I run my fingers over the tarnished metal. I gave this to her. I found it at an abandoned construction site. The thought of giving it new life through need fulfillment was nice, but I'd laughed when I passed it off. "Don't know what the heck you're going to do with this, but here you go," I'd said. She took it without comment and threw it into her bag.

I take a deep breath. Maybe this isn't what it looks like.

Because it *looks* like Deja was afraid or had something to hide. But the police came here. They saw this. I press and turn the lock on the doorknob, then wiggle it on the other side. It works fine. Why would Deja install the chain lock? Malcolm's voice trails up the stairs again. I turn and give the room another once-over, now positive there was something going on in Deja's life that she never shared.

At least not with me.

CHAPTER 18

. . . .

Malcolm waits until we reach the end of Ms. Jasmine's block to bombard me with questions.

"The bathroom trip was a front, right? You went up to Deja's room? Did you find anything?"

I wipe my sweaty palms on my jeans. "Um. Did Dej ever talk to you about stuff?"

"No. We had staring contests and sent blank iMessages back and forth."

"You know what I mean, Colmy. Serious stuff."

"Of course she did, Ri. She's my best friend."

My next inhale is rough and shaky and insufficient because even though I know this boy's heart is big enough for two best friends, it hurts to hear him call her that. I was his first. I fiddle with the back of my earring, forcing away thoughts that maybe she'd been replacing me. Scary thoughts that her disappearance was somehow a fulfillment of my need and desire to reclaim my best friend. It's not outside the realm of possibility. Nothing is anymore.

He links his arm with mine like he knows exactly how his words hit. Like he's sorry for that. He won't say it out loud, though. He doesn't need to.

"I don't know many details, to be honest. She didn't like being at home, but ain't that true for most people our age?"

"She didn't like being at home, or she was afraid of being at home?"

He drops my arm and stops walking. "Afraid? What makes you say that?"

"Have you ever been in her room?"

He thinks about it for a few seconds. "No, actually. I don't think I have. Why? What did you see?"

I fiddle with the small stack of friendship bracelets on my wrist, still processing the last thirty minutes.

"Spit it out, Sariyah. You're making me nervous. What'd you find?"

I monitor my tone carefully so I don't freak him out even more. "She had an extra lock on her door. A chain lock." I don't mention that it was provided by me. "The lock on the knob worked fine, but there's probably a good explanation, right?" I can't think of one, but maybe I could be swayed if he can.

He scrunches up his face. "Ri, what Black mother you know gives a mess whether or not her kid's bedroom door locks? Some of us are lucky to have doors, period. Nah. A chain lock? That don't sound right."

"Yeah. You know what else doesn't sound right?"

He glances away from me. "What?"

"Derrick. Her stepdad. He needed a black light."

"A black light? Maybe I watch too many crime shows, but can't you use those to see bodily fluids?"

159

"I think so. There are probably more . . . innocuous uses for them, but the vibe was off in that house, Mal. Maybe Deja really did have a reason to run away."

"It doesn't matter if she had a reason to run away. Look at the facts, Sariyah. She used that pepper spray in the woods. She left her phone out there. There was blood out there."

"I know, Malcolm! I know that. I'm not implying that running away means she's off chilling somewhere happy and cozy." I understand better than anyone why he's so resistant to the suggestion. Once the police decided Tessa was a runaway, their effort to find her seemed to drop off a cliff. They didn't reclassify her case until the security footage and chat room logs popped up five months later. Five months too late. "We don't need to call Habib in a panic claiming Deja had problems at home. Not yet. But figuring out what was going on with her might get us closer to finding her. That's all I want."

He lets out a big puff of air. "You're right. I'm sorry. Are you thinking Derrick is involved somehow?"

"I don't know. The police likely saw everything I saw in her bedroom. More probably. And you know they questioned him and her mom."

"They did." He takes my hand. "But we're going to make sure they didn't miss anything."

"Oh!" The lock thing completely distracted me. I wriggle free of his grasp and take the Valentine's Day card from my purse. "Have you heard of somebody named J.? Was Deja seeing someone?"

Malcolm's eyebrows crash into each other and he snatches the card from me, taking a few seconds to read. "I know this can't be from Jay Peters. That boy smells like Subway and he don't even work there. Deja wasn't that desperate."

"No. I had the same thought, and no. Could it be a girl?"

He nibbles on the end of his thumb. "I don't think so, but don't quote me." He tucks the card back in the envelope and inspects the front. "No stamp or return address. Whoever it was must have hand-delivered it."

"What are you thinking?"

He shrugs and passes the card back to me. "Maybe Dej had herself a little secret love affair, but Valentine's Day was like two months ago. Her longest relationship was five weeks. If she broke the record, we would have heard about it. Now come on, because Deja willingly turning her bedroom into a bunker is a far more pressing mystery."

· · ·

I follow Malcolm upstairs to his bedroom and plop down on the corner of his ratty mattress. Miss Doretta trots over and nestles herself in my lap as Malcolm settles in on the floor with his laptop. He clicks around, types furiously, and curses at the whirring machine every few minutes for being slow.

"What are you doing?"

He pops a jumbo Lemonhead into his mouth and talks with it pushed into his cheek like a chipmunk. "Looking up Deja's stepdaddy to see if he has any priors."

"What?" I scootch across his sheets until I can see his screen. "The police wouldn't have missed anything that obvious, right?"

Miss Doretta gives me a low rumbling growl for daring to disturb her.

"Of course not. But it's not like they are going to tell us if they found any dirt."

"Wouldn't he be under arrest if they did?"

"Not if they didn't find a straight-up smoking gun. Not if they are trying to build up a case against him or something."

He immediately goes to the Georgia Sex Offender Registry website. I gasp.

"Sariyah, she had a chain lock on her bedroom door. Let's get the extreme stuff out of the way first."

"But you don't think—"

"No, I don't."

We both let out an enormous sigh of relief when his name turns up nothing. Malcolm even uses his address to search in case Derrick Henry isn't his legal name. Nothing.

"I feel dirty for even going there." He pumps some hand sanitizer into his palm and clears his browser's history.

"If you won't get your hands dirty for a friend, who else would you do it for?"

"You right. Onward?"

"Onward."

For over an hour we scroll through court records, DMV stuff, even old voting records. By the end, what we've actually discovered is Deja's stepdad is a pretty stand-up citizen. Abrasive in person, and old-school in an annoying way, but on a paper—a decent human who donates much of his time to local charities.

"How did you even know about all these sites?"

He shrugs. "I'm a nosy bitch with a missing sister."

I sink back against the wall, deflated. "Derrick was rude as hell today, but I think Ms. Jasmine was telling the truth. He's taking this hard. Maybe he wanted the black light to do his own investigation."

"Maybe so." Malcolm closes his computer and slides it

under his end table. "What'd you do after the rally yesterday, other than leave me on read?"

I grimace. "I'm sorry."

"Not asking for an apology." He stretches and yawns loudly. "I get it."

"I kind of can't stop thinking about Danny, to be honest."

Miss Doretta begins to snore. Malcolm rubs her head but doesn't say anything to me and I'm brought back to the abrupt way he ended the conversation about Danny in the bathroom at Retro. A quiet voice in my head says to drop it and talk about something else, but I need to get these thoughts out. "You know Charlie McKinny from school?"

"Yeah. I have graphic arts with her."

"Well, Danny was her uncle." I skip how I learned that for now. "Her mom started a fundraising account for his medical expenses and it hasn't really taken off. I want to help."

"I didn't realize you were cool with Charlie like that."

"I'm not, but I don't really need to be cool with her to want to help, do I?" I hope he hears what I'm not saying. Plenty of people who didn't know Deja well are supporting the effort to find her. So many people searched and continue to search for Tess. The work of thousands of strangers closed Casey's case.

"Of course not," he huffs. "I didn't mean it like that. But how'd you know about her mom's fundraiser? She told you about it?"

"No. I was looking up some stuff about Danny. I can't shake this sense of guilt over what happened. Helping financially feels like the least I could do."

"He had heart disease, Sariyah," he says, sounding bored as ever.

"I was thinking about making a donation." Another donation. A more significant one.

He pushes his shoulders up near his ears. "Okay, so make a donation. You need my permission or something?"

I roll my eyes.

"Oh? What's all that about?" Malcolm stands and I can tell he is more than ready to fight. Like he's been holding something in and has had enough. And that's fine. Maybe I want to fight, too.

"Look, I know he had heart disease, but you're acting like you can't possibly understand why I feel some piece of responsibility. Like it's absurd for me to be caught up on it. Like you wouldn't be caught up on it if you were in my shoes."

"I can't ever be in your shoes, Sariyah. But from where I'm standing, right next to you, no, I don't get it. Why are you more worried about your potential three degrees of separation in the death of some random dude than Deja? That's how it goes. These girls disappear into thin air and no one cares. Not for long. They forget. They get wrapped up in other shit."

"I can walk and chew gum, Malcolm. We just left Dej's house. You wouldn't have even gone if I didn't drag you there. You're projecting."

"Hell yeah, I'm projecting and why shouldn't I? I'm angry, Sariyah. I'm pissed off. I actually thought things would be different with Dej. But it's been five days and already her own friend has new priorities. Why do you want to raise money for that man when you could raise it for Deja? For Tessa? For all the other missing people who might still actually have a shot at life?"

"Malcolm, you need to chill out. For real."

He laughs. "No, I don't. Ms. Jess laid you and Jude off.

You don't have any money and it sure don't sound like you'll be satisfied with throwing ten bucks at the fundraiser, so put it out there. How are you thinking about helping out? Go ahead and say it out loud so you can stop looking all confused about why I'm so mad."

I set my jaw and refuse to meet his eyes.

"Okay. I see you. Go ahead and pimp out your ability, but don't come crying to me when the gnats start swarming."

I'm angry at him for knowing, for guessing, for having the nerve to look down his nose at me over it. "Why are you acting like you haven't suggested I do exactly that at least once a month for the past three years?"

"Why are you acting like you didn't know I was joking?"

"Because I didn't!"

He looks genuinely surprised—and irritated—by this.

"Maybe the first ten times, but when someone makes the same joke five hundred times, you start to wonder if they mean it. You're always talking about hustling and grinding and making money. What was I supposed to think?"

"You were supposed to think I would never honestly suggest you do something that could get you hurt. Folks out there are unpredictable, Sariyah. We know that personally. Too personally."

I pick at my chipped nail polish. Over this conversation. Over this day. This week. He can suddenly act all high and mighty if he wants. I'll leave him out of it. Gladly. "I gotta go."

He turns his back to me. "Bye, then."

I storm out of his bedroom and leave the door wide open because I know he hates it.

Any building anger fizzles as soon as I step outside. Only hurt is left in its wake and I'm sick of hurting. I pull my phone from my bag and go to my recent contacts.

"Hello?" Jude's voice is deeper and scratchier than usual.

"Did I wake you?"

He clears his throat. "I fell asleep on the couch. What's up?"

"Malcolm and I had a fight. Can I come over? I don't want to go home."

CHAPTER 19

. . . .

Jude is sitting on his front stoop when I get to his place, his legs stretched out in front of him, black socks and slides on his feet.

The gate to the fence enclosing his tiny front yard squeals when I push it open.

"Hey." He points over his shoulder with his thumb. "Let's go around back. It's nice out."

I follow him to the side of the house. It's weedy and barely wide enough for us to walk through single file, but my jaw hangs slack when we get to the backyard. There are twinkly lights strung back and forth across the small, shrub-lined yard. A beautiful patio made of stone pavers. A firepit. Lounge chairs. It's gorgeous, and it smells like a whole-ass flower garden, even though I don't see anything in bloom yet. "What's this secret oasis you've been hiding?"

He rubs his neck and holds back a smile. "I set it up for my mom."

"Jude, you did all this? You could start a business. This is amazing. Was it her birthday or something?"

He laughs. "No. A son can't do nice things for his mother for no reason?"

"I mean, yeah, I guess." A drop of piping-hot shame courses through me. When's the last time I did something nice for my mom just because?

"Nah. You called it. It was an apology and thank-you wrapped up in one." He squats near the firepit, fiddles with some kindling, then pats his pockets until he comes up with a lighter. "Good night for some flames."

"You wouldn't have a little something else we could light up, would you?" I take another look around the yard. "Doesn't look like there's any poison ivy back here."

He chuckles. "Are you sure? Definitely got the impression it wasn't your thing," he says as he pulls an Altoids container from the pocket of his sweatpants.

"I don't think it is. Tried it once thinking it would quiet the needs. Opposite effect."

"Then why do you want to do it?"

"There aren't any needs to quiet right now, but there's plenty of other stuff going on in my head that I'd like to shut up. Maybe it'll be different this time."

"Maybe." He removes a finger-length, tightly rolled paper from the container, lights it, and takes a long draw. His thin gold-framed glasses slide to the end of his nose and he looks up at me over them, fire glinting in his eyes. My pulse quickens and my stomach fills with butterflies. For the first time, I don't shame myself for reacting to him this way.

He takes another puff before passing it to me and I copy him, only I'm not nearly as smooth with it. I choke and cough and pass it back, waving the smoke from my face as we walk to the large, circular lounge couch.

"Are you going to tell me what you did?" I ask once we're both seated and comfy.

He pushes his beanie back on his head. A few chocolate curls spring free. "Hm?"

"All of this. The yard. Why'd your mom deserve such a big apology?"

"Because I was a really bad son for a really long time." He flicks away some ashes. "And I'm still no saint, clearly. But I've come a long way. I'm kind of scared to tell you about the old me, if I'm honest."

"Why?"

He leans forward, knee bouncing anxiously. "Because I want you to think good things about me."

"Well, it's too late for that," I tease. "But seriously. I supplied the weapon that caused the injury that led to a fatal heart attack, and you still give me the time of day."

"Malcolm's right, you know. That doesn't sound as bad as you think it does. But either way—what you do, that's nature. You can't impose morality on nature. It just is. All you can do is respect it. Be gracious when it blesses and humble when it doesn't."

"Give me that." Obviously not on his level yet, I reach for the joint—or blunt, I sure as hell don't know the difference— and take another drag. "I'm human, Jude," I say, holding back another cough. "Morality is the only thing that makes us any different from the other animals."

"You're human and . . ."

"Oh, you've definitely been hanging around Malcolm too much. And what?"

He blows out a puff of smoke, smirking. "Just and."

I roll my eyes and shove his shoulder with mine. "Tell me your secret. You know mine."

169

"Your ability isn't a secret, though."

"It is to most people. Even gnats don't know about the headaches, or my inability to hear the people closest to me." I stop there, hoping he'll remember that he is one of only a few people on this planet that fall into that category.

"Fair enough." He lies back, exposing a thin strip of his stomach and the dark gray elastic band of his underwear.

I lie next to him. It's rare to see stars in the city sky, and tonight is no exception. But the fairy lights twinkle and the leftover smog from the day gives the clouds a purple haze that draws our attention almost as much as the stars would.

A few minutes pass before Jude speaks. "I'm not from Florida. I mean, I was born there, but we left right before I started first grade. My dad got a new job."

"Where'd you move to?" I ask, instead of *Why'd you lie to me?*

"Texas."

I stay perfectly still. I don't want him to know that I've googled him. If he is going to share, I want to hear exactly what he has to say.

"I'd forgotten how green the East Coast is. So many trees. So different from the places we stayed in Texas. Mom grew up here and was so excited to come back. Kept talking about getting a garden set up, but I knew that was never going to happen. She works too much."

"Why did you guys move here?"

"It's not the only reason, but my parents got divorced. Their marriage started falling apart once I started high school. Couldn't be in the same room without screaming and cursing each other out. I stayed out of the house as much as I could, but we didn't live in the best area. Made friends with some guys I shouldn't have." He looks at me, a sad smile on his face. "We stole so much shit. And most of them—they did it so they could help keep the lights on and feed their brothers and sisters. Both my parents had solid jobs and I'm their only kid. They legit would give me almost anything I asked for. You know, so long as I kept my grades up, helped out around the house. I have no excuse for the stuff I did."

"So why'd you do it?"

He fiddles with the thin chain around his neck. "Devil finds work for idle hands," he says in a voice I assume is meant to mock his mother. "My parents put me in this after-school program. I started tutoring some of the younger kids there. Actually kept me out of trouble for a minute."

I turn on my side and study his profile. "Only for a minute?"

His cheeks color some. "They had to close the center for a couple of days because there was some stomach bug going around. I met up with my boys and we did what we always did. Stole some sneakers and stuff from these dudes playing basketball. They saw us running off with them, but we had a good head start. Turns out one of them went to my school. He recognized me, and I ended up getting into a really bad fight with him."

"Over some sneakers?"

"You sound like my mom," he says, amused. *"Over some sneakers, Jude? Really?"* he says with that same mocking voice. "Anyway, so we're fighting and a teacher comes running down the hall, shouting at us to break it up. It was in one of the back halls during lunch, so there weren't that many people around. The teacher kept screaming at us. I couldn't make out anything she was saying. I was getting my ass beat, to be honest." He looks at me and puts his hand on his chest. "Lover, not a fighter at heart, promise."

"Was she able to break it up?"

171

He laughs. "Yes, but not in the way she hoped. She grabbed my shoulder and it distracted me for half a second. Dude got a good one in." He pushes his curls away from his forehead and taps a slightly raised scar near his hairline. "I stumbled back and knocked her over. Fell on top of her. She broke her wrist, her skirt came up. I know it looked horrible, but the way she screamed, the way the assistant principal yanked me off her, the way they were looking at me like I . . . I don't know. People started talking shit, straight-up lying for no reason. Saying I pushed her. Saying I hit her. Saying—" He swallows hard. "Saying I touched her when she fell, which is absolutely ridiculous. Only a bunch of high school kids could twist that up like that. She publicly denied that part, but not the rest of it. And she didn't speak up right away. The school called the cops. Worst day of my life. By the time my mom and dad got me from the police station, all sorts of crap was plastered all over the internet. When she finally spoke up, the damage was done."

"Weren't there cameras or something?"

"When you know you want to fight someone, you track him all day. Wait for him to walk into a blind spot. Wait for a time when other kids won't really be around to record it. He wasn't fighting for clout." He offers me another hit.

I shake my head. "Still not my thing, I think."

He puts it out and pops a couple of Altoids.

"What happened after the teacher spoke out?" I accept some mints, which immediately cool my mouth and open my sinuses.

"I changed schools, but the rumors followed me. Mom told my dad she wanted to go home to Atlanta and give me a fresh start. Dad thought it was best if we went without him and filed for divorce two weeks later. We moved here three months after that. Stayed with my aunt Naomi while some repairs were being done on this place. That's when I worked on the backyard."

"I'm sorry you went through all of that."

"Brought it on myself. I was a bad person."

"You did a bad thing, and it got blown out of proportion." I wait until the silence forces him to look at me. "I still think good things about you."

His eyes search mine, trying to fish out any hint of uncertainty or dishonesty. I make sure not to look away from him. He won't find what he's looking for, and he smiles softly when he realizes this.

"Tell me what happened with you and Malcolm."

I roll onto my back and let out a dramatic groan. "I was insensitive. I should have known better than to talk to him about Danny. He's not in any space to understand why it bothers me so much."

"I don't think you need to be in any special space to empathize with why that's upsetting for you."

"It's not that he can't or doesn't empathize, but after Tessa, and now Deja—I just shouldn't have brought it up around him. They are so much bigger in comparison. I know that. I feel that to my core. But . . ."

He props himself up on his elbow and looks down at me. "But you feel other things, too?"

I nod, playing with the string of his hooded jacket, wanting to tug him closer.

"That's okay, you know." He lets his gaze linger on my mouth before returning to my eyes.

"I know." I swear I can hear both our hearts pounding as I raise my hand to his face and gently run my thumb over his scar. He stays completely still, eyes warm and steady on mine

173

as I trail my fingertips down his cheek and across his jawline. My mind is hazy, like a cloud, and it feels so good to lean into it. To let all my complex and conflicting emotions swirl together until there's nothing distinct left. To allow my body to act without running through some infinite list of pros and cons. I position myself so my face is only inches away from his. Crickets whisper from the bushes and a light breeze tickles the back of my neck as I lean in close enough for the skin of my bottom lip to graze his. Pillowy soft. I pull away with a slight grin. "Carmex game on point."

He exhales a laugh, blowing the strong, minty smell of Altoids over my face.

"Breath too."

"You forever got jokes, huh?"

"Not just jokes." I want him to ask me what else and make this moment perfect.

His lips curve upward. "What else?"

I kiss him, slowly, and all the little demons that have been plaguing me flutter away.

For now.

CHAPTER 20

• •

Friday afternoon, Jude and I post up inside the Five Points MARTA train station. Last night I told him about my idea to make some extra money and he didn't have any of the hang-ups Malcolm did. Of course he didn't. He hasn't seen any gnats in action. I insisted he accept a 20 percent cut for help-ing me. Made it seem like being my assistant and keeping me organized was going to be the most painstaking job he's ever done. He'd joked that he'd tutored me for free so he can han-dle anything. I was glad to have him distracted with teasing me. Because telling him the truth, that I'm scared to do this alone, would have for sure deterred him. And we have no time for that. I have until 5:00 P.M. Sunday to submit the payment for Josiah's camp. He's stopped texting me about it, so I know he thinks it's a lost cause. That'll only make his reaction a hundred times better when I tell him he's going. I need to see that reaction. And I need to see that progress bar on Danny's fundraiser move. And I need to help Ms. Jasmine raise money to hire a private investigator. These are things I have control over. These are things I can make happen. But to eliminate the skeevy feeling of exploiting my ability for cash, I'm making this a tip-based endeavor. If I get lucky, someone will find use for their object quickly and tip heavily. And maybe even spread the word.

It takes twenty-two minutes to get lucky, and then I have a steady stream of people coming to see what I might have for them. A tall, brown-skinned man in need of socks approaches. I fish around and hand him a fresh two-pack.

"Socks? I just bought me some new ones yesterday." He extends his arm to give them back when a guy on a skateboard zooms between us, knocking a McDonald's Sprite from the hand of a little kid. The drink spills all over the tall guy's Crocs.

He rises onto his tiptoes and settles back down again, the moisture in his socks causing a squelching sound. Then he bursts out into laughter, wagging an index finger at me. "Did you set that up?"

I toss up my hands, happy to let people wonder if I'm putting on some kind of gimmicky magic show. "Well, sir, I—" The logo on his T-shirt catches my eye. I point at it. "You've been to Shug Mama's Diner?"

He looks down at his chest. "Sho have. Best peach cobbler in the state of Georgia."

"So you've been to Chefly?"

"Been there? I grew up there. And there's only one Shug Mama's." He sits down on the bench and removes his shoes.

"Watch out!" I warn before he places his Sprite drenched socks on top of Deja's flyers.

He drops the socks on the ground and points at the stack. "I know her."

"What?" Jude asks, suddenly paying attention.

The man picks up a flyer. "Well, I don't know her, but I seen her."

"Seen her where? When?" I ask.

"In Chefly, actually! Bout two, three years ago. Think she was living over by the high school with her parents."

I deflate. Deja definitely never lived in Chefly and even if she had, sightings from years ago are useless.

"Hey, you got anything else for me in that bag, Bag Lady?"

"No, sorry." I fulfill the needs of a few people who witnessed the sock thing. Some of them pout when nothing immediately happens, but tip anyway, deciding that eye drops, plastic baggies, and a phone case are worth a little something.

"You sure about that, Bag Lady?" the man from Chefly asks when I finish. "You ain't got something else for me?"

"She said no," Jude answers firmly.

The man backs away, hands raised, and leaves his dirty socks on the ground.

Two hours later, I've passed out fifty-two Deja flyers, fulfilled thirty-two needs, and made ninety-six dollars. Fifty of which came from one person. I'll have to use a chunk of my earnings to restock Santa Bag, but even considering that, I made more money than I would have for the same time spent behind the counter at Sweet Pea's. I hand Jude a twenty. "Let's do it again tomorrow."

He studies the bill. "I feel like you paid me for hanging out with you."

I hold out my hand. "I mean, if you don't want it . . ."

He smirks and pushes the cash into his pocket. "Hey, I'll be taking advantage of this until you finally wise up." He stops in front of one of Deja's posters and tries to stick the sagging top-left corner back to the wall. "You have some tape?"

It's in my hand before he even turns around. We fix the sign, but the fact that we needed to shifts the mood.

"Hey, I know this might be a big ask, but . . ." Jude trails off, chewing his bottom lip. "Remember my aunt? The one I was telling you about last night? I was hoping we could stop over there with Santa Bag and maybe you could do your thing for her."

I laugh in disbelief. "Your aunt?"

"Yeah. She's been kind of down on her luck. Maybe a little mystical intervention would help her out."

I stare at Deja's sign, the corner of which has come untacked again. I use my fist to press it back against the wall. "That's what you're thinking about right now, Jude? Your aunt?"

His chin drops toward his chest and I realize I'm doing to him what Malcolm did to me. Insulting him by implying there's only room in his head to care about one thing. Yesterday, I knew what it was to be in Jude's shoes right now. But today, I understand Malcolm's point of view a little better. When you're consumed by one thing, it's painful to hear someone else talk about anything else with any kind of conviction. "I'm sorry. That wasn't fair."

He gives me a wary, hopeful grin and grasps my hand. "It'd mean a lot, Sariyah. You can keep my cut from today. I'll even throw in an extra twenty."

I sort of hate that he's asking this of me, but who am I to pass up some extra cash right now? And who am I to help strangers, but not my friends? "Sure. But let's keep it low-key. It's going to be pretty freaking awkward if your aunt goes all gnatty on me. And that's if I even pick up on anything. No guarantee, you know. And no guarantee it'll be the life-changing thing you're thinking it will be if I do. You saw that guy use the T-shirt I gave him to wipe dog poop off his shoe."

He smiles. "How do you know he didn't get on the train and meet the love of his life right after that?"

"Jude, who is meeting the love of their life on MARTA?"

"Hey, you never know."

I force all signs of amusement from my face. "I can't do this if you have some unrealistic expectations. I'm not a miracle worker."

"Sometimes you are."

"Jude, seriously."

"I know." He meets my eyes. "It's been a hell of a week, Ri. And I know it's had you questioning things about yourself. But I hope the fact that I'm asking this of you shows you what I think." He nudges my shoulder. "Good things. Only good things."

I turn away, hiding my smile. "Fine. When?"

"Um, right now? It's her birthday and she's having a get-together at her place."

"Are there going to be a bunch of people there?"

"I mean, yeah. It's a birthday party, but you can ignore everyone but her. We'll be in and out in like five minutes."

"It's difficult for me to ignore needs, Jude. They pester me until I deal with them. On any given day I have a rotation of at least five unfulfilleds that I sit around worrying over. I don't want to do that with your family."

He shifts uncomfortably from one foot to the other, rubbing his arm. Thinking. "Right. I'm sorry. I shouldn't have asked."

I sigh heavily and dig around in my bag until I come up with a clown wig and squeaky red nose. "Forget plan low-key." I pass the wig to Jude. "You're helping me."

• • •

179

Jude bursts through the front door of his aunt's house with Santa Bag tossed over his shoulder. "Heard it was somebody's birthday!"

"The hell you got on your head, cuz?" a girl with long twists and a Solo cup in hand asks.

"Magic cap." Jude opens Santa Bag so I can search inside.

"For you," I say, presenting her with a packet of morning glory seeds. "From Random and Ratchet Gifts Emporium." I squeeze my big round red nose until it honks.

"Thanks?"

I elbow Jude hard in the ribs and whisper, "Your family is going to think there is seriously something wrong with me."

"Random and Ratchet was your idea."

"Shut up."

He grins and points across the room. "There's my grandma. Big Mama!" He waves at an old woman sitting in a recliner, casually observing everyone else. A tiny old white man wearing a kippah and huge Coke-bottle glasses sits next to her, holding her hand.

We walk over to them, and Jude gives the old man's shoulder a squeeze. "Hey, Saba." He kisses Big Mama's cheek.

"Hey, baby." She smiles at him, then looks me up and down. "Now, who is this here?"

"Big Mama, this is my friend Sariyah."

"Sariyah?" She sucks her teeth. "You sure got a bunch of little girlfriends, don't you?"

"Nah, Big Mama, you're thinking of Cousin Drew, not me." He points at a guy in the corner with a girl hanging on each arm. He does resemble Jude—if he were six inches taller and fifty pounds heavier.

Big Mama adjusts her glasses. "Is that right?"

180

"That's right, Big Mama. I am not good with girls at all."

She points at me. "You got one to come here with you, didn't you? You're doing all right, baby." She takes his hand in hers. "Just keep out of trouble."

Her words are suggestive, and I can imagine how Jude would feel if she'd said that before he got to share what he did last night.

"For you." I give Big Mama a shiny black pen.

"Well, it's about time! I asked somebody to bring me a pen for this crossword about an hour ago. Thank you, sugar." She slips on her reading glasses. "Now, y'all go on and say happy birthday to Naomi. She's out back."

Jude kisses his saba's forehead and we go out into the yard. His aunt is far from the noise of everyone else, pulling a few weeds from her garden. I take a random business card from my bag and pass it to Jude. "Give her this."

"Juju," she drawls. "Good to see you."

Juju? She pulls him into a big hug and I stare at him impishly from behind her head.

"Hey, Auntie. Happy birthday."

"Thank you!"

"This is my friend Sariyah."

"What a pretty name!" She gives me a once-over. "And a pretty person!" She points a finger back and forth between me and Jude and raises her eyebrows.

We both stammer and laugh awkwardly.

"Oh, I see." She winks. "To be young again! Y'all enjoy it while you can."

Her words snap me back to reality. The reality where not all young people get to enjoy their youth. I think his aunt catches her error because she lets out a small gasp.

"I'm so sorry. I heard . . . I know. Wow. All this must seem . . ." She looks around at everyone lounging, drinking, and talking. Not a care in the world.

Jude squats a little so his eyes are in line with hers. "It's okay. We contain multitudes. Isn't that what you always say?"

She pats his cheek. "That's right, baby."

"Well, we aren't staying long, just wanted to say hello." He passes her the business card. "Put this somewhere safe."

She reads it, flips it back and forth a few times. "What's this?"

"Don't ask questions because I don't have answers," he says truthfully.

"Strange as that mother of yours." She slips the card into her pocket. "Well, I don't want to hold y'all up. Thank you for stopping by. And, Juju, you know I'm here if you need me, right?"

"I know, Auntie." He squeezes her hand. "Bye."

I give him a playful shove on our way out. "Juju? Jojo is going to love that."

"I'm sure he will. You should go home and tell him all about it right now. And after that, you should call Malcolm."

I agree, and he takes me home. But I don't do what I said I would. Not right away. I stall by cleaning the apartment from top to bottom. When I finally sit on my bed with my phone, it rings. Malcolm got to me first.

"I'm sorry," I blurt as soon as I accept the call.

"For what?"

I smile a little because him giving me a hard time like this means he's already forgiven me. "Really, Mal. I shouldn't have—"

"Yeah, cool. I'm sorry, too. Onward?"

"Onward."

"Okay, so I'm starting to see more about Deja online. People from school have been putting in work. They are showing up for her, Ri. The posts from Afro Alt were a catalyst, but she isn't viral yet."

We brainstorm other ways to attract attention, wondering how much it will take to get her name on the national news. We don't say another word about our argument. It might not be the healthiest thing. In fact, I know it isn't. All we've done is tighten the cap on a shook-up bottle of Coke. But this is how we do. This is how we've always done. And these days I take comfort in the familiar.

CHAPTER 21

. . . .

Josiah spends Saturday morning moping around the house. He goes back and forth to the fridge, holding the door open way longer than Mama would ever tolerate, hoping for new food to appear. He plays his video games for only a couple of minutes at a time before getting bored. What tugs on my heartstrings the most is when he asks to borrow my computer and I later find my YouTube account recommending nothing but animal videos. It's hard to watch, but I can't tell him I'm going out later to scrounge up the remaining cash I need to secure his spot at camp. I don't think his nine-year-old body could handle the letdown if I told him I was trying but ended up failing.

Both of us start when Mama's bedroom door opens. She shambles into the kitchen but only leaves with a glass of water. "Need you to go to the grocery store for me this weekend, Sariyah. Break is about over and Josiah needs stuff for his lunch. There's cash on the table by the door."

"Yes, ma'am. Do you need anything?"

"No." She goes into her bedroom and closes the door.

"Is Mama okay?" Josiah asks.

"She's . . ." I wonder, for a second, what the age-appropriate response is. "Depressed."

He stares at her closed door, considering the word. "She was depressed before."

"Yeah. It happens to everyone sometimes, but for some people, it happens a little more."

He frowns. "Why? Did we do something?"

"No. Not at all. Sometimes there's no good reason, but I think certain things can make it worse."

"Like Deja being gone?"

A hard lump forms in my throat. "Mm-hmm" is the best I can get out before taking a huge gulp of water. "But she'll be okay. And so will Deja. And so will I."

His face is wrinkled with uncertainty.

"And guess what?"

"What?"

"I'm signing you up for zoo camp."

• • •

I sit at the dining table for my daily social media rounds. It's hard to believe I once did this for fun. This time last week, we were all getting ready for the festival. It's been one of the longest and shortest weeks of my life. My first stop is Afro Alt's Facebook page. The post there is the same as the one on all their other platforms. It's mostly strangers in the comments, but a few people from school who never even speak to Deja have chimed in talking about how much they miss her and want her to come home. About how they had this class or that with her. How they can't believe what happened and they just saw her a few days ago—as if seeing someone

185

prevents bad things from happening. Their words feel grossly performative, but I can't be mad. The engagement on the post is a good thing.

I'm switching over to the Atlanta Police Department's page when I get a notification from Instagram. Jedidiah Jones has requested to follow you. Fitz's friend. I casually wonder if my phone heard me talking about Chefly with that guy at the MARTA station yesterday and if that somehow influenced this follow request. Then I realize that sounds like something Philly would think up, and I push it from my mind.

I scroll through Jed's feed. His face is barely familiar, but Fitz has mentioned him enough that it feels like we're old friends. Looking at those two and Ella and other random kids from town—fishing, hanging around bonfires, four-wheeling—I can't help but wonder what my life might have been like if Jojo wasn't sick. If I'd gone to Blueship High. Do people get stabbed with nail files in Chefly? Do girls go missing? I scroll back up to accept his request, but my heart stops when I reach the top of the page. There. Under his bio.

Followed by DejaDej.

I immediately check, but he isn't following her back . . . or isn't following her *anymore*. His following-to-follower ratio is really unbalanced. That's how it usually is for guys who look like him—fresh cut, chiseled jaw, smooth brown skin, deep dimples. I call Malcolm.

"Hey," he answers.

"Colmy, did Deja ever mention a guy named Jedidiah Jones?"

"Jedi what?"

"Jedidiah Jones. He's a friend of a friend from Chefly."

"Why all your friends down there got grandaddy names?"

"Says Malcolm Frederick Hawkins, brother to Winifred and Contessa, dog daddy to Miss Doretta. Answer my question."

"No. She most definitely did not mention a Jedidiah. I don't think Dej could even *say* Jedidiah. You know she got a little lisp."

"There is not one letter in Jedidiah that's affected by a lisp." But man, do I miss her voice.

"Said what I said. Why you asking anyway?"

"I don't know. It's stupid. His first and last name start with J, she follows him on Insta—"

"And you think he gave her that Valentine's Day card you stole out of her bedroom?"

I sink low into my chair. "Honestly? No, not really. He lives three and a half hours away and has a girlfriend. I think I just needed you to talk me down."

"Well, consider yourself laid out on the ground. Jedidiah don't sound like her type."

"Go look at his IG. JedJones14."

A few seconds pass. "Oh dang, never mind. He's everybody's type. But I don't know, girl. If you're worried about it, talk to him. He's probably your cousin. Ain't everybody from Chefly, related?"

"Bye, Malcolm."

I accept the follow request and request to follow Ella while I'm at it. Fitzgerald's page is public. He hasn't updated in years, but I can't judge—neither have I, except to share info about Dej. Fitz only has two posts. One of a record player and one of him and a girl with their backs turned, looking at the sunset. Crystelle, his ex-girlfriend, soon-to-be fiancée, I assume. I follow him and he follows back right away, then sends me a DM.

Fitzdavy
You're spoiling me now. A phone call and
social media contact all in the same week?
Jed was just telling me he found you on here

> **Me**
> Is it bad I kind of forgot
> what he looked like?

Fitzdavy
haha no. He spent almost every
summer at football camp in South
Georgia. I think y'all met like once.

A new message pops up at the top of my screen.

JedJones14
HOW COULD YOU FORGET
A FACE LIKE THIS?

> **Me**
> You and Fitz are together, I see.

A few seconds later and I'm part of a new group chat with
Fitz, Jed, and Ella. I catch up with all of them for a few, wondering how soon is too soon to ask Jed about Deja. The conversation transitions to Blueship track and field and I can't
wait any longer. I send him another private message.

> **Me**
> Fitz told me you helped hang posters
> for my friend, Deja. Thanks for that.

JedJones14
no problem! Really hope she turns up soon

He takes over five minutes to reply.

JedJones14

Whoa. Hey, I had no idea she was following
me. That's wild. She never sent me a message
or anything. I'm sorry I can't be more helpful.

Me

No worries!

I'm not even sure I can believe him, but if he's lying
about interacting with her at all, he definitely isn't about
to confess to a secret relationship with her. I choose to play
it cool and return to the group thread. The escape with
old friends is nice, but Jojo bursts my happy little bubble
after only a few minutes. He stands over me, panting and
sweaty.

"Ew, back up." I shove him away. "You stink."

"What do you expect? I was playing outside. I need to get
conditioned for camp."

"Conditioned? Josiah, it's zoo camp, not soccer camp."

"Yes, but the brochure said we'll be taking field trips to
the botanical garden and the aquarium and to be prepared
to spend most of the day outdoors. There's even an overnight
day." He paces excitedly. "We'll be sleeping by the giant pandas. Giant pandas!"

Not if I don't make the rest of the money to pay for it. I
text Jude and tell him I'm ready. "Sounds fun, Jo. Did you
need something?"

He stands there, hands on his hips, still panting, and suddenly I'm nervous.

"Josiah, did you take your medicine this morning?"

He gives me a vigorous nod.

"You need some water?" I'm in the kitchen filling him a glass without listening to his response. I pass it to him and he drinks it all without coming up once for air. "Don't push yourself too hard."

"I wasn't. Not until I saw Deja's mama."

"You saw Ms. Jasmine? Where?"

"Outside. Around the corner. She was talking with a man."

"What man? Mr. Derrick?"

"Nope." He grabs a pack of Oreos from the cabinet. "That big man you told me not to talk to cuz he sells drugs to little kids," he says, teeth black with cookies. "Ms. Jasmine looks like she does drugs."

"Josiah!"

"What? I'm telling it like it is."

"What do you know about drugs?"

He shrugs. "I been out in these streets."

I snatch a pillow from the couch and chuck it straight at his peanut head. He runs away laughing and goes into his bedroom, Oreos in hand. I go to my own room and sprawl across my bed, taking a few deep breaths. It wouldn't be the worst idea in the world for Ms. Jasmine to talk to that man. No doubt he sees and knows things going on around the city that most people don't. I roll onto my side and grip Tibby. But then again, Jojo's not wrong. Malcolm and I fought before we could start looking into her, but Ms. Jasmine has been setting off red flags for days. I won't let myself be distracted from it for even one more.

CHAPTER 22

· ·

It's hustle for cash round two. Jude calls when he's outside, but I ask him to come up for a minute. I open the door before he can knock because I didn't ask Mama if I could have a friend over. I'm not worried about getting caught. She's already left her room once today. Jojo and I aren't likely to see her again until Monday.

"Come on in."

He steps inside and slips out of his jacket. Looking at him makes my armpits sweat and I'm not trying to deal with my awkward bodily reactions to him right now. "Want something to drink?"

"Sure."

I lead him to the kitchen, and he sits on one of the barstools at the tiny peninsula.

"I want to go back to Five Points Station like we planned, but I was hoping you would help me with something first."

"What's that?"

I pour him a glass of water, stalling. "Can we drop Jojo at his friend's house? It's on the way."

He laughs like the question is a joke. "Of course. No problem. Why are you acting so funny?"

I scrunch up my face, embarrassed to say. "I want to find out more about someone."

"Who?"

"Deja's mom." It comes out like a question.

He points at me and whispers, "Is this about her interviews? The crocodile tears?"

"You noticed, too?"

"YouTube is the only place people have been brave enough to point it out. YouTube commenters have no shame."

"Well, neither do nine-year-old little brothers. Josiah thinks she's the devil incarnate."

"I do not!" comes a muffled voice from down the hall. Then more clearly, "What's in-car-ate?"

I take my brother by the shoulders and direct him back to his bedroom. "Mind your business."

"If you're talking about me, it's my business."

I dig my knuckles into the top of his head until he calls for mercy. "Go take a shower. Jude's going to drop you off at Eddie's house in a little while."

Jude stands at the end of the hall watching us. I motion toward my room. He gives a nervous glance at my mom's bedroom door.

"You don't need to worry about that, but I'll leave my door open."

He hesitates a moment more before walking down the hall and making himself comfortable on a pouf in the middle of my floor. I sit cross-legged on the bed. "Back to Ms. Jasmine."

"Right," he says. "She's a little extra sometimes, but maybe she feels like she has to be? Maybe she thinks people expect her to act a certain way?"

"Yeah, but I'm not only talking about the fake crying. I feel bad for even going there, but don't you think she always seems kinda—"

"High?"

My eyes dart across the hall to Jojo's room. "Exactly," I say, notably quieter than he did, but relieved we're on the same page.

He absentmindedly drums his fingers on the side of his thigh. "Do you blame her if she's self-soothing a little?"

"Yes," I say without pausing to think about it. "I do. She needs to be in her right mind right now."

"Sure, but is that even possible, considering?"

"I think it's possible for her to make decisions that make everything worse, yeah. And to be clear, I'm not talking about a little weed. Deja never said anything, but I think there's some heavy stuff going on with her family. I didn't mention it the other night, but when Malcolm and I visited her house, I saw something really weird." I show him the Valentine's Day card and tell him about the chain lock and the research Malcolm and I already did.

He runs his finger over the dark peach fuzz on his upper lip. "You're right. It's weird. Especially the lock. But what are you thinking? That Ms. Jasmine is hiding Deja somewhere? That she did something to her? Because she's on drugs?"

"I don't know about all that, but I am thinking maybe Dej had a reason to run away. That things weren't great at home. I already told Malcolm as much. And before you say it, I know. Horrible things can, and do, happen to kids who run away." I roll my lips together and inhale, preparing to share a hopeful thought that I couldn't share with Malcolm because this hopeful thought isn't realistic for Tess. Not with as long as she's been gone. "Horrible things happen, but not always. Sometimes runaways go to friends. Or extended family. Or a shelter. Or to live with a secret love interest whose name starts with *J*. I want to keep exploring all of the possibilities."

"Okay. Where do we start?"

"The internet. Ms. Jasmine."

He takes a seat next to me and pulls out his phone. "The internet tells lies, you know. Or at the very least leaves a lot to be misinterpreted."

I know he's speaking from personal experience, so I promise to take whatever we find with a grain of salt. "To be honest, I'm looking for any reason to drop the feelings I've been having about her. I don't want them to be true."

"Fair enough."

I do like Malcolm did and use Google to search for court and DMV records tied to Ms. Jasmine. The only hit I get is a few unpaid parking tickets. My detective work will need to be more grassroots. I sign into Facebook and navigate to her page. She makes half a dozen posts a day and shares a dozen more. I scroll through post after post of Bible verses, quotes about independence and self-care, and videos about wig installs and intermittent fasting. I come across some parenting content here and there, but one post catches my eye. There's a video of a humiliated child standing on the sidewalk outside of a barbershop holding a sign that says *I stole money from my mom's purse*. She shared it to her feed and wrote, "Proof that you can spare the rod without spoiling the child. I don't hit my kid, but this house knows discipline. Actions have consequences. Most kids these days don't understand that. Bravo to this mom!" If Ms. Jasmine is that kind of disciplinarian, I wouldn't want to live under her roof.

"Look at this." I push the laptop toward Jude with my foot.

He watches the video for a few seconds and browses the comments before taking off his glasses and rubbing his eyes. "Did Deja ever say anything about outrageous punishments?"

I take my laptop back, deflating a bit. "Am I grasping at straws?"

"If that woman is Ms. Jasmine's idea of gold-star parenting, she definitely has some issues to work through. But I'm not getting child abuse, mistreatment, or endangerment vibes off her, Ri. All I'm getting is a forty-five-year-old woman who needs to take Facebook off her phone."

"But what about the lock?"

"Wish we could just ask Deja." Jude leans back and his stomach growls so loud I almost think it's thunder.

"You don't have to scream at me." I laugh and close my computer, stand up, and stretch.

"Sorry." He places a hand over his belly. "Skipped breakfast."

I check the time. It's almost noon. "No. That's my bad. I'll throw some pizza rolls in the oven, then we can go."

While the oven preheats, I take a jumbo bag of pizza rolls from the freezer and dump the whole thing onto a baking sheet.

"To hold you over." I pass Jude a bowl of purple grapes, which he starts in on immediately.

"What's with all the pills?" He points at the stash of bottles under the cabinet by the toaster.

"Bold of you to ask. You could find out things you don't want to know."

"I want to know everything about you."

He says it so casually, so easily. It makes me want to hide. But I don't. I tell him about Jojo's sickle cell and Mama's depression, and more about my ADHD and migraines.

Josiah emerges from his bedroom right as I take the pizza rolls from the oven and grabs one of the exploded pockets right off the pan.

"It's hot!" I warn, but he shoves it into his mouth anyway.

Jude and I look on, laughing as Jojo chomps at lightning speed, mouth open, sucking in huge gulps of air, and fanning his face. A moment later, we put ourselves through the same torment because did you really eat pizza rolls if the roof of your mouth is intact after the fact?

. . .

There are people waiting when we return to our spot at Five Points. The sight ties a few knots in my stomach. The guy from Chefly is back, and he's brought friends. Malcolm was right about attracting gnats, and it's not that I doubted he would be, but I didn't expect it to happen so fast.

"Bag lady!" the tall man from yesterday shouts. "What you got for me today? Any lotto tickets in that stash of yours?"

I grip Santa Bag protectively.

"We can leave," Jude whispers.

We could, but he paid well yesterday and is waving a few twenties.

"I don't have anything for you," I say. It's the truth. I sense no fresh need coming from him. "But you—" I point at the woman next to him and draw a tea candle from the bag.

The man elbows her a few times, grinning widely. "Your lucky day. Wait and see."

She studies the candle like I handed her a piece of garbage, but the man stuffs two twenties in the tip jar on her behalf. "Name's Tim, by the way."

I thank him for the tip, then scoot by to find an open bench where Jude and I can look like we're innocently waiting for a train. The others follow.

"You ain't going to tell me your name?" Tim asks as I give an empty cookie tin to a woman from yesterday and a baseball cap to her friend. No sooner than she tries on the cap, a pigeon in the rafters poops right on her head.

"Well, I'll be." She inspects the liquid waste. "You some kind of magician?"

"Something like that." I smile and pass a roll of gauze to an onlooker. Jude makes sure everyone gets a Deja flyer.

"What's your mobile pay info, sugar?" baseball cap lady asks.

I give it to her and my phone dings with a five-dollar tip.

"I said, you ain't going to tell me your name?"

I'd forgotten Tim was still standing there. I pass a little boy a small stuffed frog. Jude studies it, then tells Tim that my name is Tiana.

I squint at him. He thinks he's cute. "And this is my partner, Frog."

Jude's face drops, and it's impossible for me to hold back my smile.

"What kind of name is Frog?" Tim asks.

"She's joking. My name is Naveen."

"Well, what kind of name is Naveen?"

Jude frowns. "Tim, I think you might be throwing off Tiana's focus."

I glare at him, but play along, rubbing my temples.

Tim looks unsure, but backs away, only to lurk nearby for the next hour until the MARTA police catch on and shoo us away. We pass him on our way to the escalators.

"Picking up on anything now?"

"No, sorry."

"When can I see you again?"

"What?" Jude snaps, and I appreciate it. This guy is doing way too much.

"I mean, when will you be back?"

"I'm not sure." I made one hundred and forty-eight dollars and twenty-seven cents this time. That, plus yesterday's earnings, and everything in my piggy bank is enough for Jojo's camp dues, but not enough to make a sizable donation to Danny's medical fund. And definitely not enough to help Ms. Jasmine get a PI. If that's even what she really plans to do with the money.

Jude looks over his shoulder at Tim, who watches as we walk away. "That guy's strange."

"He can be strange all he wants. We made bank. We need to find a new spot next time, though."

We both stop short when someone steps out from behind a column and blocks our path.

Nurse Rincon crosses his arms and taps his foot.

"Oh, hi!"

"Don't *oh, hi* me, miss. Not all creeps are as obvious as your little friend over there." He scowls at Tim, who is now eyeing us from a train window. "And I know your mother taught you not to talk so loud about how much money you got in your pockets. Are you trying to get robbed? And what use are you?" He gives Jude a once-over and frowns even harder.

"Don't make that face," I say. "We both tried traditional employment, and look what happened."

"The pharmacy is hiring. Why didn't you come ask?"

Because this is easier. More immediate. And to be honest, way more money. But I don't say that. I say the other truth. "I didn't think of it."

"I missed my train looking out for you two. I wanted to let you make your last street dollars under the safety of my watch."

"Last?" He's cool and all, but who's he to make that decision for me?

"Yes, last. La vidente, the game you are playing is dangerous. You are young and too trusting. Both of you. And it's beautiful. I don't want to take that away from you. The trust you have, even after all you have been through. But this cannot continue."

"I just needed to make some quick money."

"Like I said, come by the pharmacy. Both of you. We can work something out. And I'm not sure I agree with it, but if you are committed to this side hustle, there are safer ways. I can look into getting you a little booth set up at a farmers market or something, you know, somewhere legitimate where you don't have to hide from security"—he scrunches up his nose—"somewhere that doesn't smell like cat piss. But until then, if you need help with your finances, you have people who care for you who are more than willing to assist."

He pats my shoulder and slips a crumpled bill sporting Benjamin Franklin's face into my tip jar. It's majorly generous, but it'll pay for like one hour of an investigator's time.

"Put that in your bag right now and carry it in front of your body all the way home," Rincon says. "If I see you two out here again, I'm calling both of your mothers. Consider that a token of appreciation for all the times you've hooked me up." He walks off down the platform. "Stay safe and see you both at school on Monday morning!"

Jude watches him leave, face all screwed up.

"He just tipped one hundred dollars, Jude. Think you have to forgive him for giving you a hard time."

199

"I don't have to do anything."

"Whoa. Where's that coming from?"

"You don't think it's strange how he just pops up everywhere?"

I laugh, confused. "What?"

"He works at our school. He was at the festival that night. He was just watching us for who knows how long. Now he's offering jobs and dropping big money to get us to stop hanging around here. I don't know. He seems a little too invested and a little too . . . present."

"Jude, come on. Rincon's a good guy. He's the one who brought up talking to the police in the first place."

"People do that all the time to make themselves seem innocent. How many times have you heard about the nice guy that no one ever suspected actually turning out to be a trash human?" He starts walking again. "I'm looking him up."

We exit the MARTA station into the bright afternoon light, Jude hotly tapping away on his phone.

"Find anything?"

He grunts and keeps on scrolling.

"Jude?" I prod after another minute or two.

"Look!" he shouts suddenly, thrusting his phone in my face.

I take a step back and use my hand to shield the screen from the sun. He has the faculty and staff page of our school website pulled up. "What?"

"Look! His name. Jahir Rincon. *J.* That is one coincidence too many, Sariyah."

I search my mind, grasping for something to definitively prove he had nothing to do with this, but I don't find anything. What I do find is a heavy regret over not bringing up the card to the police sooner. "I—I should talk to Detective Habib. I need to give him the Valentine's Day card. I should have done it the moment I found it. Why didn't I do it the moment I found it? What if . . ." I start to hyperventilate.

"Here. Let's sit down." Jude leads me to a concrete bench and places his hand on my back, rubs large circles there. "Take some deep breaths."

"Do you really think Rincon could have been involved with Deja somehow?"

"Look. Seems like everybody and they mama's name starts with *J* right now. It could be nothing. The whole Valentine's Day card angle could be nothing, but I agree that we should call the detective."

Once my breathing settles, I do just that. The line rings so many times, I start thinking up what to say on his voicemail, but then a gruff voice comes on the line.

"This is Detective Habib."

I glance at Jude and he gives me an encouraging nod.

"Um. Hi, Detective. This is Sariyah Bryant. I'm a friend of Deja Nelson. You told me to call you if I thought I had something important to share."

"Yes I did and I'm glad you've done that. What do you have for me?"

I clear my throat. "I was wondering if you've spoken to someone named Jahir Rincon."

The line is quiet for a second too long. "Tell me what has his name on your radar."

I talk to him for ten minutes, sharing everything I can remember about my interactions with Rincon at the festival that night. I tell him about the card and what just happened in the MARTA station. It doesn't feel good. If Rincon didn't have anything to do with Deja's disappearance, the police are going to go sniffing around him for no reason. If he did, I befriended a monster and my judgment can't be trusted.

"Come on," I say once I end the call. "He wants me to bring the card to the station."

"Do you have it on you?"

"Yeah." I dig it out of Santa Bag and take a few pictures so I can still do my own research. I don't know how things will play out with Rincon, but I'm not taking my foot off the gas pedal. If he is innocent, and I pray he is, then there is someone else out there who has answers. We need to keep things moving while the police look into him.

CHAPTER 23

. . . .

As soon as I parted ways with Jude, I called Malcolm and updated him on everything. He'd been surprisingly quiet, then rushed off the phone. I bet he went straight to his laptop and started looking into Rincon. He won't trust the police to do their job and I'm glad. Deja needs us all in on this.

I stop by the ATM to deposit my cash, feeling dirty when I take the hundred-dollar bill from my pocket. But money is money. The first thing I do when I get home is hop online and sign Josiah up for zoo camp. It's only after I hit the confirm payment button that I realize I never actually confirmed with Mama that he would be allowed to go. There's no reason she shouldn't let him, now that the cost isn't a factor. The sign-up form had a space to explain medical conditions and everything. Still, I walk down the hall and chance a knock on her door. It's about time for her to be getting ready for work anyway. She doesn't answer at first and I give another hesitant knock, muscles tense like I'm stirring a hibernating bear.

"Mama?" I call through the door. "Can I come in?"

She's good about making it very clear if the answer is no,

so I take her silence as a good sign. I crack open the door and peek in. She lies on her side, awake but motionless.

"Hey, Mama."

"What do you need, Sariyah?" Her voice is soft. Sad.

I take a few cautious steps inside the room. "You know how Josiah and I went to the zoo the other day?"

She exhales loudly. "I already told him no. Heard about it last year. Too expensive."

"Yeah, but—" I almost tell her I have the money. That I've already paid. I almost forget how prideful my mother is. "Jude has a cousin who works there. Josiah can do the camp for free." The lie slips from my mouth effortlessly. There will be hell to pay if she takes a close look at my bank statement.

Mama continues to lie there, blinking too infrequently.

I rub my arm, afraid to say the wrong thing. "Can he do it? It's during the first week of summer break."

"Yes. Make sure he tells Jude and his cousin thank you."

"Great! He's going to be so excited."

"Where is he?"

"At his friend Eddie's place. He wanted me to ask you if he can stay the night. Eddie's dad said it was okay."

"That's fine," she answers without looking at me.

I glance at the clock. "Don't you have to work this evening?" I make sure the question sounds mildly curious, not like I'm worried about her being late—even though I'm definitely worried about her being late. Especially seeing as how her hotel clothes are currently balled up on the floor.

She mumbles something.

"Ma'am?"

She scratches her calf, leaving grayish streaks on her dry skin. "I said, I don't have a job anymore."

"What do you mean?"

A laugh pops from her mouth, sarcastic and nasty. "It's no wonder you're barely getting by in school." She sits up and downs what remains of a glass of water on her end table. "I got fired."

"Fired?" I ask, eyes stinging from her comment about school.

"You going to make me say it again?"

"But why? I thought things had gotten better. I thought they understood you—"

"You thought wrong."

"But what are you going to do?"

"Maybe if you leave me alone, I can go on and figure it out. Close my door on your way out," she says to the floor. When I don't immediately move, she hurls a box of Kleenex my way. "I said close my door!"

I back out of the room and pull the door shut, resisting the urge to open and slam it shut over and over and over. Resisting the urge to scream obscenities through the thin wood. To kick a hole through it. To tell her it's not fair to dump whatever she's going through on me. But then her cries filter through the walls and I realize that's all she's been trying to do. She made her bedroom a dungeon to contain herself and I forced my way in. Then had the nerve to be shocked when I got bit.

My head throbs with the effort to hold in my emotions. My nasal passages swell until I can no longer breathe through my nose. The lump in my throat is actually painful. And my eyes burn, begging me to moisten them. But I can't let any of it loose until I'm behind my closed bedroom door. Mama and I, we'll mirror each other. We'll rain tears on opposite poles of the apartment. And it's better that way because crying within her earshot will only throw the world even more off-balance. Crying within her earshot feels like asking her never to heal. To fall deeper into her loop of despair. She knows she hurt me, but I won't ever let her know how much. Tibby is the only one to witness the depth of my breakdown. He does more than witness. He feels it. I squeeze him so hard a seam in his stomach pops. A grape-sized ball of stuffing reveals itself. I graze it with my index finger before forcing it back through the hole, but as if spring-loaded, it comes back out. A metaphor for my life. The stuffed pig shouting, *"You can't escape this. You can't fix this."* It goads me until I'm ready to tear all the stuffing out and throw the remains across the room.

But I don't do that.

I just cry. I cry from hurt, from frustration, from uncertainty. What are we going to do if Mama doesn't get help soon? How can she find another job in her current state? I rest my face in my hands and a laugh breaks its way through my tears, because I just made some money. And not two minutes after blowing almost all of it, Mama drops her wonderful news. I feel a twinge of guilt for even thinking of Jojo's camp as blowing the money, but considering our current situation, it's fair. The brochure said they offer full refunds for cancellations made at least thirty days before the start of camp, but that would destroy Josiah. He would hate me. He's at the stage in life where he has an awareness of money, but no real concept of its value. Of how hard it can be to get. I can't cancel that camp. I've got my last Sweet Pea's check coming soon and hustling with Santa Bag is still an option. What I won't do is call Daddy. He's been on disability for years. If he had more money to give us, he would have been giving it a long time ago. What he does have to offer us is a paid-off house in Chefly. Our other home. Our original home. And while I might have daydreamed about what a life there would be like, Atlanta is the best place for Jojo and I don't want Dad to bring up moving away. This problem is for me to figure out.

I take Tibby to the bathroom and put a Band-Aid over the opening in his stomach. I have to press hard to get it to stick to the textured fabric, but I manage it. I turn out the lights and run a bath. Something I do maybe twice a year. The water is at my favorite temperature—the one that feels like nothing. Not hot, not cold. Just me, sliding into myself. A few unshed tears force their way from my eyes. I let them run down my cheeks, drip from my chin, and drop into the tepid water. My phone illuminates and vibrates on the small stool next to the tub. A puddle forms on the floor when I remove my arm from the water to check it. Malcolm. When I confirm it's nothing urgent, I set it back down without replying and sink so low into the water that only my nose and eyes are above it.

Long after my fingers and toes go pruney, I wrap myself in a towel and go to my room to lotion my legs. Malcolm texts again, this time a long paragraph that makes my stomach tense up. That makes me want to hide under my covers and never come out. I don't read it. I can't. I can't give him whatever he needs right now. I can't anything.

• • •

I spend most of Sunday in bed, phone on Do Not Disturb, almost too exhausted to feel guilty about it. Almost. I only force myself out of my pajamas when it's time to go pick Josiah up from Eddie's. I walk to meet him there, then we hop on the bus to the grocery store.

"Did something happen, Sariyah? Why are you so quiet?" Josiah's eyes are big with worry.

I sit up straighter, try rearranging my expression, but I know it won't fool him. There's no masking how I feel right now. "I'm not ready to go back to school tomorrow," I say.

"Me neither. Spring break was way too short." He crosses his arms.

"Sorry it didn't go the way you expected."

He drops his head. "It's okay. It's not anyone's fault."

"You're right. It's not, but you can still be upset about it." I pull up my email on my phone and open the camp confirmation from Zoo Atlanta. "You can be upset about it and excited about this at the same time."

He takes the phone and hugs me when he realizes what it is. "Thank you, Riyah."

Inside the store, Jojo uses his right foot to kick off and goes rolling down the bread aisle on the back of the shopping cart. I scan the price tags for the best deal on whole wheat when I sense someone behind me. Not their needs. Their body. Musty and way too close to mine.

"Bag lady, Bag lady." The smell of liquor and stale breath washes across my ear and up my nostrils. The person breaks into a chorus of Erykah Badu.

I turn around and there are only a couple of inches between me and Tim.

"Remember me?"

I take a step back, not sure how to engage. Has he been following me? "Yes, I remember you. I just saw you yesterday."

"Yeah, but you were acting like you were a little too big for your boots. Thought maybe you would have forgot me by now."

"I didn't."

"That your brother you with?"

I want to tell him no, but for all I know, he's been hovering around somewhere, watching. Maybe for days.

"You got something for me? I got your groceries tonight if you do."

"No." I shoot daggers at him.

"No? But I'm sure I heard you telling your brother y'all couldn't afford the Lunchables. A young boy like that deserves some Lunchables, don't you think?"

He does, but joke's on him if this dude thinks he's getting anything else out of me ever again. "There's nothing. I'm not picking up on anything for you." It was the truth when I started the sentence, but by the time I finish, something is taking shape. It makes my skin crawl, to feel a need as it develops. Like the universe is unsure and figuring it out involves injecting me with a million tiny worms.

He tilts his head to the side. "You sure about that?"

"Yes," I say confidently, as the word still hasn't taken shape. I want to get away from him before it does. I don't want to know what he needs.

"If you say so. But if you're really strapped for cash, I can take you to a spot. Know some folks who will pay good money for what you can provide. They might not look like they can, but once they see, they'll pay. Of course, I'll expect a certain cut for the hookup."

"No."

"What? You too good to hustle now, Sariyah?"

I flinch at the sound of my name in his mouth. How'd he figure it out?

"Well?" He takes another step toward me and I bump into the display behind me, knocking some items to the ground. The noise turns a few heads.

An employee in a blue vest catches my expression and shouts, "Can I help you, sir?" *Is there a problem here?* masked as a courtesy. They make a beeline for us.

"I see you," Tim spits. He backs away, then jogs for the exit. As he reaches the end of my range, his need comes through. It whispers over me, making the hairs on my arm stand on end. *Pocketknife. Pocketknife. Pocketknife.*

I let out a wavering breath. Before Ms. Jess, I never could have imagined something from Santa Bag being used in a violent way. I can't know for sure how Tim would have used a pocketknife, but I'm secure in being unable to provide it.

"Are you okay?" the sales associate asks, still looking toward the exit.

I want to say yes, but I am not okay. I'm scared. I want my mom. I want my dad. I want to feel like I have some semblance of control over anything that happens in my life.

Jojo appears next to me. "What's wrong, Riyah?"

I ignore my brother, mumble thanks to the clerk, and direct the cart to the frozen food aisle.

CHAPTER 24

Jojo is tired when we get home, so I send him to get ready for bed while I unload the groceries. I tidy up the kitchen while I'm at it, eager to keep busy. I collect pens, napkins, and sauce packets and walk them over to the junk drawer next to the fridge. It's overstuffed with papers. Old mailers and bills mostly. *Bills*. It's the beginning of the month, and I wonder if Mama paid everything before she spiraled. She hasn't had trouble keeping up with things like that in the past, but she's also never been fired. Not as far as I know. She was a nurse before she started at the Wilhem five years ago. I never thought much about her sudden and drastic career change. Nothing seemed important next to Tessa's disappearance.

I sneak Mama's work bag from the coat closet and tiptoe down the hall. Jojo's in his room streaming an Atlanta United match when he should be asleep, but it works to my benefit. If Mama wakes up, she'll get on to him first and it'll give me time to hide my snooping. Her laptop is heavy and slow. It creaks when I lift the screen and groans when I boot it up. Her password for everything is my first initial and birthday, followed by Jojo's and an exclamation point. I type S518j1002! and I'm granted access. This isn't personal, I tell myself. I'm not trying to discover her deepest secrets. I just want to make sure our bills are paid and can't—would never—insult her by asking.

I open the browser where Mama's online banking account is saved to the bookmarks toolbar. Her last direct deposit from work was a little over a week ago, so there should be at least one more coming soon. But even if so, there's only enough money here to get us through two months tops, and that's if we stick just to necessities. I could continue to hustle needs and we wouldn't want for anything, except after tonight at the grocery store, I'm terrified. But Daddy once told me desperation can melt fear. So I hold the fright in my mouth. Suck on it like a throat lozenge. And it soothes just as well. Because as long as the fear is there, things aren't dire.

Mama will get through whatever she's going through. I hope. She always has before. But I wish I didn't have to be responsible in the meantime. I want to rewind to last summer. To when me, Josiah, and Malcolm spent long balmy days in Chefly, walking around barefoot, not a care in the world. No new missing girls, not on our radar at least. Tessa was still on our minds, she always will be, but after so many years, grief for her had made itself at home. Unfortunately, I can't rewind. Not one week, not five years. I have to sit right here in the present. And while our family finances may not be dire yet, that on top of everything else has my brain at the jumping-off point. But there's one problem that, if favorably resolved, could make almost all the others dissipate. Make everything else seem trivial.

Deja.

My yearbooks are tucked away in a box under my bed, along with other high school memorabilia from over the years. I choose the one from tenth grade because that was when I peaked on the social ladder. The last year I made homecoming court. I run my fingers across the sash and crown. An entirely different person wore these things. But it wasn't like it is in the movies. I can't pinpoint one specific event or groundbreaking decision that removed me from that path. There was no fight, no bad breakup, no massive betrayal or a humiliating night at a party. And it happened long after Tess and long before Dej. My fall from favor was quiet. Uneventful. It was more like I got distracted by something at a rest stop during a road trip and everyone else left without me. Except, I don't feel left behind. Not at all. I'm just somewhere different.

I sit on the bed with the yearbook and compare the hundreds of autographs in the back of the book to the writing in the photos of the Valentine's Day card. There are a few that make me do a double take, and a couple that make me squint, comparing loops and points, even word choice and language. But none of them are right. Next, I go through names. Everyone whose first and or last name starts with *J*. There are dozens of people who qualify, many of which I'd already ruled out by their handwriting.

When the yearbook leads me nowhere, I grab my phone and open Instagram. I go back to Jed's page and stare at the *followed by DejaDej* under his bio, like looking at it long enough will make it less weird. I scroll through his posts, tapping here and there. It takes a few minutes for me to realize what I'm doing—scanning the likes for Deja's name. I find what I'm looking for on a post from February. It's a photo of Jed and Ella. She sits on his lap, her hands pressed against either of his cheeks as she kisses him. The caption reads: *My ride or die*. I tap to view the comments.

Ella_Davis1: I love you, Jedidiah Jones. Forever.

Fitzdavy: *vomits*

DejaDej: adorable

My phone slips from my hand. The comment was left only three weeks ago. Does Deja have a habit of commenting on random people's photos? Does she follow just anyone? I snatch my phone back up, take a screenshot, then go to her page.

Followers: 411 Following: 409

I scroll through the list of all four hundred and nine accounts. Most are celebrities or people I recognize from school. It doesn't make sense. I can't find a single connection between Deja and Jed, other than me. But Jed and I weren't even connected on social media until yesterday, and I sure as heck never mentioned him.

I get ready for bed, still trying to find logic in any of it. I wonder if part of me is just desperate to rule out Rincon. He's a grown man. That's likely to be a much darker path than this one. But even if Jed is J., and he and Deja had some kind of fling, it's obviously over—she wouldn't be leaving comments about how adorable Jed and his girlfriend are if it wasn't. The comment doesn't make sense either way. Jed should be a stranger to her. He said he never spoke to her. And if he was lying, I'm afraid to know the reason why.

My anxious thoughts trigger another lucid dream. I've never had them so close together. But things are exactly the way they've been every other time. Tessa sits on the floor, painting her toenails, humming quietly to herself. I sit next to her.

"Hey, Tess."

"Hi, Riyah."

I watch her paint until all her toes are electric blue—the last color I ever saw them. My eyes are watery when I bring myself to speak. "Tessa, who was that man you were talking to?"

The scene rearranges itself. Her answers always come from my memories, so I know what's coming. And I don't want it to. I hate reliving this. But if there's a chance I could get some insight that might help Deja. I have to. If there's a chance I could get it right this time, I need to.

I'm on the school bus, looking out the window. Tess wasn't at school that day and I remember being so excited when I saw her waiting for me at my stop. I waved at her, but as the bus turned the corner, I noticed she wasn't alone. There was a man with her. It's hard to say how old he was, but I do remember thinking he was a *man*. I frowned when I couldn't get her attention. The bus stopped half a block from where they stood, and when I got off, he was gone. The scene replays around me, our words muffled until we make it to the part of the conversation I resurrected by asking what I asked.

"That guy? He's just someone I know."

Twelve-year-old me had accepted that answer. Twelve-year-old me never told anyone what I saw that day. Fifteen-year-old me did. But it was too late then. If that man at the bus stop was the same man in the security footage outside of the convenience store, I could have saved Tessa. All I had to do was tell her mom, my mom, the bus driver, anyone. No one was angry with me when I shared it years later. Not even Malcolm. Because I wasn't the only one who ignored something that could have made a difference. Almost everyone had. But what I didn't share with anyone, is that I heard that man's need. A rock. My insides curdle when I think about why he might have needed it. How he might have used it. I prefer to imagine myself throwing one at him. Right out the window of the school bus. Watching it hit his temple. And then waking up, cuddled right next to my best friend in her eighteen-year-old form.

CHAPTER 25

· ·

My walk to school Monday morning is quiet, aside from the light thudding of Santa Bag against my hip with each step. I woke up at 3:00 A.M., replaying memories of Deja over and over in my head. Looking for clues that took too long to surface with Tessa. By 6:00 A.M., I was sure she'd been communicating with someone she didn't want to tell us, or me, about. It's not just the card or the comment on Jed's post, but the more I think about it, Deja was skittish with her phone. My most distinct memory being the way she'd acted in the library after our math quiz. It was the day before the festival. I'd caught her smiling at it and she'd shoved it deep into her book bag. She'd gotten defensive. I have to find out who she was talking to.

I get called to the counselor's office at the start of third period and I don't fail to notice that Rincon's office is dark and empty on the way up. Ms. Huxley welcomes me inside and I sit in the egg-shaped chair across from her desk.

She analyzes me, all sad eyes and sympathy. But there's something else behind her expression—a certain eagerness that makes me uncomfortable.

"Do you know why I asked you to come see me, Sariyah?"

I wait a few seconds, hoping she doesn't actually want me to answer that question, but apparently she does. "You asked me to come here because my friend went missing. Because I was with her that night. Because a guy got stabbed at my job, then died. Because you probably think I'm going to crack at any minute. Like I've never dealt with anything hard before."

"Have you?"

"Have I what?"

"Dealt with hard things before?"

I sit back in my chair, defiant. "No."

"No?" That hungry look shows through her concerned mask again. "Are you sure?"

I know she knows what I'm not saying. I know she wants me to talk about Tessa, but I won't. I can't.

"Sariyah?"

"My problems are minor compared to Deja's."

"I don't care if they are small. Maybe letting them out will make room for processing the bigger things."

"Do I have to?"

"No. But you'll be here with me for the next twenty minutes at least. I don't mind silence, but I'd quite like to talk with you."

No way I can spend twenty minutes with this woman just staring at me. "My mom got fired. She doesn't have a job anymore and neither do I. And seeing as how I might not even graduate on time, finding decent work might be kind of hard."

She blinks and clears her throat, like she didn't expect me to dump all that on her. Like she didn't want me to. Like she didn't ask me to. Someone prepped her to talk to me about missing girls. Not about broke moms and bad grades. Not about that everyday crap she deals with as a school counselor.

She shakes her mouse to wake up her computer. "Let's start with graduation." Her nails click-clack against her keyboard as she types. "Okay, so it looks like you need three more credits to graduate and"—she types some more—"based on your current grades with a half credit for each course, you're on track to earn two . . . if you can maintain that seventy in history."

Tell me something I don't know, Huxley.

"Have you spoken to Dr. Stone about getting some help in physics?"

"No. Bigger things on my mind than science."

She rests her forearms on her desk and clasps her hands. "Listen, Sariyah. We want every senior at East Lake to graduate. That includes you. Your teachers know Deja is a close friend of yours and I'm sure they will be more than willing to work with you to get your grades up." She smiles with her eyes, little happy creases forming at their corners.

"So my teachers are going to give me special treatment?"

She shakes her head lightly. "Education has never been one-size-fits-all."

"Right. I have an IEP. I know that. But it sounded like you were saying I get to graduate because Deja disappeared."

"That's not what I was saying at all."

"Good, because I'm not looking for some silver-lining BS happily ever after out of this."

"I didn't think you were." Her mouth twitches, and she removes the lightweight scarf from her neck. "In fact, let's keep it real." She code-switches so quickly it's like a whole new person teleported into the room and replaced her. "You trying to martyr yourself? Is that it? Another Black teen without a high school diploma? Are we adding to that statistic? You're worried your friend has become one, so you think you need to match her?"

"I—"

She holds up her hand. "Let me finish. You're almost an adult and have been going through some things that most adults never will. I sure haven't and I hope that remains the case. But you can't ride this self-pity train to the end of the line. Life happens for you, not to you. Have you heard that quote?"

I don't even try to answer this time.

"It's easy to get caught up in the awfulness around us. To ride it like a raft down the Chattahoochee and let it drop you off wherever it wants. But you have oars, Sariyah. You have oars to force your life in a different direction from the current. You have a life vest to keep your head above water. You have people around you to lift you up, to fight with you. Those rapids, these rapids, that bang you up and try to throw you off course—they are shaping you. But the final product is up to you." She seems proud of herself. Like she's been waiting to deliver that Disney Channel–movie, coach-in-the-fourth-quarter-down-ten-points speech her entire career.

I hold back my eye roll. I know she meant well, but her words had strong-Black-woman vibes dripping from each letter. What if I don't want to battle rapids and get tossed up and down a raging river my whole life? I was raised by a self-identified strong Black woman and I saw her break. I don't want that for myself. I don't want to fight.

"That was really . . . inspirational, Ms. Huxley. Thank you. You've given me a lot to think about. Is it okay if I go back to class now?"

She smiles, clearly pleased with herself. "Yes, Sariyah. My door is always open."

I grab Santa Bag and leave her office. It might earn me another call home, but I stop resisting the urge to fulfill needs. I don't want to fight.

Deck of cards. Peppermint. Watch. Teddy bear. Magnet.

• • •

"Jo?" It's oddly quiet when I enter the apartment after school. No cartoons or video games going, no microwave beeping or chip bags crinkling. "Josiah?" I cross the living room and peek out the window that overlooks the neglected basketball court—cracked concrete, two rusty hoops with no nets. Sometimes he and his friends play kickball out there, but not today. I check his room, the bathroom, and my room before cracking open Mama's door.

"Mama, where's Josiah?"

"What?" she mumbles.

"Josiah. Your son. Where is he?"

She sits up and squints at the alarm clock on her end table. "Where's my phone?"

I spot it at the foot of her bed and pick it up. There are several missed calls from the elementary school and two from Children's Healthcare of Atlanta. She has the number for the blood disorder center saved. "Mama, I think he's at the hospital. I thought you were going to put my number down as an alternate!" The rooms grows hot and I can hear the blood whooshing in my ears. I pat my pockets for my own phone, scared I missed something, but I had it in my hand all the way home. Nothing.

Mama, alert now, slips into her house shoes, grabs the keys from her end table, and snatches her phone from me. "Come on."

We run out to the car and she speeds for the hospital, voicemails playing through the car Bluetooth.

"Mrs. Bryant, this is Nurse Monica St. Clair from Pine Brook Elementary School. I'm calling because your son Josiah is in quite a bit of pain this afternoon. I gave him the medicine on file this morning, but I have it in my notes here to call you if it doesn't provide him with any relief. Give me a call back when you get this, please."

Pain. It's a part of life for people with sickle cell. Jojo has a high tolerance for it and, unlike me, he's actually good at school and hates missing class. If he went to the nurse, he must have been hurting badly. My head fills with all the worst-case scenarios. Blood vessel blockages cause the pain. What if he had a stroke? "Mama what—"

She shushes me so we can hear the next voicemail, whipping the car in and out of traffic.

"Mrs. Bryant, this is Nurse St. Clair again and I'm growing quite concerned." She pauses to comfort a crying Josiah in the background. Both our hearts audibly shatter. Two hearts that were holding so much worry, the car is immediately flooded with palpable distress. I crack my window to stop us from drowning in it. Mama skips to the next message.

"He's okay" is the first thing out of Dr. Kumjari's mouth. The plug has been pulled from the drain. The elephant lifted off my chest. "The school told me they were having trouble reaching you and I know you'll be in a panic when you get these messages, but he's okay." Dr. Kumjari is not Josiah's doctor, but she's a friend of Mama's. "My shift just ended. I'll stay with him until you get here."

Mama repeatedly forces the heel of her palm into the steering wheel when the traffic comes to a halt. The streets and interstates passing through Atlanta become soul-sucking

222

demons between the hours of four and seven each weekday. Mama can barely keep her grip on her phone as she picks it up to call Dr. Kumjari back.

The line rings only once.

"Hi, Maggie. Are you on your way?"

"Yes. How is he?"

"He's with the doctors now. Severe pain crisis. They'll likely transfuse him."

"Do they know what caused his count to drop so low? Acute chest? Splenic sequestration? Talk to me."

Mama goes into nurse mode—a job that a former version of her loved into the ground. She and Dr. Kumjari swap medical terms back and forth. I know them all. These are words I've known since I was nine years old. But I don't want to hear them right now. Over Bluetooth. On the interstate. I shove some earplugs in my ears and let the needs of the people in the cars around us take over my thoughts. Usually I hate this. The staticky way needs come in and out while driving. But it's okay today. It's exactly what I need to survive the rest of the ride to the hospital.

Baseball. Chopsticks. Speaker. Sponge. If Jojo were here. If I could hear him. *Blood.*

CHAPTER 26

· ·

Mama and I move through the halls of the hospital on autopilot and without speaking. Dr. Kumjari stands in the hall outside room 310. No words are exchanged. Only thankful and reassuring glances.

Mama reaches Jojo's side first and lays five wet kisses on his forehead. "Hi, baby."

"Hello, Mrs. Bryant, Sariyah." Dr. Inglewood, Jojo's hematologist, enters the room along with Dr. Kumjari, who goes over to hold Mama's hand.

I pull up a chair next to Jojo. "I can't believe you used your phone to text me about zoo camp, but not an actual emergency."

His mouth twitches into the smallest, sleepiest smile.

"Will you do an MRI?" Mama asks his doctor. "I've been reading about silent strokes."

"We're going to cross our t's and dot our i's, but we need to get him some blood first."

Mama fusses over Josiah, smoothing his blankets, fluffing

his pillows. "It's been a while since we've had to do this. Any idea of the trigger?"

"Nothing stood out in our initial workup. How have things been at home? Any stressors? Trouble at school?"

Mama and I lock eyes.

"Why don't you go take a walk, Sariyah?" Mama suggests. "I'll catch Dr. Inglewood up on everything."

I nod and go into the hall, content to leave the adulting to her for the first time in days.

• • •

After watching an hour of Nickelodeon in the waiting room, I get up to take a few laps around the floor, stretch my legs. I'm making my fourth pass by the vending machines when someone shouts at me.

"Excuse me, miss! You're disrupting patients with those squeaky-ass sneakers."

I turn around to find Malcolm and Jude giggling like they're the absolute kings of comedy. They are so dumb, but I can't help but smile.

"What are y'all doing here? How'd you—"

"Your mother texted me." Malcolm pulls me into a hug.

"My mom?" I ask into his shoulder. My heart warms just the slightest because Mama thought of me in a moment where I wouldn't have blamed her for forgetting I existed.

"Yes, your mom. She said he's stable, but what's up?"

I wiggle from his grasp so I can breathe and talk normally. "He's getting a transfusion. It was another pain crisis, but they're still trying to figure out what led to it. He'd been doing so well with his new medication."

"Things have been intense lately. It's probably a lot for him."

Another wave of shame hits me. The only special thing we did for his spring break was go to the zoo. He loved it and wasn't expecting fireworks every day or anything, but he's a kid. I wish I'd made more time for him. "Thank you guys for coming." I look at Jude, who I've yet to acknowledge. "Both of you."

"Where else would we be?" Malcolm asks.

"I don't know. You zipped off so quickly after school today. I thought maybe you were upset with me."

"I'd just got out of my meeting with Huxley is all. I don't have anything to be upset with you about."

His expression makes me feel like there's something he's not saying, and when his phone dings, I remember. I've got to be in the top five worst friends on the planet. "I got your text the other day. I haven't had a chance to read it."

"You haven't had a chance?" he asks, rightfully skeptical, but his eyes are . . . hopeful?

"I mean, I had the chance, but—well, I was going to and then—"

"Girl, stop." He rolls his eyes and slips my phone from my pocket. A few quick swipes and he's in. He memorized my passcode a long time ago.

"Here." He passes the phone back to me. "The texts no longer exist."

"Malcolm, why'd you do that? What was it?"

"Hey. We all get overwhelmed by a block text. I was just venting about everything. We can talk about it later, but more importantly—Rincon is off the hook."

"What? That fast? How'd you hear?"

Again something is off about his expression, but I let it go. He literally just said he has stuff he wants to talk about later.

"My dad got an update from Derrick not too long ago. Rincon was live streaming almost the entire day at the festival with his friends. Apparently there's even a moment when he spotted the four of us and beelined for the other side of the park."

"Oh. I'm relieved, I guess. But—"

"But it means we're not any closer to answers," Malcolm fills in.

"Ruling someone out is progress," Jude says. "And maybe that little bit of video Rincon had will be helpful."

"I feel bad for giving up his name."

"Don't," Malcolm says. "At least you were out here trying to connect some dots. Shouldn't have to do their job for them." I swear I hear his teeth grind and a vein pops out in his forehead as he continues to think on it.

"Hey!" Jude says a little too loud and cheerful. "Is Jojo awake? I brought Uno."

The mention of Jojo calms Malcolm down and the three of us head to his room. He beams when he sees us, then mimes that Mama is asleep.

"No, I'm not," she says, one eye barely cracked open.

"Mama, why don't you go find some coffee? The young people want to hang out," I say, knowing how much Jojo will love it.

He tries to hide his smile. "Yeah, Mama, you seem like you need some coffee."

"I wasn't sleeping. I was praying. You all should try it sometime." She stands, knees popping. "But coffee sounds nice. And I think I'll stop by the house. Need to pick up a few things."

She leaves and we play the card game until Josiah can no longer keep his eyes open.

"Hell, I'm wore out, too, and haven't been through a tenth of what Jojo has. Not today." Malcolm transitions to the plastic sky-blue love seat under the window and curls up. It's only a couple of minutes before he's asleep, too.

"I have good news," Jude whispers.

"We could all use some of that. What's up?" I pick at my cuticles, then ball my hands into fists to hide the crusty remnants.

"My aunt Naomi found a job." He grins. "She starts next week."

"Really? That's great! Tell her I said congrats."

"I will." He ruffles his curls and adjusts his glasses. "But I haven't told you the best part."

"Go ahead, then." I resume mission destroy cuticles.

"It's all thanks to the business card you gave her."

"For real? I was betting she'd use it to pick food out of her teeth. What's the job?"

"Manager at the Wilhem Hotel."

All the muscles in my body tense. "Which Wilhem?"

"The one downtown."

I laugh out loud. Even harder as the confused expression spreads across Jude's face.

"What?" He smiles a little, eager to be in on the joke.

I continue to laugh and he shushes me, warning that I'll wake my brother.

"Sorry. Let me make sure I have this right. I gave your aunt a business card for the Wilhem Hotel?"

"Yes?"

"Figures. That's what I get for not looking at it."

"What do you mean?"

"I mean I wish I didn't do that stupid favor for you. I wish your aunt didn't get that job."

He shrinks away from me. "What's your problem?"

"Nothing. No problem at all. We're just sitting here in the hospital while my brother gets a freaking blood transfusion. Oh, and Deja is still gone. Tessa is still gone. Danny is still dead."

He turns his palms up. "I know. But you just said you could use a little good news? I'm confused. I thought you'd be glad. You helped someone."

"You thought I'd be glad," I sneer. "Of course you did. Why wouldn't you? How could you know I'd give her the business card to my mother's place of employment? How could you know they'd fire my mom and hire your aunt in the same position? Nah, that's one hundred percent my fault. It's my fault because I didn't listen to my gut. It's my fault for thinking I have to do every little thing people ask of me. Because I told you—" I clench my jaws to keep my building rage inside me. Where it belongs. "I told you I didn't want to do it. I told you I don't do those sorts of favors for friends because it always, always backfires somehow. I ignored my gut because you said please."

"Sariyah, I'm sorry. I don't even know what to say. I'm sure there's some other . . ." He trails off and says sorry again.

"Don't be." I scoot my chair closer to Josiah's bed. "I am not lying to you when I say the only person I'm angry at is myself."

"But you shouldn't be. All you do is try to help people."

"Jude?"

"Yeah?" His chocolate eyes are big and sad and hopeful.

"Can you leave?"

"Sariyah. Come on."

"Please. Seriously. Can you go? I'm not angry with you, but I want to be alone."

He doesn't move. He just sits there, gaping at me.

229

My sinuses burn as I hold back an ugly torrent of emotions. "Jude, please go."

"What about him?" He points at Malcolm, still asleep on the couch.

"He's family."

His face crumples, and I know he hears it in my voice. Sees it in my face. The meltdown that's about to come. I know it hurts him that I'm pushing him away right now. But he stands, grabs his jacket, and leaves without a word.

I pull the neck of my hoodie over my face and cry into my chest.

CHAPTER 27

. . . .

Malcolm and I meet at a coffee shop for an extra early breakfast before heading back to the hospital to visit Josiah. He complains about his neck and back every few steps on the walk over.

"What are you, sixty?"

He does a dramatic shoulder roll. "Sixty? Your mama's knees sound like a bowl of Rice Krispies at forty."

"Your mama? Really, Malcolm?"

"What? I feel a way about you letting me nap on that small ass plastic couch last night."

I drop my head, done teasing him. He stayed with me until visiting hours ended. "You didn't have to stay, you know."

"Yeah, I know." He sips his iced matcha latte. "But do you remember Jojo's face when he saw me? I'm nothing without my fans."

I shove him. "Shut up. Are you going to school after this?"

He contorts his face, getting another whiff of his favorite mystery foul substance. A silent *What you been smoking?*

We stop at an intersection with a bunch of people in business attire waiting to cross the street. I frown as I'm assaulted by needs. *Safety goggles. Button. Post-it notes. Pillowcase.* I fulfill a few while a woman jabbers loudly on her phone. Malcolm glares at her after she releases a boisterous cackle directly into his left ear.

"People in this city are rude as hell," she says into the phone, eyeing Malcolm right back.

Malcolm points at her and looks to me for confirmation that she is, in fact, the rude one.

The woman laughs again, though she has put some space between us now that we've started moving through the crosswalk. "No, girl, they found her this morning. Pulled her out of Lake Lanier."

The world seems to move in slow motion as I hyperfocus on this woman's conversation.

"Yeah, it's real sad. They been looking for her for over a week now, though. We already knew what it was."

The words enter my ears and fall straight to the bottom of my gut, but Malcolm's oblivious. He shakes his drink, mostly ice now, and pulls at the straw, which makes a grating squeak against the plastic lid. I move to the other side of him, closer to the woman, trying to hear more of her conversation. Trying to latch on to anything that might take my brain off the course that it's on.

"Excuse you." The woman presses her phone against her chest and looks me up and down.

Malcolm's a few paces ahead now, looking around confused.

"Sorry," I say. "Did you say they found someone in the lake?"

"Mm-hmm." She hesitates, assessing me, before continuing. "You would think by now people would know to stay the hell away from that thing. It's cursed!" The person on the other end of the line laughs loud enough for me to hear, and I want to slap the phone out of her hand. In my head, I'm back in the car with Jude, giggling about the cursed lake. Here, right now, my skin goes cold and my head gets light.

The woman's face softens as she gives me yet another once-over. Her eyes linger on my East Lake High School hoodie. She brings her phone back to her ear. "Let me call you back."

Malcolm finally joins us and places a hand on my shoulder. "You okay? What's going on?"

I don't speak. I just wait. Wait for this woman to tell me that the *her* that got pulled out of the lake was anything but a human body. Anything but—anyone but—

"I guess y'all went to school with her, huh?" she asks, any trace of hardness gone from her face.

"Went to school with who? Who was it?" I'm frantic, invading her personal space even more. A few other people on the sidewalk have slowed down or straight-up stopped to watch our interaction.

She takes a step back, but stays calm, looking to Malcolm for help, but Malcolm just stands there, lips slightly parted.

"The girl who went missing at that music festival last week. Da—De . . ." She searches for the name.

"Deja Nelson?" one of the random observers fills in. "Yeah, they found her this morning, bless her heart."

I release a loud groan or whine, I don't even know, but I can't form words. Only animal-like sounds. My heart thumps

233

so fast I'm sure it'll disintegrate into a million pieces. I press my hand against the cool brick of the building next to us to stabilize myself.

"Ri," Malcolm says, shaking my shoulder. "Ri. She's got something wrong. They all do. It's not Deja." He shakes me again. "Look at me."

Slowly, I shift my gaze to meet his eyes.

He raises his phone. "No calls. No texts. Nothing. It's not her."

I stare at the black screen. I stare and watch as it illuminates with an incoming call from his mother.

He looks at the screen, surprised. "Bad timing. It's just bad timing."

"Answer it."

"I'll call her back in a minute."

I straighten up. "Answer it."

When he opens his mouth to make another excuse, I snatch the phone from him and accept the call.

"Hello?"

"Oh. Sariyah, is that you?"

"Yes, ma'am."

"Are you with Malcolm?"

I can't read anything from her tone. "Yes, ma'am. He's right here."

"Listen, I know your brother is in the hospital, but you two should come over to the house as soon as possible." There's a loud rustling in the background.

"Is it about Deja?"

The rustling stops, only leaving the light sound of her breathing.

"Mrs. Hawkins, is it Deja?" My hand tremors violently. "Is she dead?"

The line goes so quiet I have to make sure we are still connected.

"We don't know yet. But it doesn't look good, baby. It doesn't look good."

• • •

"It's. Not. Her." Malcolm enunciates each word as we speed walk down the street. "How many times do I have to tell you that?" He texts furiously on his second phone. His main one is still tight within my grasp.

"I thought your mom took that from you."

"What?"

"That phone. I thought your mom took it from you."

He pulls an ugly face and rolls his eyes. "She gave it back."

"Why would your mother give back a phone that exists solely for you to defy her?"

"Why are you so pressed about that right now? And if you must know, I got a lot of shit to keep organized in this search for Deja, you know, since I been carrying most of that weight."

I let his sentence hang heavy in the air and I know it's crushing him. Because if what that woman said is true, all that effort—all *our* effort—was for nothing.

The walk from his driveway to his house feels longer than the half mile we've walked from the bus stop. Malcolm knocks on his own front door, even though he has his keys, and I appreciate the few extra seconds to live in limbo. His mother opens the door. Face stony and unreadable, like always.

"What's going on?" Malcolm asks when we join his father in the living room.

I sink into the couch, listening, but making a distinct effort not to look at anyone's face. I'm scared their expressions will give away something before I'm ready to hear it. Scared I'll read into every twitch of an eyelid, every crease in the forehead.

"They found a body early this morning," Mr. Hawkins says. "It—it wasn't in the best condition."

"What does that mean?" Malcolm asks.

"It means it'd been in the water for a couple of days." His voice sounds far away. Almost drowned out by his persistent and cawing need for a stamp.

"It isn't her," Malcolm says resolutely.

"Her mother is on the way to make the ID, son. The description matches."

"Okay, and?" Malcolm shouts. "What description was that? A Black girl with braids? That fits half the teenage girls in Atlanta."

His father sighs deeply. I still don't look at his face, but I track his feet to the love seat where he rests against the cushy arm. "It was the outfit, Malcolm. You two gave them photos from earlier that day."

"She bought that thing at Target. It doesn't mean anything."

Mrs. Hawkins pops the cork out of a bottle of wine. It's barely nine in the morning. "At least closure is within reach for her family. At least they get that."

"I'm going to be sick," I say before running for their half bath. The room spins and I'm overcome by wave after wave of nausea. Nothing comes up. Nothing comes out, except tears, and they are explosive. Malcolm barges in and lifts me from the floor by my arm. He pulls me up the stairs to his bedroom. Both our phones go off in sync as we receive multiple texts from Jude.

"Can you answer him?" I have to be some new degree of awful for still not wanting to talk to him. Even now. Or maybe I'm just embarrassed, I don't know.

Malcolm texts back and forth with Jude while I scroll through dozens of social media notifications. Almost all of them are comments that include #RIPDeja, dove emojis, and prayer hands. I throw my phone across the room. It hits the wall and lands at the bottom of Malcolm's mattress.

"We don't even have confirmation, but #RIPDeja is taking off faster than #FindDeja did. What's that say, Malcolm? What's that mean?"

He puts his phone down, takes me by the hand, and leads me to his bed. We both lie down facing each other like we have so many times before.

"It doesn't mean anything except they are going to look real dumb in a few hours. The body isn't hers. It can't be." He lifts my chin so I'm looking into his eyes. "You hear me?"

I know he believes it with everything in him because he hasn't shed a single tear and Malcolm has never been afraid to cry.

"I hear you."

He pulls me into a hug and we hold each other for a long time. Long enough for his breathing to grow slow and heavy. He really must have slept horribly last night. I slip out of his now-slack grasp. Watching him lie there, so relaxed, fills me with energy. Anxious energy. Paranoid energy. I nudge him gently, testing the depth of his sleep. When he doesn't react, I nudge harder, say his name at a normal speaking volume. It gets me a sleepy mumble, but his eyelids don't budge. I feel around for his phone. The other phone. The one that, for some reason, he lied to me about. I pat the blankets and carefully squeeze his jacket pocket. Nothing. I try pushing him over and he furrows his brow and swats at me. But that's fine. I have full access to the rest of his room.

I inch my way off the mattress, stand, and look around. He doesn't have many places to hide stuff, not that I even know what sort of things he'd want to hide. Not that I want to know, for the most part. But I'm positive there's something important he's keeping from me. I'm also positive that Deja was keeping something from me. And I'm getting the feeling that the *something* was shared between the two of them. I tiptoe to his closet. Malcolm doesn't live in the kind of house that has squeaky floors, but he has a dog. Miss Doretta perks up from her bed and lets loose a growl. I put my index finger over my mouth and shush her, but she doesn't like that. The hair on her back stands on end and she starts to yap. I put my hand on my forehead and sigh as Malcolm sits up.

"Quiet," he says to Miss Doretta.

The dog gives me another growl, but then takes a few turns and settles back into her bed.

"What are you doing?" he asks sleepily.

"I'm going to go home. Called an Uber." The last part is a lie, but I add it on so he won't offer to drive me. He hates getting behind the wheel, but after yesterday and today, I know he'd insist.

"Oh. Did they discharge Josiah?"

"No. He'll be home tomorrow, but I need a shower and a change of clothes."

He picks up his iPhone. "How long was I out? Any updates?"

"Not long. And no. Nothing."

His hand goes to his pocket, the one he'd been lying on, but he doesn't remove the burner phone. I want to tell him I already caught him in the lie, so he might as well tell the truth, but I don't. Whatever he's hiding will come out when it's meant to, or I'll figure it out on my own.

"See you later."

CHAPTER 28

. . . .

Later that evening, I sit on the end of my bed and FaceTime Fitz. I need to talk to someone other than Jude or Malcolm. Calling him still feels like it might disrupt the organization of the universe. And maybe that's why I try him again right away when he doesn't answer the first time. I want this universe disrupted.

He accepts my call this time, grinning. His round face is dim, only illuminated by streetlights as he walks down the road. "Atlanta! What it do?" He uses his dirty tank to wipe sweat from his forehead.

"I'm just . . . here."

His face drops. "Still no word on Deja?"

I pause, debating how to answer. "They found a body."

He stops short, mouth falling open. "Oh, shit." He stutters through his next question. "Was it her?"

"Not sure yet"—I blink quickly to keep tears at bay—"but maybe."

"Wow, man." He climbs up some steps to a porch with

much better lighting and sits down. "I don't even know what to say, Sariyah. I'm sorry."

"Malcolm doesn't think it's her."

"Do you?"

The question throws me because, somehow, I hadn't paused to consider what I think. "No. No, I don't." I sit up straighter, finding more resolve. "I think she ran away." I can't make the blood and the pepper spray fit the story I'm forming, but I put it together anyway. It's still a dark narrative, but it's more hopeful than all the others and I have to cling to it. "I think her stepdad is too strict. I think her mom has a drug problem. I think she has a secret boyfriend. I think she ran away from her parents and ran to her boyfriend."

"And you think her secret boyfriend is Jed?"

"I don't know if—Wait, why do you think I think it's Jed?"

"He told me you were asking him some weird questions about Deja."

"Oh. I did ask him some questions, but I don't think they were weird. Deja follows him on Instagram. I wanted to know if he ever spoke to her. He said he didn't."

"Well, he's a liar."

"What? Are you saying he did talk to Deja?" I shift the phone to my other hand, as if somehow it will make me see and hear him better.

"No. I don't know. All I'm saying is he can't be trusted."

"I thought he was your best friend."

"Yeah. He was and I don't even know why. He's been trying to sabotage my relationship with Crystelle for years. Then I found out he cheated on my sister."

I want to ask how it is he is so put off by Jed cheating on his sister, when he forgave Crystelle for what she did, but I doubt he could give me any logical answer. "Did they break up?"

"Yep. Straw that broke the camel's back. It's for the best. They'd been having other issues. He's got a temper on him."

I swipe away from our call so I can check Jed's Instagram. Sure enough, all the photos of him and Ella have been deleted. Including the one that Deja had commented on. I'm glad I still have the screenshot. "Who did he cheat on her with?"

"Ella said he made a Facebook account to help boost posts about Deja, like you asked, but then she found some really flirty Facebook messages between him and some girl."

I immediately search Facebook for Jedidiah Jones. There's only one in Chefly, Georgia. His profile picture is of a dock at sunset and the rest of the page is equally bland. But we aren't friends. There may be things I can't see. I send him a request.

"You still there?" Fitz asks.

"Yeah, sorry. What was the girl's name?"

"Not Deja, if that's where you're going. It was Willa? Willow? Something like that. Didn't catch a last name. But hey, I'm sorry. I gotta go. Supposed to meet up with Crystelle in a few."

We hang up and I feel even less at ease than I did before I called him. I grab my laptop and sign into Malcolm's student account. He lets me know every time he updates his password so I can always have access to his class notes. He doesn't have the patience to be a good tutor, but that never stopped him from finding other ways to help me with school. And that's why I don't open his email expecting to find anything earth-shattering. But he and Deja had several classes together and maybe there's a clue about what was going on with her in one of their exchanges for school.

There's one email in his inbox. It's from his social studies teacher reminding him and Deja to submit their project proposal. Malcolm was so excited to work with her on it over break, but they didn't even get a chance to start. I'm about to close his email when I notice a message in his drafts folder written three days ago. I click away when I see it's addressed to Deja, thinking I've stumbled upon some therapeutic exercise where you write letters to your missing friend. I've already invaded his privacy, but reading something like that feels like a step too far. But I glimpsed enough to see that whatever he wrote was very short. Which makes it very unlikely to be some emotional diary entry. I hover my cursor over "no subject" for a solid thirty seconds before clicking it once again.

Notice anything?
M.

There are eight attachments. All articles. Two about the disappearance of Contessa Hawkins. Four about the disappearance of Casey Sullivan. And two about the disappearance of Deja Nelson.

I open all the attachments, so much adrenaline coursing through me it's difficult to see straight. Why would Malcolm draft this when he knows Deja is missing? Why would he send her any of it, period? I try to rationalize. See from his perspective, but I can't make it make sense. Unless he meant to send it to someone else. Maybe me even. That has to be it. I laugh away some of my nervous energy. It's not a long shot that he'd accidentally type Deja's email in the recipient line. It's like when you accidentally send a text to the person you're trying to talk shit about. Right? I click through the articles. I've seen all of them before, but I comb through them as if Malcolm's message was absolutely meant for me. I comb through looking for anything out of the ordinary, but there's nothing. The reporting style in Deja's and Tessa's articles differs from Casey's in a grating sort of way, but that's not unusual. It's sad. It's infuriating. But it's not unusual.

I close my laptop at ten o'clock on the dot and crawl into bed, hoping to dream of Tessa. Malcolm doesn't come up in our conversations often, but tonight I wish I could tap into their twin connection through her. But Tess doesn't grant wishes. The Tessa in my dreams can't tell me anything I don't already know. And I don't know anything. I think Malcolm's hiding something related to Deja. I think Jed and Ms. Jasmine are, too. I'm afraid to find out what, but I have to. For Dej.

Sleep doesn't provide reprieve or answers. Only nightmares of teen girls being pulled from lakes, cold and lifeless. I startle awake to Mama pushing my hair from my face. It takes a few seconds for my mind to work normally, but once it does, I shoot upright. "Is Jojo okay?" I squint in the darkness. Palm around for the switch to my bedside lamp.

Mama clicks it on. "Shh, baby. Your brother is fine. I'm bringing him home in the morning."

The sight of her face doesn't calm me. Her eyes are red and puffy. "What's wrong? Deja?" My brain assaults me with flashes from the dreams I'd been having. "Was it her?"

"No," she says. "I just got back from Ms. Jasmine's. It wasn't Deja."

I don't react. I'm too scared I've heard her wrong.

"You hear me? The body they found. It wasn't Deja."

I surprise myself by crashing into her. Wrapping my arms around her soft middle. Squeezing.

She rubs my back. "I knew you would want to know as soon as it was confirmed."

I pull away enough to look up at her. "Does Malcolm know?"

"Mrs. Hawkins was there, too. She'll tell him. But it's late, baby. I promise we can talk more in the morning. I called the school and told them you'll be using one of your remote learning days tomorrow so you can be here to welcome your brother home." She takes my bonnet from my nightstand and slips it over my head. "Try to get some rest."

I hold on to her tighter because I don't know what mood she'll be in tomorrow. *It wasn't her. It wasn't her. It wasn't her.* I tell myself over and over, like if I go without thinking it for more than a few seconds it will somehow be untrue. And maybe it would. Because someone out there was wishing it was her and not their daughter. Their sister. Their friend. Mama continues to rub my back until the next thing I know, the sun is up and Josiah is calling my name.

I pull on a sweatshirt and pad out to the living room where he stands taking in the place, like he expects something drastic has changed in the two days he was gone.

"Welcome back."

He passes me an overloaded paper grocery bag. "It's nasty healthy stuff."

"Where's Mama?" I stick my head out the front door, looking for her.

"She said she was going to the dry cleaners down the street to pick up a suit."

"To pick up a what?" I ask, sure I heard him wrong.

He powers up his Xbox and sits on his knees too close to the screen. "That girl they found they thought was Deja, wasn't really Deja."

"Mama told me." I plug my dead phone into the charger. I need to call Malcolm. In the meantime, I open my laptop and sign into my school's learning platform to knock out my assignments for the day. When I finish, I start closing out the twenty open tabs on my browser, but pause when I see that Deja's missing person Facebook post has a flood of new comments.

Belinda Atkins: Thank God it wasn't her, but let's keep the family of whoever it is in our prayers.

Sharon Easley: She's still out there!

Patrice Martin: Does anyone have information about what happened to this poor young woman they found?

Roderick Thomas: Deja Nelson has been gone going on, what? Ten days now? Still no updates! They did my niece the same way. SMH!

Katie Ellwood: I go to school with Deja. I cried when I heard they might have found her body.

I feel bad for rolling my eyes at Katie's comment, like she isn't allowed to feel grief over her classmate. But she was in math with me and Deja for eight months and never even made eye contact with either of us. Now her comment has a dozen likes and four old ladies comforting her in the replies. I click back to my home page and that's when I notice the red dot by my notification bell. Jed. He accepted my friend request. I go to his profile. There's not much more to see than there was in the public view, but this isn't a freshly made account. There are some photos of the creek that runs through Chefly uploaded two years ago. A post about fishing lures shared ten months ago. Nothing more recent than that. He hasn't used this account to boost any posts about Deja. I click on the blue message button at the top of the page.

Me
Hey Jed

A green dot appears, showing he's now online.

Jed
Hello.
How are you?

I begin to type, but another message pops up right away.

Please. I am having a hard time. Can you
send me $50 right away? I will accept
PayPal or Venmo. I thank you very much.
Please, you are very beautiful. I will repay you.

Relief bursts from me in the form of a laugh as I close Facebook. I certainly don't know him better than Ella, but maybe in the shock of finding the flirty messages, she failed to ask herself if they really sounded like him. Abandoned Facebook pages are prime targets for hackers and Jed getting hacked makes way more sense than him cheating on Ella Davis. He and Ella and Fitz will work things out in a few days, and if not, I'll send them screenshots of the non-conversation I just had.

• • •

My phone illuminates as it powers back up. A flurry of notifications overtakes the screen.

Malcolm
Answer the phone! Did you hear?
My mom said your mom was there,
so I'm assuming you're ready for
this big fat I TOLD YOU SO
It's not her, Ri.

Mama comes home from the dry cleaners and calls me into her bedroom. I stand and pump out a couple of texts. Playing it cool until I figure out which thread I'm going to tug on next. I've followed Jed's as far as I can for now, and that only leaves Malcolm's or Ms. Jasmine's.

Me
You can rub it in later. I'll call you tonight.

Malcolm
Okay. And we can discuss whatever
is going on between you and
Jude later too. He's a mess.

Mama calls me again, patience audibly thinner this time. I go to her room. "Yes, ma'am?"

"Close the door."

I do as I'm told, then perch on the end of her bed as she arranges a few shopping bags on her dresser. She rests her palms against the dark cherry wood. "I know I haven't been my best self lately. I know you know it and God help me, I know my son knows it. But I'm not as far gone as you think. I've never been so far gone that I missed a night of making sure my children were in their beds. Not with girls disappearing the way they are. Not with Josiah's health issues. But I know I've been failing you lately. I know you need more from me. I know you need to talk. But it's hard to explain how I could know that and still struggle to act on it."

"You don't have to explain, Mama. I understand." I scrunch her comforter in my fists, scared to ask my next question for fear of rejection. Fear that I'm misinterpreting what she expects from this moment. "Could we talk now?"

She looks at me in the mirror, eyes a little less hollow. "Of course we can. I promised we would."

I tell her about the nail file. About the pepper spray. I tell her I did the thing she always warned me never to do with my ability. I tell her I'm so worked up that I'm suspecting my best friend of something nefarious.

She cries. We both do. When there are no tears left in either of us, she speaks first.

"I'm sorry, baby. I can't believe you were out there hustling for money."

"More than anything, I think I needed to keep busy and I didn't pick the best ways to do it." That's not exactly the truth. I really wanted to make us some money, but I'm not trying to make her feel worse about things she couldn't help. "It's okay, Mama."

She gently places her hand on mine. "You know you can be angry with me, right?"

"I'm not angry."

She smiles softly. "Okay. But when you realize you are, know that's okay, too. And about Malcolm." She taps my jaw with her index finger so I'll look at her. "Take how this situation makes you feel and magnify it by ten, baby. Malcolm has earned a secret or two and I'm sure it's nothing as wild as you're worried it is. He'll come to you when he's ready. For the sake of your friendship—and it's a worthy one—wait until he's ready."

I eagerly accept her advice, ignoring the niggling that persists in my stomach.

Mama stands and stretches. "I have a job interview this afternoon."

"What? Where?"

"It's for a teaching position at your high school, actually. Healthcare science."

I sit up straighter. "Wait, is this some scheme to guarantee I graduate on time? Because I love you, Mama. But I'm not going to school with you."

"I won't lie. That crossed my mind." She opens the dry cleaners bag and pulls out a pantsuit. "It's only part-time and doesn't start until August. I'd have some paid trainings here and there over the next couple of months, but no huge commitment and I think that'd be best for me right now."

"I'm happy for you, Mama. You'll do great."

"Thank you." She kisses my cheek and goes to the bathroom to get ready.

CHAPTER 29

. . . .

I find Josiah knocked out asleep when I leave Mama's room. One foot hangs off the bed and a fresh stream of drool glistens on his cheek. I tuck him in, close his door, and grab Santa Bag. I need to go to the convenience store and pick up a few things we'll actually eat. Mama goes on these extreme health kicks every time Jojo has a hospital stay and I'm not living off brussels sprouts and chia seeds.

It's cool out. Overcast, like it may storm later. I open Instagram as I walk and go straight to Deja's page. This time I don't look at the comments. I already know what they'll say. People expressing their relief, their sympathies for the other girl, their renewed hope for Deja. Just like Facebook. I don't want or need to read that stuff again. This time I look at her pictures. Really look. Before now, it was hard for me to do. Like somehow she could see me through the photos. Judge me for not doing more to avoid all of this. Plead with me to find her. But her pictures do none of those things. Her most recent one is of the four of us at Afro Alt. It's a photo that begs to be printed and put in a frame. She's kissing my cheek, and

I'm pretending to be irritated by it. Malcolm's on the other side of her, posing for the gods. Jude's on the other side of me, looking away, laughing. Behind us, blurs of smoke and color and life. She's written a mushy rhyming caption, which I'd read days ago, but only now strikes me as odd. Deja's not the sentimental type, and she doesn't have any special way with words. But as I swipe through her other photos and read the other captions, they all have a similar vibe. A lovey, sometimes romantic vibe that started right around New Year's Eve. Jed might not have been her secret boyfriend, but the secret boyfriend exists.

I'm nearly at the convenience store when a need whispers at me. The walk had been completely silent until now.

Clothespin. Clothespin. Clothespin.

It's faint and I don't see anyone. They must be right on the edge of my range. I slow down, hoping they will put enough distance between us to silence it, but it doesn't help.

Clothespin. Clothespin. Clothespin.

I look around, expecting to spot a frustrated person trying to hang laundry on a line when a kid, maybe thirteen, emerges from the trees. He jumps when he sees me.

"Sorry," I say, even though he's the one randomly popping out of foliage. "Um, this might seem a little odd"—I fish a clothespin from Santa Bag—"but you should hold on to this."

He holds the pin in his open palm, glancing from it, to me, to Santa Bag. I know what he's about to do a half second before he does, but I can't react quickly enough. The boy throws the clothespin aside, snatches Santa Bag from my hand, and takes off running.

"Oh hell no!" I shout, taking off after his scrawny behind. "Hey!"

He sprints down the sidewalk and takes a right at the corner. I curse under my breath and pick up my pace. I turn the corner and run smack dab into a low-hanging branch, a broken twig slicing my cheek right below the eye.

Footsteps on the pavement draw near and a few seconds later, that dumb kid's face is hovering over mine.

"Daaaaamn," he says, fist over his mouth. "You bust yo—"

"Drop the bag!" shouts another voice from out of view. It's deep. Intentionally intimidating.

"Who are—"

"I said drop the bag. Don't make me say it again."

Santa Bag clatters to the ground and the boy takes off. I wipe the blood dribbling from my wound and sit up.

"You okay there?" comes the voice again, softer and closer.

Goose bumps erupt across my arms because now it sounds familiar. I know this man. The need follows a millisecond later. *Pocketknife. Pocketknife. Pocketknife.*

Tim.

"Get away from me." I grab Santa Bag and leap to my feet, patting my pockets for my phone.

"Looking for this?" He waves my phone in his hand, a fresh crack across the screen. "You dropped it back there. Here."

He extends his arm, but snatches it back when I reach for the phone.

"Aht aht. This can't be the only thanks I get for saving your hide." He tilts his head to the side and takes a few steps toward me. "I think you've got better ways to show your appreciation. Unlike ol' boy just now, I don't want random things out that bag. If that's what I wanted, I would have been had it. I know that's not how this works, though."

I walk backward, looking up and down the street for someone who might help me. There's no one. My entire body quakes with fear as I scramble for a way out of this. Tim's from Chefly, and people down there are very superstitious. There's a good chance I can scare him right back. "You think you know how this works, but you have no idea. I have something for you, but are you sure you want it?"

His eyes shift from left to right.

"Are you sure?" I shout.

He takes a nervous step back, hands in the air.

I laugh bitterly. "Oh, are you afraid of me?" I take a quick step forward and he flinches. "Your type always is. You think I'm gonna curse you, don't you?" This is exactly how things took a turn for Grandma Bryant. Saying stupid stuff to the wrong people, but I don't have any other ideas. "You think I'm a witch, huh?"

"I ain't about to find out, tell you that much." He lengthens the space between us.

"No. It's too late for that."

"Hey, now. What you mean too late? What'd you do? Undo it. You can undo it."

"It's. Too. Late." I savor the opportunity to flip this dynamic. To make *him* uncomfortable. Nervous. Fearful.

"Nah. Look, enough is enough. This wasn't even my idea." He drops my phone in the grass and jogs away. When there's considerable distance between us, he shouts, "You can send that curse on down to Chefly where it belongs!"

I blink away the tears that have filled my eyes, making the blood on my face go watery. What the hell was that supposed to mean? I swallow down the urge to call after him, demand he explain himself. I'm fortunate I got him to back off at all. I won't be pushing my luck any further tonight.

• • •

I ended up spending the whole evening alone in my room replaying my encounter with Tim and that kid, feeling embarrassed and foolish for attracting a gnat. I never got around to calling Malcolm back, so I'm not surprised when his name pops up on my phone first thing in the morning.

I accept the call.

"You don't read my texts. You don't call when you say you will. And now you're skipping school without even telling me?" A bell rings in the background.

"I'm sorry. I took another remote day. Mama has an appointment out of town and Josiah needed another day to recover."

"No, I didn't!" Jojo shouts from his bedroom.

I get up and close my door.

"I told you it wasn't Deja."

"You did." I lean against my closet and stare at the dusty ceiling fan. "But she's still not home."

"She will be soon."

"How do you know?"

"I was right before. I'm right now."

"But is there something specific that makes you believe it?" Just because I won't be outright asking him what he's hiding doesn't mean I can't try to guide him into it.

"No. Not really. But let me guess, something specific has made you into a believer."

"I was looking through her posts on Instagram again. I really think she was dating someone. All of her captions—"

"Are song lyrics. Yes. Next?"

"Huh?"

"Oh my God, Sariyah. I know music isn't your thing, but I'm going to need you to keep up with everything that comes

255

out of Lizzo's mouth, okay? Tess isn't the first teenage girl to quote her favorite artists on IG."

"Tess?"

"What?"

"You said Tess when you meant Deja."

"No, I didn't."

"Yes—" I take a deep breath and choose to drop it. Because of course Tess is on his mind and I don't need to rub it in. "There's something Deja didn't tell us. Or something she didn't tell me, at least. All of it is too weird, Colmy. The locks, her mom, her stepdad, the card—"

"Why are you so obsessed with that card? It's months old and the police already know about it. You aren't the Black Nancy Drew, okay?"

"So you want to leave it up to the police? Since you trust them so much?" Tessa's name doesn't leave my mouth, but it's heavy in the silence after I speak. "Sorry. I didn't mean anything by that. I just feel like you're being really damn choosy about what is and isn't a good thing to look into. You went all expert-investigator when you thought something was suspicious about Deja's stepdad, but now you won't even hear me out."

"Look," he says, a little less abrasive now, "if it'll get you to drop this, I'll go with you to Deja's tomorrow afternoon. We can search her room for signs of that J. dude or some box of super-secret items she wanted to keep locked inside while she slept."

"Really?" I ask, ignoring the sarcasm he injected into his words.

"I guess. It's that or let you get up to God knows what by yourself. Or worse, drag your little boyfriend into it."

My face heats. "I know you aren't talking about Jude. He's not my boyfriend."

"Should I assume you've already gotten him involved since you ignored the other half of my sentence?"

"I mean, not really."

"I swear you meddle like your life is one big episode of *Scooby-Doo*."

"You're saying I can be Shaggy, but not Nancy?"

"Haha, no. Shaggy and Scooby are legit. They are the only ones on that show that have any sense. But you? You're Daphne."

"Then I guess you're that blond dude."

"Shoot, that's all right, with his fine orange-ascot-wearing ass."

He gets a laugh out of me with that. "Seriously, Mal. I thought the whole point was to meddle."

"No. It never was. That's where you're mixed up. The point was to disseminate. Disperse. Get people talking. Make people see her. That's what worked for Casey. Not digging up dirt about her family or romantic life." He takes a loud swig of a drink. "But listen, I'll talk to you later. I need to get to art. Oh, and by the way, your not-boyfriend is about to skip the rest of his classes for the day and go surprise you with lunch, so I don't know, fix your hair or something."

• • •

I don't bother changing out of my tank top and pajama pants, but I do tie a stretchy headband over my frizzy twists and force myself into the bathroom to brush my teeth.

Jude knocks on the door to our apartment and Jojo runs down the hall shouting, "I got it!"

"Take it easy, Josiah! You just had your blood replaced with someone else's."

"Yeah, and that made me feel better, not worse!" he hollers. "Juju!"

There's some rustling, laughter, and muffled voices before Jude pokes his head into my room. His expression drops right away. "Hey, what happened to your face?" He takes a few quick steps over to my side and gently runs his thumb across the scabbed-over, but puffy, scratch under my eye.

"She ran into a tree," Jojo says casually as he passes by my room.

"Sounds fake, but it's the truth," I say with a reassuring smile, not wanting to get into everything that happened before and after that.

"Looks like it hurts," he says, face still contorted with concern.

"It's fine. Promise. Can you close the door?"

He pushes the door until it's as close to being closed without actually being closed as possible and I love that he automatically knew that's what I meant. His mom must not play that game, either. There are no mothers present right now, but old habits die hard.

He jabs his thumb over his shoulder. "I brought you some tacos, but Josiah snatched them and ran."

Of course he did. "I don't have much of an appetite anyway. Thanks for bringing it, though. He was probably minutes away from destroying the kitchen trying to make himself a peanut butter and jelly sandwich." I sit cross-legged on my bed.

"I'm sorry," we say in unison.

"I overreacted," I say.

"I shouldn't have asked you to do it in the first place."

I shake my head. "No. I struggle with . . . what I do. Is it good? Is it bad? You know. Malcolm said I meddle too much earlier, and it's true. I meddle every time I fulfill a need, and

I've seen amazing things come from it. But I can't help it—the bad is what stands out in my mind."

"I know. I'm sorry," he says again.

"Me too. And the thing with your aunt and my mom. I think maybe it'll turn out good for both of them."

"What do you mean?"

"I mean, my mom had an interview for a job she's really excited about. It's part-time and doesn't start for a while and she needs that kind of flexibility right now. I don't know if she'll get it, but the opportunity put a little life back into her, I think. Maybe that wouldn't have happened if she never got fired."

He gives me a hesitant smile. "I hope she gets the job."

"Me too. It'll be even more motivation for me to graduate on time or else we'll be in the halls together next year."

"Oh, shoot. It's a job at the school?" He unzips his book bag. "Should we make this a study session?"

"Yeah, we should. But first, I need to catch you up."

"Sounds serious."

"It is. It's about Deja." I pull up her Instagram and pass my phone to Jude. "Malcolm said her captions are Lizzo lyrics, but I still feel like she was trying to communicate something about someone she was seeing."

Jude scrolls up and down her page, clicking photos here and there. "Wait, what?" He laughs. "These aren't Lizzo lyrics."

I look over his shoulder, as if I'd actually be able to tell the difference. "Those are her own words?"

He laughs again. "No. You know she's got quirky taste. They're Willow Smith lyrics."

"Willow?" My heart rate skyrockets as I recall the last conversation I had with Fitz. "Give me. Pass me—" I gesture wildly at my laptop.

He passes it to me, eyes wide as saucers. "What's wrong?"

I'm so worked up it takes me three tries to hit the F key and get Facebook to autofill in my browser. I hit enter and go straight to Jed's profile. I click his "friends" tab and type "Willow" into the search bar. One result pops up.

Willow D. Nelson.

CHAPTER 30

. . . .

"We can't know for sure this is her," Jude says. "The profile is blank."

"Willow. D. Nelson. Jude, what more evidence do we need? Jed cheated on his girlfriend with someone called Willow. Deja posts mushy Willow Smith lyrics on her Instagram, where she just happens to be following Jed. Now this?"

"You think Deja is hanging out in your hometown with Jed? Wouldn't she have been seen by now? Hasn't your dad been hanging posters?"

I shrug, frustrated by questions I can't answer.

"How well do you know Jed? Would he . . ." Jude pauses, choosing his words carefully. "Is he dangerous?"

I shrug even harder. "I don't know. I don't think so."

"You don't think so?"

"I don't know him well, but I'm friends with his best friend and I don't think he would hurt her. But he knows something." Maybe something valuable enough that he'd pretend to be a hacker on his own Facebook account. He could have ignored my message. That he didn't proves he's trying to write his own narrative. Best-case, that narrative is all about convincing Ella he didn't cheat and winning her back. Worst-case is something I don't want to think about.

"What do we do? Call the detective?"

"I'll update him, but I'm not holding my breath waiting for them to do anything. Malcolm said he'd go with me to Deja's tomorrow. I want to check her room one more time. See if there's anything related to Jed we might have missed. And if it comes to it"—I stand and rest my hands on my hips, contemplating if I really mean what I'm about to say—"I'll go down to Chefly."

"What? You can't do that. We don't know what he could be capable of, Sariyah."

"My dad would be my first stop. I wouldn't confront Jed alone."

He considers this. "Say the word when you're ready. I'll drive you down."

• • •

Malcolm doesn't show up at school Friday. I text him through-out the day, confirming more than once that we're still on to meet at Deja's. So I'm pissed to high heaven when he doesn't show. I call and text back-to-back for fifteen minutes before giving up and catching a bus to his place.

The garage doors are up, but his parents' cars aren't inside, only his dusty little hooptie. I let myself inside the house. He's out on the deck, French doors wide open.

"Your mom is going to trip over you letting all her AC out."

He pockets his phone. The burner one he's been lying to me about. "Do you see my mom anywhere around right now?"

I jerk my head back. "Excuse me. If anyone has the right to have an attitude right now, it's me. You stood me up." I lean against the pollen-coated grill. "What happened? I've been calling you nonstop."

He checks the phone again, then rubs his hand back and forth across the top of his head, knotting up his tiny coils.

"I know you don't want to hear it, but Colmy, I found out some stuff. Let's go over to Deja's now. I can tell you everything on the way." I start walking back toward the house.

"There's no point, Sariyah."

I stop walking but take a second to fix my face before I turn around. He's irritating the mess out of me. "Yesterday you said it wouldn't hurt to go look around." The words come out stiff, not at all disguising my annoyance.

"Yeah. It wouldn't, but I got a lot on my mind right now, okay?"

I know he does. We all do, but I still don't understand. "You could've—"

"Sariyah, please. I need to think." He paces and once again checks that stupid phone.

"Malcolm, what's going on? Talk to me."

His Adam's apple bobs up and down. "I messed up, Ri."

"What do you mean?" I move closer to him, wondering if this is the moment Mama told me to wait for. I hope it is because he has one more time to touch that phone before my patience runs out.

"Something's wrong," he says more to himself than to me.

"Yeah, Malcolm, a lot of stuff is wrong. Can you be more specific? What happened?"

He laughs, but his eyes are watery. Tormented. "I just think it's funny how the video of me quitting Sweet Pea's went viral with no effort. People, even our own damn people, won't hesitate to share a video of a Black person popping off, but a Black girl who's missing? Nah, that's too much. They want a minstrel show, something to laugh at. Not a thirteen-year-old dark-skinned girl disappearing quietly into the night. Not even a seventeen-year-old one disappearing under suspicious circumstances."

"Mal, you want something to make this viral, I got it. That's exactly what I've been trying to tell you. We could have searched Deja's entire house by now."

He takes out that phone again, and I slap it from his hands. He barely reacts. We both watch it clatter and clunk across the deck, unmarred in the end.

"She stopped answering my texts," he says to his feet. "I haven't heard from her in a day and a half. Maybe her phone died. I don't know. But I'm worried. She should be home by now. I held out because I knew it was the last day, but something's not right."

"Malcolm, what the fuck are you talking about?"

"Deja."

• • •

Malcolm leans against his windowsill, wringing his hands as I pace in front of his bedroom door.

"Do you remember that current issues project Deja and I were excited about doing together?" he asks.

"What's that got—" I freeze in place. "Do not. Malcolm, I swear to God. Do not sit there and tell me you two faked her disappearance for a social studies project. Tell me you didn't."

"We didn't," he snaps. "It started the conversation, but we did it for Tessa. And Deja's cousin Amari. And every other

Black and brown girl the world let disappear without a second thought."

"Are you seriously going to act like you did someone a favor? That you helped anyone by doing this? You made a mockery of those girls. You made a mockery of Tess. Turned it all into some big fat joke. And for what? What was the end goal, Malcolm?"

"Change! To see if anything had changed. Casey's case was still fresh on everyone's mind. We wanted to see if people would keep that same energy if the girl wasn't blond. I needed to know. If Tessa disappeared today, instead of five years ago, would she have had a better chance of making it home? And if the answer was no, I wanted the world to see it. I wanted it right in everyone's face. I wanted people who shared Casey's posts and not Deja's to look in the mirror and ask themselves why."

"Oh, be for real, Malcolm. Some ill-conceived social experiment wasn't about to change anything. What were you going to say when she came back, huh? That she ran away? You chewed *me* out for even considering that possibility while y'all were out here literally creating a whole new data point for that statistic. You thought that would make things better for Black missing kids? And what if the truth about all this gets out? Our people don't get the benefit of the doubt as it is. What do you think will happen if they catch us crying wolf?"

Malcolm turns his face away from me. Stares out the window.

"Did you even consider how many resources, how much time and attention, this would suck from people who actually needed it? If you could have guaranteed that Tessa would walk through your front door at the end of it all, no one would blame you. And I know. You're angry, you're hurt. I

265

hear you. But do you know how much trouble you could get in for this? How much trouble Deja might be in right now?"

"Yes, I know! But don't tell me you hear me. Don't lie to my face like that because you haven't heard me in a long, long time, Sariyah. If you did, if you'd really been listening to me, you'd understand why we had to do this despite all the risks."

"You didn't have to do anything, Malcolm." I scan his body from head to toe. "You knew she was alive and safe and said nothing. Not even when we thought they pulled her body out of the fucking lake."

"I told you it wasn't her."

I clench my teeth so hard my jaw aches. This betrayal has pushed my heart through a fine-mesh sieve and I can't even begin to consider how to repair it. "You're sick, Malcolm. Sick."

"Oh, I don't disagree with you there, but illness don't come from nowhere do it?"

I think about my mother, and I want to say yes. Sometimes it does come from nowhere. Sometimes there's not a good and clear reason. But that's not the case here.

Malcolm stands there, eyes reddening. "Ask me what made me this way." He beats his chest. "Ask me!"

I don't need to ask him. "How does throwing your own life away help Tessa or anyone else?"

"I'm not throwing anything away. We had a plan."

"Yeah. Exactly. How's that going, huh? How's it going if you don't even know where she is?"

"Who said I don't know where she is? You. Don't. Listen. You forever stay caught up in your own head and, on God, I know you can't help it. I know that, but sometimes I can't stand your ass for it."

"Yeah, well sometimes I can't stand myself, either!" I turn my back to him so he can't watch me fight back my tears.

"She's in Chefly," he says quietly.

I spin around. "Chefly?" There's no hiding the panic in my voice. "Is she with Jed?"

"There you go again. Still not listening. I have told you over and over I don't know nothing about no Jed or no stupid behind card."

"Okay, and you just confessed that you've been lying to me for almost two weeks. I don't know what to believe. Where in Chefly is she, if not with Jed?"

He looks away from me. "The rental in the back of your dad's property."

"Wait, what?" I replay his words in my head, hoping to arrange them in a way that makes sense. "Malcolm, what the hell is wrong with you? My father is a Black man who lives by himself. Do you know what could happen if they find her there? Are you confident enough in our police force, in the police force down in Chefly, Georgia, to believe they'd give him a chance to explain? Did you think about any of that?"

"No!" he screams as tears gush from his eyes. "No, Sariyah, I didn't think about any of that because it's not about you or your daddy. It's about everyone the world was content to forget about." He sobs. "I just miss my sister. I just want someone to care. I want the police to care. I want the country to care. I want the world to care. I want you to care."

"Malcolm, I do."

"Then why couldn't you see? Why couldn't you see what that news about Casey did to me? You're supposed to be my best friend on this planet and you didn't see. How come you can help everybody—how come you can give everyone what they need except me?"

"I don't know." I'm crying freely now, too. "Malcolm, I wish I could. You know that. You know it kills me. But I don't even know who you are right now. How could you hurt everyone this way? With this lie? How could you hurt me this way?"

He dries his face. Composes himself. "Because there are bigger and more important things than your temporary pain. And is it absurd to think a taste of some hurt would do some good? Let it hit close to home. That's the only time people give a damn. So, nah, I don't feel bad that we made people sad for a week. Half of them were performing anyway. But Tessa? Me and my family have been living with that for five years."

"Really, Malcolm? Like I don't love Tessa, too? Like her being gone hasn't tormented me, too?"

"You're still making it about you. But since you want to do that so badly, let's do it. What you feel about Tessa and what my parents feel are not the same. What I feel and what you feel are not the same." He raises his voice. "The very cells that made me were next to her before I even formed a consciousness, Sariyah. There's no comparison because you don't have a twin, but if Josiah disappeared today and you didn't see his face, hear his voice—if you didn't know whether he was dead or alive for five years—you couldn't see yourself driven to extremes? If you saw it happen over and over to other little boys who look like him. If you saw different, better outcomes for the ones who don't, that wouldn't break you? That wouldn't have you ready to do anything in the world to make people see how wrong it is?"

Him talking like this makes me want to hit him. I want to rush him and feed his words back to him. Shove them back down into whatever ugly part of his body created them. But I don't. Because he accomplished exactly what he intended to. Everything that was black or white two minutes ago is now gray. I'd go to even further extremes than Malcolm has if anything ever happened to my little brother.

"Point made." I have one hundred more questions, but this isn't the time for them. Deja might be in trouble. "Did you and Deja have a fail-safe? What to do if you lost contact?"

"I'm supposed to go to the police with the truth if I don't hear from her in six hours."

I look at my watch and snatch up Santa Bag.

"What are you doing?"

"Make up something to tell my mom. I'm going to Chefly. And I'm taking your car."

"The hooptie?"

"Do you have another one?"

"No, but it—"

"It's a car. Where are the keys?"

He takes out his phone. "Sariyah, maybe we should go ahead and call the police now."

"And let them roll up on my father and accuse him of snatching Dej? I don't think so."

"Then I'm going with you."

"No. Our parents will flip if both of us are gone. My phone is fully charged and I'll share my location. Text or call me randomly over the next six hours. If I don't answer or respond within five minutes, then you can call the police."

CHAPTER 31

· ·

Now that I'm sitting alone in this musty car with three hours of driving ahead of me, I regret not asking Malcolm more questions. He said Deja was supposed to come home today but didn't say how she was planning to get there. I consider calling him but think better of it. I can't help Deja if I crash this car because I'm arguing with Malcolm. And I don't think I can speak to him without it turning into another fight. The details don't matter right now anyway. I just need to get to Dad's and hopefully find Deja in that rental with a good reason for not coming back as planned. A reason that has nothing to do with some stupid boy.

A nasty storm is brewing by the time I reach the halfway point of my drive. The farther south I travel, the angrier and angrier the sky gets. Not the tee-hee-hee kind of angry. The mess-around-and-find-out kind of angry. It's hard not feeling like I should take it as some sort of omen. When the sky finally cracks open, it brings with it winds that make me grip the steering wheel until my joints hurt. The rain gets heavier and tiny bits of hail bounce off the windshield. The wipers are dry rotted and no match for a storm like this. I pull over and Malcolm texts me only a couple of seconds later.

Malcolm
Checking in.

I react to his message with a thumbs-up.

Malcolm
Still haven't heard from her

Me
I assume she has a burner too? Text me the number. I'll be there soon.

And I will. The storm is moving quickly. I wait another few minutes, then get back on the highway. The sun is just starting to set when I arrive in Chefly. It's a miracle I made it. The hooptie was on E for the last thirty miles. I stop at the first of two gas stations in town. The car put-puts and groans all the way to the pump. No way it would have made it the three remaining miles to Dad's. I call him on my way inside to pay, but he doesn't answer. A cowbell dings as I push open the door. A door that I notice is not covered with Deja's missing person posters.

"Now wait a minute," the clerk says when I'm halfway to the coolers for a bottle of water. "I know you ain't Ennis Lee Bryant's daughter come in here not speaking to nobody."

Tweezers. Tweezers. Tweezers. I take a deep breath and turn around, forcing a smile.

He presses his fist to his forehead. "What they call you? Maggie is it?"

"No, sir, that's my mother." Another need joins his, but

271

Santa Bag is in the back seat and I don't have time for this. *Tweezers. Matches. Tweezers. Matches.*

"Sariyah?" comes a voice from behind me.

I look over my shoulder, and standing there, with a Mountain Dew and a bag of pork rinds in hand, is Jedidiah Jones. I watch as he fulfills his own need and plucks a box of matches from a s'mores display. I can only assume he must have a use for them that he is currently unaware of.

"What are you doing here?" He glances out at the pumps and scratches his arm.

I scan the shop, half expecting Deja to emerge from the aisle behind him with a bag of sour candy. "I think your Facebook got hacked." I don't believe that at all anymore, but I don't want to reveal that I suspect him of lying. All I want is to find Deja and bring her home.

"Oh yeah, it did." Jed adds a pack of sunflower seeds to his snack pile. "You here visiting your dad, or . . . ?" His forehead is sweaty and he, once again, glances out at the hooptie.

I walk to the counter with my card and continue to avoid the question he so desperately wants me to answer. "Twenty on pump one, please." I open my text messages and tap the number to Deja's burner that Malcolm sent me. The call connects and as soon as it begins to ring, a buzzing starts up behind me. A vibrating phone. I turn and stare at Jed and he stares back dumbly. My eyes drift to his backpack, where the sound seems to be coming from. A coincidence? Do I believe in those? My muscles tense. "Are you going to answer that?"

"What?" He pats his pockets a few times before freezing in place.

I end the call. The vibrating stops. And we both know what this is.

Jed's face goes dark. He drops everything in his arms and sprints out of the gas station.

"What in the ever-loving heck got into him?" the clerk says, handing me back my card.

I snatch it from him and race out to the car. Jed is gone, but the hooptie was the only vehicle in sight when I pulled up. If he's heading to Daddy's rental, I can beat him there. I fill the tank with just enough gas to get there and speed off down the road.

The five-minute drive feels like an eternity. What used to be a dirt path leading to the small rental house has turned into mud and swallowed the whole yard with it. I can't risk getting the car stuck in that mess, so I drive another ten seconds and turn onto the gravel road that leads to Dad's house. In the yard are several missing person flyers covered with sheet protectors and taped to paint stirrers stuck in the ground. The rain has made a mess of them, but I'm glad they're there. Dad's truck isn't out front, but I can't wait around. I text Malcolm to let him know I got here safely and then go inside.

"Daddy!" I shout over the squeak of the screen door that he never keeps locked. I don't expect an answer, but I get one in the form of an irritated bark. Otis, Dad's toothless English bulldog, comes trotting down the hall like he's gonna do something. He gets a whiff of me and spins around in an excited circle, but there's no time to greet him. I need to find Deja and get out of here.

I run straight through the house and out the back door to the shed where Dad keeps the four-wheeler, praying the thing is functional. The key hangs on a nail above the toolbox. I put it in the ignition, hold my breath, and turn. It starts. I reverse out and drive it as fast as it will go toward the rental.

Mud splashes up to my waist, but I'm there in a flash. I cut the engine directly across from the long staircase Daddy built that leads down to the creek. Those banks used to be the most peaceful place on Earth to me, but today the sound of rushing water sets me on edge.

I dart up the ramp that leads to the side door of the house. It's locked, but the window next to it is wide open. It's too high for me to reach from the ground, so I climb onto the rickety railing. I balance there for a few seconds, debating the best way to transition inside, before taking my chances and bunny hopping through the window. All would have been well if the floor wasn't rotted out. My right foot breaks through the decaying pine. I clench my jaws to avoid shouting out in pain and carefully remove my foot from the hole. My lower calf is bloody, muddy, and full of splinters. "Deja!" I shout, forgoing my plans of a gentle approach. I lurch over onto all fours and use the wall to straighten up to my full height. "Deja!" I call again, but there's no answer. If she were here, she would have heard that grand entrance I made. Still, I hobble around the small space, looking for any sign she was here at all. I find a promising bag of fresh trash in the kitchen.

In the bedroom, I find the flower crown and romper she wore to Afro Alt balled up in the corner. My stomach drops as if I'm free-falling on a roller coaster. She was definitely here, but there's no telling where she, or Jed, is now. I need to find my dad. It's time to call the police.

I limp my way back to the side door and accidentally drop the keys to the four-wheeler as I fumble with the doorknob. They land at the edge of the hole I created with my foot. When I reach down to grab them, I sense something.

A need.

CHAPTER 32

· ·

Water. Water. Water.

I get down on all fours and peer into the hole in the floor, but the little remaining light of the day doesn't extend far. The need persists, but no one answers when I call out. I take another lap around the house, feeling the clarity of the need wax and wane. In the end, I'm drawn back to the hole. The flashlight on my phone doesn't help much, but I stick my arm as far in as I can without blocking my vision. I slowly rotate it, getting a glimpse from every angle. Something brushes against my wrist and I flinch, dropping the phone out of reach. It rests sideways against a rock, illuminating some of the space I couldn't see before.

Illuminating a set of long, honey-brown box braids.

"Deja!" I scream. It's guttural. A sound I've never heard leave my mouth. I have to tell myself three times over that she isn't dead. If she were dead, I wouldn't be hearing her need.

I try reaching for my phone again, but all I do is knock it over, sending the crawl space back into darkness. *Crawl space.* There has to be an entrance to it somewhere. I run outside and scan the perimeter of the house. Nothing on the outside. Covered in mud, I go back in and reassure Deja I'm going to get her out. I don't know if she can hear me, but I promise her over and over.

I spot the hinge of the crawl space hatch door on the floor of the bedroom closet, partially concealed by renovation supplies. A sour taste builds in the back of my throat when I find several Walmart bags filled with snacks and drinks stashed beneath a sheet. I push the junk aside, only to find the door padlocked. It's old and cheap, like something a middle school kid would put on their locker. A measure clearly taken to keep Deja in rather than any worry about keeping someone out. I scan the closet for something to open it with. A rusty toolbox sits on the top shelf. I rise onto the tiptoes of my good foot and take it down. There's no hammer inside, but there is a tiny key. My hands tremble so badly, it takes several seconds to get the key into the hole. Once the lock pops open, I snatch a bottle of water from the case to my right and throw open the door. A strong, mildewy odor smacks me in the face. I never thought I had issues with confined spaces, but the distance between the floor and the earth below can't be more than three feet high. I don't allow myself any more time to think about it. I wiggle down into the space and crawl to my friend.

"Deja!" I nudge her shoulder. "Deja, can you hear me? It's Sariyah."

I get only a few shallow moans in response.

"Hey." I give her face a few firm pats. "Dej, it's me. We need to get out of here."

She slowly opens her eyes. Blinks a few times. Gasps. "Sariyah?" She reaches out and touches me. "I thought I was dreaming."

Tears wet my cheeks and I twist open the water. "Here. Drink."

The recycled plastic crinkles and crunches as she gulps it down.

I feel around for my phone. The air is warm and thick, like a bathroom after a shower. It's hard to breathe.

"Where is he?" Deja asks, voice small.

"Where is who?" I ask, wanting her to confirm what I already know.

"Jed."

"I don't know. That's why we have to hurry." I find my phone, but it's caked with mud and glitches wildly. Refuses to make a call. I shove it into my pocket.

"Can you move? Are you hurt?"

Deja grunts as she rolls onto her stomach and begins to crawl. I move ahead of her.

"Something's wrong with him," she mumbles through tears. "He thinks I'm someone else."

"We can worry about all that later. Let's get to the main house and call the police." I grip the edges of the entrance to the crawl space and hoist myself out. I squat down to help Deja, but then there's a noise. From down the hall. A door opening and closing. Boots across the wood floors.

I look down at Deja and press my finger to my lips. If it were Daddy, he would have called out to me. I would have heard him hollering all the way from the house. The footsteps stop. I grab a wrench and slip into the bedroom, pulling the closet door as close to shut as I can without making a sound.

On a deep inhale, I take one step and glance down the hall to my right. Someone stands there, a massive figure looming in the shadows.

"Sariyah?" He takes a step forward into the light.

277

Fitz.

I drop the wrench. "Oh my God, Fitz. Call 9–1–1–!"

He whips his phone from his pocket as I dart back to the closet to get Deja. I have her halfway out before I realize I don't hear Fitz talking. An icy chill spreads across my body.

"Fitz?" I call.

There's no answer. A song starts up. Something old and jazzy. I look around for the source and spot a Bluetooth speaker on the shelf. Deja's arms are wrapped tightly around her chest, her lower half still in the crawl space, fresh tears pouring from her eyes. I've heard this song before. She played it by accident in the library at school.

"Don't cry, cry baby," Fitz sings along.

"Jed, please. Let us go," Deja begs as he appears in the doorway.

I stay squatted on the floor, looking back and forth between them, trying to piece this together. "His name isn't Jed," I whisper.

"I was hoping she'd arrive at that conclusion on her own." He turns down the music and crouches to my level. "I sent her a whole playlist of Ella Fitzgerald's classics. Wrote love letters inside of *The Great Gatsby*. Felt like a whole narcissist, but I figured she'd think it was cute once she got it."

"Fitz, what are you—why?" I adjust myself, discreetly creeping closer to the toolbox.

"Why? For Crystelle, of course."

Deja sobs behind me. "My name isn't Crystelle!"

"I know that!" Fitz bellows, eyes bulging, nostrils flared.

I don't have time for whatever twisted shit is going on here. I grab the toolbox and flail it, smacking him across the side of his head. Deja screams as a bit of blood spatters the wall and Fitz collapses backward onto the ground. His phone slides across the room, coming to a stop under the windowsill. I scramble for it.

A need begins to form in the back of my mind. Staticky and unstable.

"Ri, watch out!" Deja shouts, right as I reach the phone.

Fitz is on his feet, blood dripping down the side of his face, eyes fixed on me like an angry bull.

"Run!" I shout to Deja as I force the window open and hurl half my body out in one motion. A second later his arms are wrapped around my legs like a vise. I resist, doing all I can to grasp the slick siding on the outside of the house. He yanks. Hard. My chin clips the windowsill on the way back inside and all goes black.

CHAPTER 33

· ·

When I come to, I try to sit up but smack my head against something hard. My thoughts jump to the most horrifying, extreme possibility first. That I'm in a box, a coffin, buried alive. But Deja's hand against my skin makes the image dissolve. Reality isn't much better. I'm closed in this damn crawl space with her. She removes her hand from me and curls into a tight ball on her side, whimpering softly. Hopelessness in her eyes. Hopelessness she has earned after thinking I was about to save her, only to end up right back at square one. But I'm not hopeless. I'm pissed off. We won't be rotting away down here without a fight. We won't be a pair of forgotten missing girls.

I check my pockets for my phone, but it's gone. "Fitz!" I bang on the crawl space door. "Fitz! Let us out of here." I whack the door until I'm dripping with sweat and my wrist aches. I collapse onto my back to catch my breath.

"He left," Deja whispers.

"You could have told me that before I shouted myself

hoarse," I snap. I lie there until my breathing returns to normal. "Why?"

"I don't know."

"I'm not asking why Fitz left. I'm asking why you came here. Why you did this."

"Malcolm and I wanted to—"

"Stop. I already heard Malcolm's reason. I'm asking you for yours."

"It's the same as Malcolm's. I've had a family member disappear, too. I know most missing people, even most white girls, don't get the attention Casey got. But—"

"But nine times out of ten the ones who do are white. Yes, I know. Everyone knows. It's common knowledge and I still don't get how this stunt was supposed to change anything. But you can explain that part later. Because I know it's not your whole truth. What was going on with you and Fitz?"

"Nothing."

"Look where we are, Dej. What's the point of lying? If we get out of this, which we will, all our dirty laundry is getting aired out. It's probably best to get the worst of the funk off now before the whole world catches a whiff."

"Nothing was going on with me and Fitz! He told me his name was Jed. I met him over Christmas break and we hit it off. Shit sucked at home. I thought I was in love with him. Malcolm's idea was my chance to escape and maybe bring awareness to a bigger issue at the same time . . . only I never intended to go back home like we planned. Jed—I mean Fitz—picked me up from Afro Alt and we were just going to figure things out together."

"He picked you up from—" I can't even get the sentence out it's so absurd. "And what? You sprayed the pepper spray and cut yourself to make it seem like something bad happened?"

"No!" She releases a frustrated sigh. "I mean, the pepper spray did seem useful considering what we had planned, but I really ended up needing it! This dog. It ran up on me. Knocked me down. I cut myself and had to use the spray to keep it from attacking me."

It feels like my skull shrinks two sizes. There's so much that's not adding up. "Wait—back up. You met Fitz in person this past winter and he introduced himself as Jed?"

"Yes."

I pinch the bridge of my nose. "And when you followed him on Instagram, you didn't wonder why he looked different and had a whole-ass girlfriend?"

"I never followed him on IG. It should have been a red flag, but he said he preferred Facebook. I made an account on there to talk to him."

"Willow D. Nelson?"

"Yeah. How'd you—"

"Doesn't matter." Fitz must have hacked Deja's Instagram and Jed's Facebook. Some kind of stunt to set him up but there's no telling why. "Dej, what was so bad back home that running off with a guy you barely knew seemed like a good idea? I saw the lock on your door. I gave it to you. What was going on?"

She sniffs, sinuses already heavy with the fluids that come with tears.

"Is it Derrick?" I ask.

"No! No, Derrick is . . . good. I was most worried about how all this would affect him. How is he?"

"How you'd expect, I guess. But if it's not him . . ." I don't want to be the one to make this accusation.

"My mother." Those two words are almost a complete story. "The lock on my doorknob works, but the door doesn't latch properly. The chain lock was to keep her out of my purse. She takes my money. Buys drugs, clothes, makeup. I was fed up. Pissed off. I don't want her in trouble or people talking smack about her. I just wanted to slip away. Erase myself from her life but keep living my own. Or start mine over, I don't know."

"Are you afraid of her?"

"No, but it's strange." She thinks for a few long seconds. "Like watching a scary movie. You know there's no real physical threat, but your heart races anyway."

"Physical threats aren't the only ones that can hurt you."

"I know," she whispers. "I'd already planned to leave before Malcolm said anything to me."

"But what about graduation? What about—"

"Hello, hello," Fitz's voice booms from above. "Are you ready to have a civilized conversation, Sariyah?"

Deja scooches over to me, close enough for me to see the warning in her eyes. The warning that tells me I better play nice.

"I said, are you ready to talk? I know you can hear me."

I clear my throat. "Yes."

"Good. I hope there are no hard feelings about"—he searches for words—"your current accommodations, but you kind of gave me no choice. You understand?"

He pauses like he actually expects me to respond in the affirmative. Deja nudges me. "Yeah" is the best I can get out. "But Fitz, it's me. You know me. What are you doing? What are you thinking?"

"Well, I thought you knew me. But that didn't stop you from looking at me sideways and knocking me across the head with that box before I had time to explain, did it?"

"I'm sorry," I say as earnestly as I can, even though it's complete bullshit. "I'm listening now."

"Ain't much to say, really. You gotta see for yourself."

There's some rustling, then he's slipping a small piece of paper—no, a photograph—in between the floorboards. It flutters to the ground and I pick it up, but it's too dark to tell what I'm looking at.

"I can't see."

He shines his cell phone flashlight into the crack. It doesn't help much, but it's enough to force a small gasp from me as I process the image. It's Fitz and Deja. I hold the picture out in front of her. Her eyes widen and she shakes her head, afraid to speak. I take a closer look and the picture is obviously old. It's outside the local high school. They both have on back-packs and letterman jackets. The girl isn't Deja. But I've seen her before. I've seen her recently. That day at the city zoo with Josiah. I think of Tim, from Chefly, who claimed he saw Deja years ago. Could it have been this girl?

"Is this Crystelle?"

"Those were good times," he says wistfully. "I reached out to her back in September when I found that photo at the bottom of the suitcase I brought to college. She laughed with me. Reminisced with me. Cleared some things up. That cheating mess at prom never even happened. Bunch of dirty rumors. Probably started by Jed. Anyway, when I came home for Thanksgiving I found out Crystelle—"

"Was in a relationship with someone else," I fill in. The kind of relationship where they take day trips to the zoo.

"Yes. She goes to Georgia State. I went up there during winter break hoping to surprise her. Convince her to drop the new dude. The ice-skating rink seemed like a romantic spot, but I wanted to check it out before I asked her. The wild part is, I was thinking of you that night. Thinking of that ability of yours. How you give people exactly what they need."

"I don't know what—"

"Careful now. I don't enjoy being played for a fool. Your grandmother is a legend down here, your auntie got a big mouth, and you and I've spent almost every summer together for the past ten years. You think I didn't notice there's something different about you? Something extraordinary about you? I bet that's the real reason your daddy sent y'all up to Atlanta. And like I said, you were on my mind that night at the ice-skating rink. I was thinking, if I could just see you, I could get whatever I need to win Crystelle back. To show her how much I love her. So I texted you. A little early for our midyear check-in, but close enough. Do you remember what I said? When you asked what I wanted for Christmas?"

"You said you wanted to be happy."

"Yep. And not thirty seconds later, I saw Deja. Spitting image of Crystelle. Maybe it was dumb, thinking you could fulfill a need over the phone. But that's exactly what I thought you did. Didn't find out y'all were friends until a few months later. Right around the time I realized a doppelgänger is no substitute for the real thing. I tried to see you in person a few days before your buddy down there was scheduled to come visit me. Waited for you at the ice cream shop, but all hell broke loose. That man got stabbed. It could have been me. I'm a superstitious guy. I respect signs from the universe. You're a good friend. I knew if I had her, you'd come right to me. Now, I did pay off that good-for-nothing Tim to try and hurry you along, and when that didn't work, I made Deja stop replying to Malcolm's texts. But I never doubted that you'd come to me and give me what I need. The giver of the most perfect things."

Sneaky-ass gnat. I know where this is going and I don't want it to go there. But trying to avoid it, trying to block a potential need from developing, only seems to encourage one to form. It's fuzzy and buried deep in the back of my head. The more I try not to think of it, the closer it comes to the forefront of my mind. "I don't have anything to give you, Fitz. And even if I did, there's nothing down here but bugs and dirt."

He cackles. "All right, you got me there. But it's not like you can't just tell me what it is."

"It doesn't work like that," I say assuredly. I've never tried simply telling someone what they need. It never felt right or possible, and in this moment, that works in my favor. "And I need to be able to see you," I add. He acts like a know-it-all, but he doesn't know shit. I'm not powerless here. Not if he wants something from me badly enough. "I have a bag of things in the car. If you let me go get it—"

"No. I'll get the bag myself. Then we can talk." Dust rains down on us as his feet drag lazily across the floor. And then he's gone.

Again I try to beat open the hatch. When that fails, I crawl to the closest vent, then turn and try to kick it open.

"They're too small," Deja says without looking at me, still scrunched in her spot near the door. "I already tried."

My eyes shift to the spot where a bit of light from outside creeps in. A hole where a vent is missing. Maybe a toddler could get through, but she's right. That's not our way out. I'm crawling back over to her when there's another sound from above. No way Fitz went to the car and back so quickly. He must have heard me trying to get out. He won't be happy. I listen carefully, but his gait seems off. His shoes sound different against the floor.

"Hello?" A deep voice, slightly irritated, echoes through the house.

My dad's voice.

He don't gotta speak twice. I scream for him as loud as I can.

"Sariyah? Where the hell are you?"

The light coming in from the kicked-out vent cuts out as someone runs by. Fitz. He probably saw Dad coming as soon as he made to leave.

"Daddy, watch out!"

The back door opens and closes.

"Who is that? Sariyah?"

"No, Daddy, we're down here!"

"Hi, Mr. Bryant." Fitz sounds totally different. Cheerful. Innocent.

"Fitzgerald? What are you doing here, son?"

I cling to the distrust in my father's voice.

"What are you doing in this house? On my property? I don't recall you asking permission."

Fitzgerald snickers. "I don't need your permission."

"Boy, where—"

There's a loud *clunk* that makes my next scream catch in my throat. "Daddy?" The word wobbles out.

It's silent for several painstaking seconds, and then there's a commotion, a struggle. Shoving and grunting and sliding and cursing. I bang on the hatch, shouting for my dad, praying my voice will keep him pushing.

A loud thump. A body hitting the floor. I scoot a few feet over to where I heard the sound and stare up at the floorboards, listening, waiting, afraid to speak. Afraid that doing so will confirm what I already know. If Dad won this fight, he'd be calling for me. My eyes cloud with tears as a drop of something dark and warm and tacky seeps through the planks and lands on my arm.

"Daddy?" I cry.

"Daddy?" Fitzgerald mocks. "He ain't dead. Just a little cut. Head wounds are dramatic. I'd know. I'll tell you what I'm going to do now, though. I'm going to go get that bag of yours and you're going to give me what I need. That, or I'll give your daddy's wound something to bleed about." He laughs at himself.

I can't give Fitzgerald what he needs. What he needs can't be pulled out of a bag. But as if in protest to my own thoughts, once again something stirs around the periphery of my mind, brews there. It's uncomfortable. I wish whatever it is was for Deja again, but I know it's not. And I don't want to know. Once I hear it, it can't be unheard. I don't want this connection to this man. Still, the sound of the first letter breaks through. *R.* "Stop," I draw out. "Stop. Stop. Stop."

Deja grips my wrist to keep me from digging my fingernails into my temples.

I turn onto my side and rock back and forth, try focusing on any random thing, but my mind bounces aimlessly. *Physics. Dad. School. Jude. Afro Alt. Ice cream. Ring. Secrets. Lies. Malcolm. Ring. Jojo. Casey. Tessa. Ring. Ring. RING.*

My nose burns, then runs, as I hold back my emotions. Why can't I turn this off? Why can't I turn it off for people like this? I want to be stingy. Choosy. Selective. Because this ability is an extension of me. I have the right to be particular about how much of myself I share with others. But this is a compulsion. And I've never been taught how to manage it. And I wonder if that means it's not meant to be managed. If I'm not meant to resist it.

Ring. Ring. Ring.

CHAPTER 34

. . . .

Fitzgerald returns with Santa Bag. His need relentlessly circles through my mind. Is he really going to use a ring provided by me to propose to Crystelle? I can't think of any other use for it. A little bile forces its way up my esophagus.

"You got some interesting stuff in here," he says. "Where do you get it all?"

"Let me come up."

He doesn't respond.

"I have to hand the item to you. There's no room down here for me to find it. I can't see."

It's silent for a minute, then the hatch swings open. Deja and I shuffle out of his view.

He laughs. "Girl, don't be scared. We go way back. There's nothing to be afraid of. Not if you give me what I need. That's the plan, right?" His voice goes dark and threatening.

"That's the plan."

"Okay. Then we don't have any problems. Come on out."

I still hesitate, eyeing the bloody spot on the floor where my father lies. "You'll let us all go after?"

"Got no reason to keep you, do I?"

I want to call him on his bluff. If this man believes he can let any of us go and not get reported to the police, he's a damn fool. But he's not foolish at all. He just thinks I'm stupid. He's one of those cocky men who think they can manipulate anyone into anything. He thinks I'm humbled at his feet. That I'll do whatever he wants, that I really believe catering to him will get me what I want. I don't believe it for a minute, but my best shot at a fight is getting out of this hole. And just like Daddy said it would, I feel my desperation melt my fear away.

"There you are," he says when I stick my upper body through the opening. There's a swollen knot and a smear of blood across his face from where I hit him with the toolbox. His devious expression looks bizarre paired with his fluffy cheeks and long lashes.

He stands a comfortable distance away while I climb all the way out. The open closet door blocks my view of Daddy, and I'm thankful.

Fitz and I both take a step toward each other. He smiles wryly and pulls some rope from behind his back. "I see you already hobbled your ankle, so this is just for your wrists. You understand, right? Can't have you getting yourself into trouble before you fulfill your end of the deal, can we?"

I hold out my wrists, unbothered. I've never been called clumsy. He can bet his ass I'll run with my busted ankle and restricted arms if it means saving my life, Deja's, and my dad's.

He scoots by me and closes the crawl space door, locking Deja in once again, then motions to Santa Bag like a showgirl. I limp over to it. "Go on," he encourages as I sift through. It's difficult with my hands bound, with him watching me.

Ring. Ring. Ring.

I know there's one in here. Josiah found it at the park before we went to the zoo. I feel around until my fingers graze a cold metal loop. Fitz rubs his dry hands together, grossly eager to accept his prize. I keep my back to him as I sneak something else out of the bag along with the ring. The steel hair comb Philly gave me. I hide it in my left hand, slip the ring onto the tip of my right index finger, and cup my hands together. He'll only have eyes for the ring.

"What is it?"

I turn around, cradling it against my chest. The gold glints in the light of the portable lamp by the door.

He looks hungry. Feral.

"I knew it!" He sticks a finger in my face. "I knew it. You're something else. This makes everything make sense, don't you see? A second ago, I wouldn't have admitted to the doubts I let creep in. But that right there. That coming from you—it's all the confirmation I need. Crystelle and I are supposed to be together. That ring is going to link us forever."

I purposely do not extend my arms. If I wait long enough. He'll come to me. And he'll have to get close.

"Let me have it, then." He opens his palm, but I stand firm. He scoffs and takes two long strides to close the gap between us.

I straighten my index finger so he can take it. While he's distracted, I lunge forward with the comb. I catch the shock in his eyes for half a second and wonder if Ms. Jess saw the same look in Danny's. The pointy, rusty teeth gash the side of his neck and we both topple over. The ring goes rolling across the floor. We viciously fight to reach it first, kicking, scratching, wrestling. But I have the advantage. My hands may be tied, but he's losing blood. I squeeze my fingers closed around

291

the ring and push myself back onto my feet. Fitz's hand is pressed against his neck. Blood trickles between his fingers, and his eyes are filled with rage. "Give. Me. That. Ring!" he roars.

I run. It hurts more than I expect, even with the help of adrenaline. Sparks of pain radiate up my leg and I'm not moving as fast as I need to, but I've got a head start. I tear out the back door, but I forgot about the mud. My feet stick in it and I can't use my arms properly for leverage. Fitz catches up to me in an instant and jumps on my back, knocking us both to the ground. He presses my face into the soft earth and I cannot breathe. I open my mouth to scream, but it's impossible. All I can do is flail around beneath him as he pins me down with all his weight. Sludge cakes its way into my mouth. Up my nostrils. He's going to kill me. I'm going to die. But he suddenly yanks my head up, ripping some of my hair out.

"Where's that fucking ring?"

I can't answer him. I'm choking.

He shoves his fingers into my mouth, clearing away the mud. Finally. Air.

"The ring!" he demands.

"In the mud," I gasp. "I dropped it."

He slams my face back down, then rolls me over before frantically flinging muck everywhere in search of it. He's so consumed by that thing. He trusted me blindly—but it's still in my hand.

I inch away, eyes on him the whole time. When I find purchase on a little patch of grass, I stand and run. This time toward the steep embankment by the creek. Daddy's neighbor has his chicken coop just across it. If I can make enough noise, it might get them going, draw some attention.

"Help!" I scream once I'm a few yards away. "Help me!"

The mud stops slinging and Fitz barrels toward me like the linebacker he once was. I continue to scream for help at the top of my lungs until he's on me again. His eyes are fiery. Greedy. Every trace of the friend I thought I knew, gone. The rope around my wrists makes it easier for me to keep my hands clasped shut. To keep the ring from him. He rips the rope away once he realizes this, taking a layer of skin with it. I cry out and hold the ring behind my back.

"Give it to me," he says through gritted teeth. "Give it to me or I'll kill you right here."

"You're going to do that either way."

His eyes go ablaze again and he wraps his hands around my neck. Instinctively, my grip relaxes and I drop the ring. He catches it and caresses it like fucking Gollum from *The Lord of the Rings* while I put distance between us and struggle to catch my breath.

"Thanks," he says, walking toward me without an ounce of appreciation or mercy in his expression. But then he trips on a root. He stumbles and the ring is flung into the air. We both look up at it. In slow motion, he grapples for it, but it bounces from his grip three separate times. Finally, he grasps it, but the embankment is slick. It breaks away beneath his feet like overly moist cake and he vanishes from my sight with a shout.

I stand there in shock. Barely believing what I just witnessed. The sound of a distant police siren reaches my ears and gives me the courage to crawl to the edge and look down. Part of me is afraid to find him clinging to a branch or stone, ready to attack me again, but he's not. He's down at the bank of the creek. Face up. Neck twisted at an ungodly angle. Golden ring glinting in the center of his palm.

CHAPTER 35

· ·

I know I'm in the hospital before I open my eyes. I can tell by the smell. By the sterile chill in the air. My throat burns when I try to speak.

"Sariyah? Mama, I think she's waking up."

The sound of my brother's voice is instantly comforting, which, if the aching in my body weren't enough, would be proof that I've been through hell.

It takes a surprising amount of effort to open my eyes. The lids are heavy and sticky.

"Ri!"

Josiah's brown face is the only thing in my field of view.

"Back up, baby. Give her some breathing room," Mama says.

I motion to the mauve cup and pitcher next to my bed. Jojo, in his eagerness to help, spills a bunch of water on the floor.

"Sorry." He passes me a cup, water dripping down the sides.

"Thank you." My voice is crusty. I take a few quick gulps of water as Mama rubs my head.

"You've been out for almost twenty-four hours. Fractured bone in your foot is the worst of it. Some ugly bruising on your neck. Cuts and scrapes. But you'll be okay, baby."

"Dad?"

"He's okay. Just a couple of rooms down. Deja was fine. A little dehydrated. She went home this morning."

I sit up quickly and wince. "Went home with who? Did someone find my phone?"

"Relax." She gently pushes my shoulder until I'm resting against the pillow again.

"As soon as Derrick heard you'd found her, he was in the car speeding down 75. Didn't even wait for Jasmine. Turns out Deja wasn't the only one having problems with her mother. She and Derrick will be staying at his mother's house until everything gets straightened out."

"What else did Deja say?" I need to know if her and Malcolm's scheme got exposed or not.

"She said that manipulative young man offered her a safe haven during a rough patch with her mom. Said he snapped a few days after she arrived."

"Is he dead?"

She waits a moment before responding. "Yes."

I turn to face her. "Good." I don't mumble. I don't hesitate. I don't stutter. "Am I in trouble?"

"Because of what happened to Fitzgerald? No, baby. That was an accident. They could clearly see where he slipped in the mud. And even if he hadn't, look at you. Not a juror in this country would fault you for pushing him."

I'm surprised by how much I don't need reassurance. For once, guilt isn't high on my list of emotions. And it's not just because he was going to kill me—and I really believe he would have. I have a sense of calmness and trust surrounding my ability that I've never felt before. Fitz asked me to give him what he needed. I did what he asked and it turned out what he needed was also precisely what I needed. What Deja needed. What Dad needed. What Crystelle needed. We needed him dead. And I can't help but wonder if that was what the nail file was about all along. Fitz was there that night. If Danny hadn't stepped in the crossfire, maybe all this would have been avoided. Even the hair comb. If I hadn't given Philly those gemstones, I might not be alive right now. I won't look at need fulfillment as an individualistic thing ever again. Seen and unseen, the ripples are infinite.

. . .

We go back to Atlanta the next day. All of us. Mama insisted Dad come, too, so she could nurse us both back to health and get Jojo back in school. I use Dad's phone to FaceTime Jude when I'm settled back in my room. I smile when I see his face, but he frowns. I adjust my hoodie to hide the marks on my neck. "Looks worse than it feels."

Jude rubs his forehead. "You said you'd tell me when you were ready to go to Chefly. I would have gone with you."

"I know. I'm sorry. I didn't have time."

He puffs up his cheeks and exhales. Waves me off. "It doesn't matter. I'm glad you're okay. I'm glad Deja's okay."

"Have you spoken to Malcolm? He's on his way over here."

He makes sure no one else is around before answering. "Yes. He called and told me everything when you didn't hold up your agreement to reply to his texts. I was with him when he called the police. He felt really guilty, wanted to confess everything, but I told him to tell them only what they needed to know to find you. I thought that might be what you'd want."

I nod slowly. I'm angry with Malcolm. Deja, too. But I don't want their lives ruined over this. "What happened when he called the police?"

"They already knew."

"What? How?"

"Jed went to them. We hit him up on Instagram and got his number. Long story short, Jed noticed the resemblance between Crystelle and Deja, and when you pointed out that she was following him, he got a bad feeling. Fitz had been acting strange for a while. Obsessing over Crystelle. He didn't want to believe Fitz would get into anything messy, but then you showed up in town and he found Deja's burner phone and a bunch of other stuff planted on him."

"Did he give the phone to the police?" I ask, truly afraid to hear the answer.

"No. He tossed it as soon as he realized what it was. Burned everything else. Fitz was probably planning to pin everything on Jed after he got what he wanted from you."

"I figured that much out."

"Any idea why he'd set up his best friend?"

"I guess because he never approved of his relationship with Crystelle. He thought Jed was spreading rumors to keep them away from each other."

There's a knock on our front door and I hear my father greet Malcolm. Jude hears it, too.

"I'll let you go," he says. "Maybe I can come see you tomorrow?"

"I'd like that," I say, and we hang up.

A few seconds later, Malcolm drums his fingers against my open door. "Hey." He wrings his hands like he always does on the rare occasions that he is nervous. "It's so strange seeing your dad here this time of year."

"It's different, but I'm happy he's close."

"Yeah, of course." He steps inside and stands there awkwardly for a moment before perching on the end of my bed, head bowed. "I knew she had a boyfriend. She told me his name was Jay. I didn't know any more details than that, but when you found the card, I got worried you'd interfere and mess everything up. I knew the police wouldn't figure anything out before the date Deja and I set for her to come back, but I wanted to at least see how close they'd get."

"I don't blame you for *thinking* about doing all of this, Malcolm. But I can't believe you actually went through with it."

"I went back and forth about it all the way until you sensed that pepper spray. It seemed like a sign. We wanted the police to suspect foul play, like they did with Casey. That's the only way it'd be a fair comparison, but we didn't want to do anything too out there. The best we came up with was for her to leave her phone behind. But after you gave her the pepper spray, I told her she should discharge it before Jay—Jed"—Malcolm drags his hand down his face—"Fitzgerald picked her up."

"Why'd you look up all that stuff about Deja's stepdad if you knew she was fine all along?"

"Because I never fully understood why she agreed to it. I felt like she was hiding something, too."

"Why didn't you tell me sooner, Colmy? Not just that she was hiding something, but all of it. Your plan. I know you were angry with me, but . . . it's me."

"I tried to." He takes out his phone and passes it to me.

298

"Go to our thread. Remember those texts I deleted from your phone?"

My thumb trembles slightly as I scroll.

"I thought, maybe even hoped, you were lying about not reading it. That you did and needed time to process it or something. But then, it was so vague anyway . . ."

He keeps talking, but I'm busy trying to locate the text.

Malcolm
Tried calling you earlier. Call me back.
Hello?
Look, there's something I need to tell you.
I really can't do it over text, but I need to
get this off my chest. It's about Tessa and
Casey and Deja. It's driving me up the wall.
I need you with me in this, Ri. I'm trying to
hold it on my own, but I don't think I can.
Feeling like I've messed everything up. Like
I'm doing too much and not enough at the
same time. How is that even possible? I
know I'm ranting at this point and none of
this makes sense, but . . . call me. Better
yet, come over. Let me get this out because
I swear it's rotting me from the inside.

Tears are gliding down my cheeks when I finish. How did I ignore this? And why would Malcolm put me in a position to feel bad about something like this?

"I was going to tell you. That day. I wanted to. But when you didn't reply, I got nervous. I regretted sending it, but it was too late to undo, so I followed up with a casual text that would be easy to ignore if you saw the message preview."

"Malcolm, I am so sorry." I'm not the only one who needs to offer apologies, but I mean it.

He holds up his hand. "I didn't regret it because you didn't respond. I got scared. Cold feet. That's when it got real for me. That's the first time I really thought about consequences or who was getting hurt in the process. I mean, me and Dej talked about that some, but our goal felt so much higher than all of that. So much bigger. So worthy. And I was angry. I *am* angry. Have been for years. I needed to make a point, and she was willing. Can't say she understood it on my level. But she understood rage. Her mom made sure of that. But you, I saw how your anger over Tess faded until only sadness and nostalgia were left. And there's nothing wrong with that." He presses his lips together, then releases them with a small *pop*. "But that's not where I am."

"So this wasn't about a project, or making a statement, was it?"

He contemplates this. "I thought it was. I really did. But maybe it was more about justifying my anger. I was overwhelmed by it, Ri. And it seemed like I was alone in that until Casey. People who didn't even know her were outraged. Like I said the other day, I needed to know if something had changed since Tess. And if nothing had, I wanted people to think about why."

"Well, mission accomplished." I hand Malcolm his phone back.

I left his browser open to a think piece that has been shared 347,000 times. Atlanta Missing Teen Held Captive and Found by Friend: Did you even know she was gone?

CHAPTER 36

. . . .

My noise cancelers cover my ears and Santa Bag hangs over my shoulder as I hobble across the stage at graduation, orthopedic boot still on my foot. It took relentless tutoring from Jude, Malcolm, Deja, Mama, my teachers—even Jojo—to pass all my classes, but together, we managed it. Rincon didn't trip when I admitted to giving his name to the police, but he did flip when he found out I had no plans to walk. A lot of things have changed over the past several weeks, but my dislike of large crowds hasn't. Our principal is all uptight about tradition and expects all students to dress uniformly for the ceremony. No bags, no headphones. But he made an exception this year. So here I am, accepting my diploma to the chorus of two thousand needs. Minus the usuals. And minus Deja's. I haven't heard any needs from her since that night in Chefly.

"Retro for dinner?" Malcolm asks me after the ceremony.

I shed my hot, scratchy gown and Mama happily takes it off my hands.

"Go have fun," she says.

I look at Dad. He's going back to Chefly in the morning and I don't want to miss out on our last few hours together.

"Go on," he encourages. "We'll wait up for you."

Malcolm smiles and waves at my family, then throws his arm over my shoulder, directing me away from the football field.

"Tess should be here with us today," he says, once we escape the larger portion of the crowd. He isn't angry or somber, just reflective.

I squeeze his left hand, still dangling over my shoulder. I'm not over what he and Deja did. My stomach lurches every time I imagine them scheming behind my back. But it's not as hard for me to understand why they did it anymore. The country may be talking more about how race, and sex, and socioeconomics affect how missing persons are handled by the police and media, but there's a gap between talk and action. A gap worth getting angry over.

Deja and Jude wait for us under a giant oak tree at the far edge of campus. They both pull noisemakers from behind their backs and clap and cheer as we approach.

"We did it!" Deja whoops.

She's the only one who can say that without earning an eye roll from me. She and I are the only ones in our group that anyone ever worried wouldn't make it across the stage.

Jude laces his fingers with mine and tugs me close enough to kiss my forehead. "Proud of you."

Malcolm looks at Deja, wagging his finger between me and Jude. "We still not going to acknowledge whatever's going on here?"

"No," I say with a smile.

Jude grins at me and I'm glad he's okay with letting whatever it is—because it's definitely something—just be.

. . .

I come home to Jojo playing in my cap and gown and Mama and Daddy cuddling on the couch. I join my parents in the living room.

"Good time?" Dad asks.

"Yeah, it was great." I hand my leftovers off to Josiah.

Mama glimpses what's inside before he makes it to the kitchen. "No, sir. You not eating all that sugar before bed."

"Oh, let him," Dad says.

Mama raises her eyebrows and twists her lips. "Don't think about nudging me when he comes in the room at three A.M. talking about *I threw up.*"

He kisses her temple. "I won't. Sariyah can handle that."

I snatch the Styrofoam container away from my brother and shove it in the back of the fridge.

He grins evilly. Mouth already chipmunk stuffed with cold pancakes.

"You sure you don't want to come down with Josiah after his camp?" Dad asks me.

"I'm sure. But tell Jed I said hey." I don't mention Ella, even though she sent me a message explaining how terrible she felt about what her brother did. She had no reason to feel bad, and I let her know as much, but I can't really imagine a world where we could be proper friends. Because I know being angry with her brother, being disappointed in him, doesn't erase her love for him. And I'm not far enough into my therapy sessions to welcome that kind of complexity into my life. Mama signed the whole family up and gave referrals to Mr. Derrick and Mrs. Hawkins. It's helping, but I think it's the kind of work that doesn't really have an end.

Mama stands and twists her body until her back pops. "Come on, Jo. Let's go pick you out some clothes for camp."

When they disappear down the hall, Dad leans forward and rests his elbows on his knees, hands clasped. "You still thinking about going to trade school?"

I laugh. I have nightmares about that crawl space and gutted rental almost every night. The thought of being a contractor isn't appealing anymore. "No. I don't think that's for me after all."

"Fair enough. What's the new plan?"

"I'm not sure." I scrunch up my face, hoping he'll accept that answer for now.

"You don't have to be sure. I'm curious is all."

"I'm starting full-time at the pharmacy next week. The pay is better than I thought it'd be." Which means I can save and still plan a proper donation to Danny's fundraiser. "But as for long-term plans"—I hesitate, nervous to share—"I don't know. I was thinking about finding an organization I could volunteer or maybe intern with. A group that helps teens going through things like Tessa and Deja were."

Dad's eyes grow shiny. "I think that's a great idea, baby girl."

He leaves me to go pack his things and I go to my bedroom, legs heavy and eyes tired. I crawl into bed just after ten and fall asleep knowing Tessa will visit me.

Tonight, her room is decorated with streamers and balloons.

"You're all grown-up!" She throws confetti in the air, happily exposing her neon-blue braces. I try to recall where the sentence was recycled from, but I can't place it.

304

"I'm glad you're here," I say.

"I'm always here." She wanders to the nail polish station.

I watch as she lifts and inspects various bottles, reading out some of the silly names. *Darker Than My Heart*, and *Lacquer of Love*, and *Let's Flamingle*. If Ms. Jess never reopens Sweet Pea's, she could make waves in the nail polish business.

Tess settles on a shade that perfectly matches her braces. I join her with a jade green. We sit there, quietly painting our toes. I'm going for my second coat when a need, soft as a summer breeze, whispers through my mind. I can't make it out and I don't want to, because there is only one person it could be coming from. And what would that mean? What would it mean if I could suddenly hear Tessa's needs? That we aren't close anymore? Or maybe it's just meant to be a slap in the face. Too little, too late.

She giggles next to me. "Relax. This is a dream, remember?"

I fake a laugh. "Of course I remember, but this dream is breaking the usual rules. Like you reading my mind, for instance."

"Is it really reading your mind if this whole interaction is happening in your mind? And like I said. You're all grown-up now. Things change."

Something about the way she says it makes my stomach knot up. Like there's something else to be gleaned from the words. I look around at all the decorations and I realize this is more than a graduation party. It's the last time she'll visit me like this.

"You're wrong, by the way," she says.

"What do you mean?"

"I'm not the only one the need you're sensing could be coming from." She snaps her fingers, which have magically become perfectly manicured. Santa Bag appears in the corner by her dresser. She opens it, shoves her arm in up to the elbow, and comes up with a scrap of something. A small piece of paper.

"Here," she says, extending it to me.

"What is it?"

"It's what *you* need."

I take it. A newspaper clipping with the words *mile marker 15* highlighted.

Tessa stares at me with her big, round eyes. "It's what you need to find me."

ACKNOWLEDGMENTS

I used to think writing a book was a solitary thing, and in many ways it is. But now that I've reached this milestone, now that I can reflect on the journey, it's the moments that involved other people that stand out the most. That mean the most. To every person who had a direct hand in shaping this book into its final form—I see your fingerprints on every page. To every person who had a direct hand in shaping *me*, you are there in every line as well. I thank God for blessing me with this opportunity and for placing each of you in my life.

Thank you to my phenomenal agent, Molly Ker Hawn, for finding this book a home. Having you on my side, with all of your experience and expertise, has been the greatest comfort as I navigate this industry. You are an absolute gem, and it is such a joy to work with you. Special thanks to Jenny Bent for knowing this book would be right up Molly's alley and forwarding it along to her.

Thank you to my wonderful editor, Tiffany Shelton, for seeing and loving these characters. For choosing to champion this book and me. Thank you for all the time, energy, and care you poured into preparing this book for publication. All my awe and gratitude to Kerri Resnick and Taj Francis for designing and illustrating the most gorgeous cover. To the entire team at Wednesday Books: you are all so hardworking, so talented, and so appreciated.

Massive thanks to Alex Antscherl, Michelle Brackenborough, and everyone at Bloomsbury UK for bringing Sariyah and her crew to even more readers around the world. Thanks also to Carla Hutchinson. We didn't get to work together long, but your deep enthusiasm for this book was evident from our first conversation.

Thank you to the Pitch Wars class of 2021 and my mentor, Karen Bao. *Needy Little Things* is not my Pitch Wars book, but I'm not sure it would exist if I hadn't participated. The experience taught me so much, but it truly is the connections I made along the way that I cherish most. Huge shout-out to my fellow mentee, Elizabeth McWhorter. You were the first to read this book, and your critique and commentary were invaluable. All the hugs and screaming cat GIFs to Megan Davidhizar. Your pep talks and camaraderie are everything. And to the rest of the There or Square squad: Emily Charlotte, Christine L. Arnold, Valo Wing, Lally Hi, Sulagna H., K.A. Cobell, P.H. Low, Sana Z. Ahmed, Laurie Lascos, and Aimee Davis—y'all are the greatest. Thank you for enthusiastically celebrating every win and for also providing comfortable shoulders to cry on. I am so grateful for your advice, beta reads, positivity passes, and friendship.

Thank you to Hannah for tagging me in all the Instagram memes that perfectly represent our friendship. There's nothing quite as cathartic as talking and venting with you for hours on end during one of our semiannual sleepovers. Let's keep them up till we're old and gray.

Tonika. My Chief Accountability Officer. Thank you for understanding on all the various levels there are to be understood. For being a safe space. I so admire you and all of your talents. Watching you nourish your creativity and chase your dreams pushes me to do the same.

Chris: I've kept every inspirational note you've hidden in my house over the years. Reading them has gotten me through so many low confidence days. You believed in me from the very start. Thank you for always being there. From ninth-grade algebra to this moment and beyond.

Thank you to my partner, Wes. You were there cheering me on when this story was just a passing thought after binge-watching *The Twilight Zone*. A day spent brainstorming, reading, and gaming with you is a perfect day. Thank you for your kindness and gentleness. Thank you for dreaming with me, and thank you for sharing your own writing with me. I have grown so much by reading your words and spending time by your side.

To my dear mama, my sweet momo. I love you and I am so honored to be your daughter. Thanks for bringing me food when I'd hole up in my room with a book for days as a kid . . . and as an adult. Thank you for ravenously supporting my dreams and for letting me be me. For our Al Green jam sessions and scary movie nights. For our DIY adventures that never fail to end with us laughing until we cry. XOXO. Always.

To my dad, my pops, my levelheaded advice-giver with the softest heart. I love you big. Thank you for your strength and steadiness. For keeping it real. For your goofy wisecracks. For answering the phone when I call and for calling me when I text. For having a fix for every technology issue I have ever had—except that time I accidentally dumped a bowl of ramen on my laptop. RIP Macadamia III.

To Stacey, Naseem, Andre, Simmi, and all the friends and family I could fill pages and pages naming. I am endlessly grateful for your encouragement, your hugs, and your love.

To all the students I've taught and athletes I've coached—you've been such an inspiration to me. Pieces of your humor, tenacity, curiosity, and joy are embedded in each of my characters.

And finally, to you, reader. Thank you for picking up this book. I hope you enjoyed it.

ABOUT THE AUTHOR

Edge Portraiture

CHANNELLE DESAMOURS is a high school science teacher from Atlanta, Georgia, who loves writing tales about magical Black girls. When she's not napping to recover from her five-A.M. writing sessions, she can be found building tiny homes on *The Sims 4* or tending to her house plants. *Needy Little Things* is her debut novel.